BLACK WIDOW

JJ MARSH

PREWETT
BIELMANN

Black Widow

Cover design: JD Smith

Published by Prewett Bielmann Ltd.

All enquiries to admin@jjmarshauthor.com

First printing, 2019

ISBN 978-3-9525191-0-3

Dedicated to MB and BH, for so many happy memories

Prologue

SIGNOR GENNAIO COLACINO
World of Wine requests the pleasure of your company for a
wine-tasting and apero.
Suppliers demonstrating their selections include: Quinta da
Gaia (Portugal), Château Agathe (France), Villa Fiori (Italy)
and Zoltan Winery (Hungary)
Date: 10 June 2019
Time: 20.00
Transport: A boat will collect you at the Hotel Zenit jetty to
take you to our pleasure cruiser at *Kopasi gát* and a water taxi
will be provided for the return journey.
Please RSVP to this email address.

Gennaio thought it over, surprised by the unexpected invitation. He hadn't made any particular plans for the evening, because he usually wandered around until a cool bar, interesting restaurant or attractive woman caught his eye. Budapest had plenty of all three so he always kept his options open. On the other hand, a wine-tasting was a great way to network and if it was dull, he could always move on to seek out some action. Where Kopasi gát was, he had no idea, but if transport was provided, what did it matter?

He replied to the email in the affirmative, made notes on the meetings he'd had that day and called his brother. Business done, he showered and dressed in his sharpest suit. The jacket strained a bit around his middle so he left the button undone. A spritz of aftershave and he was ready to take on all comers.

The boat was already waiting when he sauntered down to the jetty to greet the boat driver. He used English because he'd given up on Hungarian. That language was impossible. As he stepped aboard, his phone rang. His brother wanted more detail on the spice deal. Agusto never took anything at face value. Gennaio watched the scenery go by, reassured Agusto and sent off several messages over the duration of the journey. On arrival at this park, he looked up from his screen to see a man waiting for him. Typical security guard, suited and wearing dark glasses, he was either bald or had shaved his head that day.

Gennaio took the driver's proffered hand to ease himself onto the dock and slipped him a five-Euro tip. The guy thanked him and wished him a nice evening before sailing back in the direction they had come. On the dock, the security guy didn't respond to Gennaio's friendly greeting but asked to see ID. He spoke English but with a heavy accent. Russian, perhaps? Gennaio showed his passport and the man gave a brisk nod and walked away. These guys, with their macho attitudes, behaving more like nightclubs bouncers than VIP guides.

Gennaio followed him through the darkening park, already anticipating a glass of something cool and fragrant. He hoped there would be some food too. The security guy strode along the bank at some speed, so that Gennaio soon broke into a sweat trying to keep up. Something didn't sit right. He was the guest and his comfort should come first. When he met the hosts, he was going to mention this guy's crude manner and suggest such a welcome could put people off. Just as they approached the back of two large marquees, Gennaio slowed to a stop, took out his phone and shot a panoramic view of the riverbank and opposite buildings. The big bald donkey would have to wait.

A smack to the side of his cheek knocked him sideways, his phone flew out of his hands and a massive hand dragged him by the collar into the space between the marquees.

It had been a while since he'd used his fists, and his body wasn't what it used to be, but Gennaio had grown up on the streets of Naples. He knew how take care of himself. He twisted out of the guy's grip and threw a punch. Even before he registered the pain in his right knuckles, he threw another with his left, aiming for the solar plexus. A blow like the kick of a carthorse hit his left ear, and his feet lifted off the ground before all one hundred kilos of Signor Gennaio Colacino came crashing to earth. He lay in the dusky evening gloom, processing pain on a scale he had never encountered, his vision nothing more than white lights on a black screen.

Sight was unnecessary. One hand – so huge! – under his chin, tilted Gennaio's head to the sky, as if introducing him to God. One rapid snap to the left and the lights went out.

The big man waited several minutes, kneeling beside the Italian's body, relieving him of any identification. When he heard music begin from inside the tents, he stepped out, performed a 360° scan of the darkening area and rolled the body a few metres to the quayside. He stopped, checked once more and reached for his knife. There was only one way people would believe this was a gang killing. When he'd added the signature move, he kicked the corpse over the edge. It seemed to fall for an eternity before it hit the water.

Chapter 1

"Can I ask what you do for a living?" asked the eye specialist.

Beatrice opened her mouth, closed it again and settled on the simplest response. "I'm retired." She doubted she would ever be able to say the words 'Private Investigator' without getting an attack of impostor syndrome.

"Retired from what?" he asked, tapping the results of her eye test into his desktop computer. When she didn't respond immediately, he looked up. "I'm not being nosey, just wondering if your job involved a great deal of screen work. For a woman of your age, your eyesight is remarkably good."

"You just said I need glasses."

"You do. But many people need glasses at a much earlier stage of life. Mostly those who spend much of their time looking at computer screens. People like me."

Beatrice grew less defensive. "I was a detective inspector until last year. Working for the London Met, there was a lot of screen time, but just as much was spent out on the streets."

"Ah, that may be why your long-sight vision is so strong. You'll only need low-strength corrective lenses for close-up work. Computers, reading and so on. Here's a prescription. Take that to any optician and when you've adjusted to your specs, you'll wonder what you ever did without them."

On leaving the surgery, Beatrice did not go directly to the nearest optician. Instead, she stomped around the streets of

Exeter, feeling ancient, beleaguered and out of sorts. It was tempting to stuff the prescription to the bottom of her handbag and forget about it, but then how could she read all the case files, spreadsheets and financial details of her new business? There was no escaping the fact; she was getting old. She took a break for coffee and cake at Pasticciera Fiorentina to cheer herself up and to indulge her recently acquired taste for Italian pastries. After a good half an hour's sulk, she succumbed to the inevitable and sought out an optician. At least she could choose a light frame which would not add yet more years to her face.

The drive home to Upton St Nicholas did not fill her with her usual eagerness. In Exeter, like London, she could potter around, eat cake, browse a bookshop, buy a bottle of wine for her and Matthew or even attend a concert without meeting most of her neighbours. In the village, everyone knew everyone and observed the smallest adjustment to behaviour.

"Skimmed milk today? Are you and the professor on a diet?"

"Beatrice, will you put Heather straight? Friday's concert at the church hall was an operetta, not a musical."

"Hello, you two. Missed you on Sunday. Hear you went over to Crediton for a change."

It stifled her and she had deliberately begun to switch shops, pubs and routines simply to avoid the same faces, same comments, same dreary old habits. The exact opposite of her behaviour in London, where she clung to her connections. Adjusting to life in the country was not as simple as she'd hoped. The imminent visit of her former colleague Dawn with her partner Derek would be a blessed relief.

Her new private detective agency, the supposed dream career, provided few real thrills. So far it was all suspected infidelity, benefit fraud and one neighbourly suspicion of vegetable sabotage. All within a fifty-mile radius.

Where were the 'come to the island of Antigua urgently for

the most fascinating case of your career!' emails? The disputed will and testament case, which had already involved far too many unpaid hours of answering emails, was yet to materialise. All because the tremulous creature who 'almost certainly' wanted to employ her, was still dithering about sharing confidential information. How can you expect a detective to investigate without giving her all the facts? Beatrice was on the point of telling her to find someone else to spy on her relatives, but she'd been looking forward to a trip to Salzburg. The Austrians made awfully good cakes.

She pulled onto their driveway, keeping an eye out for Huggy Bear. Their little Border terrier had become adept at finding holes in the fence and escaping the garden to go searching for rabbits. Sunlight shone through the stained glass above the front door, throwing a rainbow of colour at her feet as she plonked her shopping in the hall. The house was silent. Matthew must have taken the dog out or she would be barking and jumping up in delight at one of the family returning home.

Beatrice kicked off her shoes and padded into the kitchen. Empty, but crumbs on the counter and the unmistakeable scent of fried bacon suggested someone had made himself a snack. She opened the kitchen door to let in some fresh air and looked into the garden, with a certain amount of pride. To her left the shrubbery shimmered in the breeze, as colourful as Rio at Carnaval. The lawn was neatly mown and her wildflower bee garden had flourished, now humming with winged visitors in the August afternoon warmth. The stream bubbled and gurgled away, swollen with last night's rain. On her right, the brand new winter garden, their favourite summer room.

Her eyes narrowed. Between two large fig plants, she could see a human arm on the rattan rug. Panic seized her. Matthew!

She raced through the house and into the conservatory, short breaths drying her mouth. On his back, snoring lightly, Matthew was dozing on a garden recliner. The newspaper and one arm had fallen to lie beside him and curled up on his stomach was a grey fur ball, observing her through eyes the colour of Dijon mustard.

Beatrice gazed at the comfortable pair enjoying an afternoon nap together. She really must stop panicking every time he dozed off. His last check-up showed his heart was in very good shape and his cholesterol at tolerable levels. So if Matthew and Dumpling were both still alive and where they should be, where was the dog? A breeze blew through the conservatory door, which was sufficiently ajar to allow a determined terrier to slip through. The house phone rang from the hallway. Neither of the old chaps moved. She returned indoors to answer the call.

"Hello?"

"Hello, Beatrice. This is Lisa from Hazeltree Farm. Just wanted to let you know we've got your dog. She wandered into the yard earlier and I thought I recognised her. Jack checked her collar and sure enough, it's your Huggy Bear."

"Really? Oh thank you so much, Lisa. I've just got home myself. That animal is an escapologist. I'll put some shoes on and walk over to get her."

"No need for that. I'm sending the girls round with a couple of jars of my homemade pickle. They'll bring the dog back to you."

"You are extremely kind, thank you. I'm sorry for the inconvenience."

"No need for that. I'd just be a bit careful, you know how these boy racers tear round the lanes. She's such a dear little thing. Give my best to Matthew and if I can have those jars back when you're done, I'd be grateful."

"Will do and thank you so much." Beatrice replaced the receiver, ashamed of her negative attitudes to village life.

While she awaited the return of the errant mutt, Beatrice set about preparing a ploughman's lunch to go with Lisa's homemade pickle. Bread and cheese were all very well, but it had to be accompanied by a decent salad. She was determined to ensure Matthew consumed his five a day, for the sake of his health. She washed some lettuce, chopped tomatoes, cucumber, celery and apple, fished out a couple of pickled onions each and arranged them around each slab of cheddar. She heated the oven and while a crusty baguette was warming, she checked her emails. She was just printing one particular query to study further when the doorbell rang.

Kayleigh and the other one whose name Beatrice could never remember delivered the dog and the pickle, with shy smiles. They seemed reluctant to say goodbye to Huggy Bear, so Beatrice assured them they could take her for a walk any time they liked. After they'd gone, Matthew came wandering into the kitchen, obviously awoken by the doorbell.

"Oh, I say, a ploughman's lunch. That looks just the ticket. I worked up quite an appetite doing the weeding this morning."

"Hence the bacon sandwich and the nap, I assume."

"Guilty as charged. Who was at the door?"

"The girls from Hazeltree Farm bringing Huggy Bear home. From now on, you can't leave her out in the garden unattended. You know what a Houdini she is."

Matthew looked down at the dog, wagging her tail at him. "Did you run off again, you naughty girl?" The dog's ears softened into the canine equivalent of a smile and the tail wagged faster.

Beatrice suspected Matthew wasn't the only one who'd had bacon for elevenses. "She always ends up at one of the farms. Full of fascinating pongs, I suppose. The problem is that means her crossing the lane at some point, which is dangerous. Do you want apple juice or water?"

"Juice, please. The thing is, I thought she was asleep beside me. The three of us had a nice sit down with the paper and I must have nodded off. I apologise for not keeping an eye on her and I'll be sure to close the door next time. How was your trip to Exeter?"

Beatrice washed her hands and they sat at the kitchen table to eat. "I have excellent long-range vision for a woman my age, but I now need reading glasses. *Bon appétit.*"

"*Bon appétit.* Personally, I think it's remarkable you haven't needed them before. I had my first pair in my twenties. All that poring over textbooks as an earnest youth took its toll. Though I wasn't asking about the optician. How did the client take your report? Was he satisfied?"

Beatrice watched him as he added salad dressing. Healthy vegetables would be a great deal less healthy if slathered with an oily sauce. He seemed to sense her gaze and limited himself to a modest drizzle.

"I wouldn't say satisfied, exactly. He accepted my findings and is prepared to pay me for my work. Yet he is still convinced his wife is deceiving him, no matter how many assurances I gave the man. These infidelity cases are an awful bore, you know. Not just the lurking around, watching people go about their daily business, but the unhealthy green-eyed monster that drives decent folk to suspect their loved ones. It's all very depressing."

"I imagine it would be. This pickle is excellent. Very fruity. Well, you don't have to do those jobs if you don't want to. You're your own boss. Choose the fun ones and pass on the rest."

Beatrice seized her moment. "There is something rather more interesting on offer, in fact. Have a look at this." She reached behind her for a print-out and passed it to him.

```
To: admin@beatrice-stubbs.com
From: BrunoStarieri@mailshot.it
Subject: Mandate

Dear Beatrice
I hope you are well. I don't know if you
remember me, the junior chef at Ecco in
```

Napoli? My sister Chantal and I have left the
restaurant now and opened our own business.
Not in the restaurant trade, but as app
developers for the tourism industry.
Earlier this year, you solved the problem of
the spy in Ecco's kitchen. Everyone was very
happy you helped us and reunited the Colacino
family. Sadly, our joy did not last long. My
uncle Gennaio was killed in Hungary a few
months later.
That is the reason for writing to you. The
police in Budapest are not pursuing the case
of my uncle's murder. Their opinion is that he
got into a fight and lost. Chantal and I are
convinced his death was connected to the
people behind the copycat restaurants. We owe
Gennaio. We want to know how and why he died.
Chantal and I would like to ask you to
investigate. We are doing well and can pay
your fees and expenses. Could you go to
Budapest and see if you can find anything the
police missed? Just to be clear, if you do
find something, we would insist the police
must re-open this case. We are not looking for
something like personal vengeance.
I look forward to hearing from you and send
you warm regards from Naples.
Bruno & Chantal

Matthew's eyes roamed over the page as he absently ate some
bread. Beatrice waited till he had finished reading before
looking at him expectantly.

"More interesting, indeed, but a bit of a leap from stalking
unfaithful spouses. This sounds like a rather dangerous
assignment. One which is more than likely to stir up a hornet's
nest."

"Yes, and with very little to go on, I'd feel bad about taking
these young people's money. If the police aren't bothered, I really

don't see why I'd be any more effective. But still ...."

Matthew watched her, biting into a pickled onion.

She focused on trying to articulate her feelings. "The thing is, this was someone I knew. When I was with the Met, there were so many bodies, so much death, I became not exactly inured to it, but I tried not to take it to heart. This is personal. I actually liked Gennaio Colacino." Her mind took her back to a café in Naples, sitting opposite the big man as he tore open a packet of sugar. She could almost smell his aftershave and feel his rough whiskers as he kissed her on both cheeks. She pictured him in his bright red Ferrari, tooting his horn in farewell.

"Not only that, it's a loose end," Beatrice continued. "I solved the Naples case and found the spy in the kitchen. After the police arrests, we assumed they were the people pulling strings. Case closed. But what if we only cut down the weeds and left the roots intact? Or only routed half the rats' nest so they could regroup and attack the deserter later?"

"Can we limit our metaphors to one theme at a time? Horticultural, zoological *or* military? I would say your hypothesis merely reinforces my point. If you only caught the foot soldiers, there is a far more powerful general steering the troops. That would be a job for an opposing army, not a single veteran without heavy artillery. Do you really want to engage with such people?"

Dumpling sashayed into the kitchen, sat at Matthew's feet and emitted a silent miaow. The signs were clear. A detective's powers of deduction could be honed at home as well as at work.

"Look me in the eye, Matthew Bailey, and tell me you have not been feeding these animals from the table."

Matthew busied himself with a forkful of salad. "There may have been one or two scraps which fell to the floor. By the way, what's the plan for the weekend and our visitors? Given Derek's model railway enthusiasm, I wondered if I might invite him along to the Railway Centre at Tiverton. Take my grandson along too and get him out from under Tanya's feet. The summer holidays can drag on a bit for working mums. The other advantage would be that you and Dawn have a few hours to chat."

"That is a marvellous idea. Derek and Luke would enjoy that enormously and I'd appreciate some quality time to catch up on all the gossip from the Met. But that deflection, deft as it was, does not address my question. Do we encourage bad habits and begging from our animals, or do we separate human and animal food, thereby giving ourselves peace at the dinner table?"

Matthew dabbed up the remaining pickle with the crust of his baguette. "Point taken. Lax behaviour on my part. Won't happen again. Do you know, Lisa's pickle is head and shoulders above any other I've eaten. I hope she enters it in the village show. Now then, what about this case?"

Beatrice thought about it, watching butterflies flitter across the garden. It was a frightening prospect to go after some sort of criminal syndicate who would coerce, bully, threaten, kidnap and even kill. "At this stage, I'll just ask for more information."

Matthew shook his head. "I think we all know what that means. Thank you very much for lunch. I'm off to research the Railway Centre and ask Tanya if I can borrow my grandson."

Chapter 2

Temple Bar in Dublin was an unholy drunken mess. Underdressed girls cackling and falling over in the street, groups of men grunting like apes as they gulped down pint after pint, clashing music from opposing bars and neon signs inviting 2-4-1 shots to help people lose their faculties as fast and cheaply as possible. The whole scene repelled him.

He took a right up a side street and unfolded his map. No location services, no satellite data, no mobile phone. Not for Davor Vida. A professional leaves no trace. If anyone needs to contact Le Fantôme, they know what to do.

The private club stood on Sycamore Street, just across from the Olympia Theatre. A small plaque announced its presence with nothing more than a number. He pressed the buzzer and gave his alias, as instructed. The door creaked open to reveal a staircase lit with green sconce lights between portraits of Ireland's literati. Of course.

He climbed the steps, ignoring sketches of Wilde, Yeats, and Synge, but stopped for a second to look at a likeness of Samuel Beckett, a face that held a thousand years and still more stories. Before he reached for the handle, the door swung open and a maître d'hôtel welcomed him in, offering to take his coat.

Davor refused and scanned the room for his host. With a jolt, he saw she was not alone. He recognised her companion and his significance. This meant one of two things: either a major job or a gold watch and lots of platitudes about many years of loyal service. He weighed up the pros and cons of both and found himself ambivalent.

She saw him approach and got to her feet for the greeting kisses, her ice-blue eyes reflecting the Art Deco table lamps. Even though it was obvious he knew the man beside her if only by sight, she performed the introductions. No one used their real names.

Davor sat, folding his coat behind him, his face impassive. None of the photographs he had seen of this man really did him justice. In real life, he was uglier than Davor had imagined. His mouth seemed permanently set in a sneer so that an attempt at a smile came across as baring his teeth. Seems money can't buy you everything.

One waiter brought champagne and another canapés. Madame de Beauvoir began reminiscing. The first time she'd hired him. How long ago that was! He must remember the Algerian job, where they barely escaped with their lives. If it hadn't been for his skill as a pilot and that borrowed Cessna, she wouldn't be here today. Davor returned every serve with an easy lob. The years had gone by so fast! How was it possible she still looked so young and beautiful? Algeria was such a crazy mission! They used to be so naïve. She surely had not forgotten the incident in Oslo? He still couldn't believe they managed to get away with that.

No one mentioned Odessa.

Her laughter and clapped hands drew unsubtle attention from the quiet tables around the room. They lapsed into silence, as if recalling more adventures from the past, while Davor waited for the inevitable. To his surprise, the man spoke first, his accent confirming his identity like a designer label.

"Monsieur Le Fantôme, I want to thank you. As an organisation, we are forever in your debt. You have been a loyal servant and we would like to offer you a token of our gratitude for your many years of service. Your most recent task was a masterpiece."

Davor lifted his chin, as if requiring clarification.

"You are too modest. I refer to the job in Budapest; the retirement of Mr Genet. That particular situation could have become very awkward for all of us. I am grateful to you and Madame de Beauvoir for tying up all loose ends."

De Beauvoir shook her blonde hair in an affectation of modesty, but her glacier eyes flashed satisfaction. "That was all Le Fantôme here. All I did was arrange the timing. He is a master of his craft. And talking of craft ..."

Her partner picked up his cue. These two were a slick team, slithery as a pair of snakes. Davor wondered if they were sleeping together. More than likely and sooner or later one would get bitten.

"We know you want to retire, and I mean that in the real sense of the word."

Everyone laughed as if killing people was the funniest joke of them all.

She took over. "We think now is the right time. It would be better for all of us if you left the scene, permanently. Go back to your country. Buy some land, keep chickens, and grow vegetables."

The unattractive aristocrat handed over a slim envelope. "This is the code to access your retirement fund. Our only request is this: should you ever find yourself the subject of questioning by any authority, you have never heard of Madame de Beauvoir, Monsieur Genet and never in your life encountered Monsieur de Maupassant. Is that acceptable to you?"

Davor scooped up the envelope and shook the man's hand. He turned to his boss and clasped her hand in some semblance of gratitude. Her nails and jewellery pressed uncomfortably into his flesh. "It has been a pleasure working with you. My memory is now wiped and I will retire to the coast, go fishing and as you say, grow vegetables. I thank you both and give you my assurance you will never see or hear from me again. Good evening to you."

Outside, people hurried for shelter from the sudden downpour. Davor lifted his face to the sky, allowing the rain of Dublin to wash him clean.

Chapter 3

On Saturday morning, Matthew and Derek left Beatrice and Dawn amongst the detritus of breakfast and departed to collect Luke for their excursion. The two women cleared up in companionable silence, then donned their walking boots. Huggy Bear danced and skipped in excitement until Beatrice eventually clipped on her lead.

"I thought a tramp over the meadows, cut through the woods and into the village, then down to the river and walk along the bank to Brampford Speke. That's where Matthew used to live. It has a rather picturesque pub where we could stop for lunch. If we're still feeling energetic after a glass of wine and some sustenance, we can walk home the direct route. Or if we've had enough, we can call the chaps to pick us up on the way back from the Railway Centre."

Dawn put on her sunglasses. "Sounds perfect. Especially the wine. Let's go!"

The August weather was kind enough to show the countryside at its most splendid. Dog roses decorated the hedgerows, butterflies skimmed the wildflowers and the sound of crickets and bees provided a busy soundtrack to their walk. The sky was a promising shade of blue with only occasional white clouds floating by, like puffs from a gigantic pipe. Once released, Huggy Bear charged ahead, sniffing and stopping and scampering about in delight. Dawn paused at the crest of a hill to survey the view.

"You are so lucky, living here. I've been in Devon, what, not even twenty-four hours and I already feel chilled out. It's so peaceful."

"It is," agreed Beatrice. "This place certainly works its magic. Although it's a different story in winter. Even then, I can honestly say I don't miss London at all. The people, yes, but the place?" She shook her head.

They climbed over a stile and followed a path into the woods. The coolness of the leafy canopy came as a pleasant relief after the warm morning sunshine, and patches of light patterned the undergrowth. Dawn pushed up her sunglasses and inhaled deeply.

She looked happy and relaxed. Beatrice smiled too, pleased her friend had found such fulfilment in life.

"Now the chaps aren't here, we're allowed to talk shop," said Beatrice. "How's the Met?"

"I'd say there's been an improvement in the last year. And before you say it, that has nothing to do with your leaving. More like Ranga is steering us in the right direction. Still under-resourced and struggling to keep on top of the paperwork, but crime figures are down for the fourth month in a row. The new DCI is a woman and we have three fresh detective sergeants on the team. Which reminds me, one of them asked me to pass on his regards – Ty Grant from BTP?"

"Oh yes, I remember him from when I worked that sex offender case. So another white rugby-playing man on the team?"

"Yeah, him and Cooper are peas in a pod. But the other two are a young black guy from Bristol and an Asian woman who transferred from Birmingham. All bright and eager, which makes for a pretty good atmosphere. It's getting better. Now I want to hear how the agency is going. Have you heard any more about that Budapest case?"

"Funny you should mention that. Yes, I have."

A volley of barking echoed around the wood and Beatrice called the dog. As they turned the corner, a woman with a muddy Dalmatian was approaching from the opposite direction. Huggy Bear barked at them as if she owned the forest. Neither the woman nor the spotty dog seemed intimidated.

"Hello, Beatrice!" The woman waved.

"Hello, Demelza! Huggy Bear, will you ever shut up!"

The woman drew closer, her long fringed dress giving her the air of an earth mother at Woodstock. She crouched down and made a fuss of Huggy Bear, who wriggled with delight and jumped up for more, all ferocity forgotten. The woman lifted her forget-me-not eyes to them. "Isn't it a glorious morning?"

"Beautiful," agreed Beatrice. "Just the way the weather should behave when one has guests visiting from London. Demelza, this is my friend Dawn, who worked with me at the Met. Dawn, this is Demelza who lives in the village and runs the local book club. And this is Poldark. Where on earth have you been, you dirty dog?"

Poldark sniffed Beatrice's hand and sauntered off to pee on an oak tree.

"Hello, Dawn, nice to meet you. Oh, he gets into that cattle crossing by the river. I keep meaning to put him on the lead when we get down there, but I always forget and next thing I know, he's up to his neck in mud and cowpats. He'll have a swim in the pond before I take him home. Are you going to The Angel for lunch?"

"We've not decided yet. Just off for a wander and see where we end up. Enjoy your walk!"

"Same to you. Dawn, I hope you like Devon. Poldark, come on now!"

Dawn thanked her and they moved on, Huggy Bear leading the way.

"Were you being vague or evasive just then?" Dawn asked. "I

thought we'd planned a route and a pub lunch."

"Both. I have an aversion to people knowing my business. Especially her. Pleasant as she is, that woman knows everything about everyone and has her very own jungle telegraph. That's one of the reasons I want to get some work outside the county of Devon. It's all far too close to home."

A stream gurgled and rushed over mossy stones, curving alongside the path as the two women turned downhill towards the village. Huggy Bear stopped for a quick drink then skittered ahead, tail aloft as if she were a tour guide with a flag.

"That's weird. I thought it would be exactly the opposite. Last week, I read an article which said one of the key factors to happiness is being a part of a community. Chatting to neighbours, getting involved in local activities, all that stuff is supposed to be good for your health. Let's face it, in London, no one cares if you live or die unless you're decomposing and causing a stink." Dawn stepped into single file behind Beatrice as the path narrowed.

"You know as well as I do that's a myth. Be honest, how many people in your area do you greet, know their names, look out for and trust to have your back? London is a series of little villages and communities, but in a city, you have a choice to form a network. In Upton St Nicholas, my only escape from enforced sociability is to take a job far from pub, market and book club."

The heat of the sunshine grew stronger as the woods came to an end and they walked in thoughtful silence into the village. Beatrice pointed out features of interest while exchanging occasional greetings with passers-by. Huggy Bear led them along a winding path down to the river and only once they were clear of dwellings did conversation resume.

"Something tells me," said Dawn, "that you're justifying yourself. That Budapest gig is a job you want. You're building an argument for taking it. Come on, Beatrice, tell your Auntie Dawn the whole story."

The whole story took them all along the riverbank, past ducks and coots threading their way through beds of reeds. It lasted as far as the village of Brampford Speke, into the pub to order food and out into the garden with two glasses of white wine and a bowl of water for the dog. Only then did Beatrice come to the end of her explanation.

Dawn took a tube from her bag and applied sunscreen to her face. She offered it to Beatrice, who refused, trusting her wide-brimmed hat and shaded position under the umbrella to protect her. She dug around in her bag and found a chew for Huggy Bear, ensuring their conversation would be uninterrupted.

"My feeling is you should see these as two different things," Dawn said, her voice soft to thwart eavesdroppers. "Naples? Case solved and filed away. The Budapest investigation? The client can afford you, the job is not particularly complicated and so long as you keep personal emotions out of it, it ticks all the boxes. What does Matthew say?"

Beatrice's gaze swept the beer garden, with an innocent air of appreciation, while ensuring no one she knew was in earshot. "He'd prefer me to investigate cases of vegetable sabotage in the village show rather than homicide in Hungary, but in his heart, he wants me to do what makes me happy. He knows my passion lies somewhere far from giant marrows."

"In that case, go for it. If you need any official stuff that I can swing without losing my job, let me know. Other than that, PI Stubbs, all I can say is good luck! Down the hatch!" She lifted her glass to catch the sunlight.

"Down the hatch! Ooh, and here's the food. That looks delicious! I fancy yours even more than mine. Isn't it always the way?"

"Yours looks pretty tasty to me. Let's share – half and half and the chips between us."

"DI Whittaker, you are one of my favourite people on the planet."

Chapter 4

For the first time in his life, Davor had a routine he enjoyed. Get up with the light, make coffee and sit on the garden chair to watch the day wake. Since retiring, he'd given up smoking and didn't miss it at all. It used to be a handy cover, while waiting for a target outside a restaurant or bar, but it was a habit he no longer needed. When the nicotine urge niggled, he inhaled the air of Mljet Island and asked himself why he would put anything else into his lungs.

While the morning remained mild, he watered his vegetable patch with a sense of pride. Duties completed, he dressed in linen trousers and a comfortable shirt, slipped his feet into sandals and walked down into town for breakfast. Neighbours and shopkeepers greeted him with a wave and a smile, unaware of the effect their casual gestures had on the recipient. He loved them. Every smile, comment and handshake was an embrace, a welcome home.

Stray cats threaded between his legs, their memories reliably informing them he was a soft touch. He bought bread, fish and oranges, ate a pastry with another coffee overlooking the harbour and joined in a debate with three fishermen beneath a café awning. Walking home, he couldn't recall the detail, but knew they were all in complete disgusted agreement about the state of the Dalmatian Coast. Cruise ships, tourism and a government whose record on environmental issues was dire all bore part of the blame. The result was shocking levels of pollution on the white sands and in the clear blue waters of the Adriatic's hottest new destination. As for Split, one could hardly move through the streets due to the swarms of tourists everywhere. Croatia was cool, apparently. Not for the residents, it wasn't.

Davor wiped his forehead. The strength of the morning sun made the uphill stroll past the church sweaty work. His fitness levels had sunk since he stopped work. Who cared? His body and his time belonged to no one else but himself.

When he got back to his cottage, he put his purchases away, showered, shaved and changed into his city clothes. Thursdays he made his weekly trip to Dubrovnik. Another routine he enjoyed. He would withdraw some cash, make some purchases, eat lunch and play chess with his old acquaintance, Tomislav. Always a pleasure. Finally, he would stop by an Internet café to check his messages and catch the ferry home.

Tomislav thrashed him. Three times in a row and so easily it was no fun, not even for the winner. As was their agreement, the loser picked up the tab. Tomislav thanked him, packed up his board and pieces and left with a handshake. They never discussed their personal lives; it was an unspoken agreement. Even if he had been a close confidant, if Davor could imagine such a thing, there were no words to describe the confusion raging in his head.

He should have stuck to his routine. Go to the Internet café *after* lunch. As it was, he'd stayed far longer and paid for more than his allotted hour, checking out website after website to find the meaning behind his online demise. He'd arrived at the café unforgivably late and was surprised to see his bearded friend still waiting. They ordered food, he played some amateurish chess and managed about three mouthfuls of his sandwich. If

Tomislav returned next week to pit his wits against the witless, Davor would be amazed.

He paid the bill and paced away towards the ferry port, barely conscious of the crowds ebbing and flowing around him. In all his years as an agent, he'd used the same point of contact. Letty Louise. A profile on a social media site, with a Photoshopped image of an older woman hugging a dog. You couldn't see her face. She'd attended an average US university, didn't engage with politics, wished people Happy Holidays and posted mainly images of flowers or quotes from classic literature. He'd crafted that persona with great care. It was his mailbox.

When they needed him, they responded to one of his literary quotes.

Letty Louise: "Conscience, my dear, is a kind of stick that everyone picks up to thrash his neighbour with, but one he never uses against himself." (Balzac)

Simone D: That is so true. Balzac's words on personal morality should be a lesson to us all. "Whoever wishes to rise above the common level must be prepared for a great struggle and recoil before no obstacle."

That was his cue. Check in and find your next job.

There would be no more jobs, at least not from them. So something cold and hard slithered through his veins when he logged on and found this message.

```
Friends, it is with great sadness we have
to inform you that our beloved Letty passed on
this morning. Letty Louise lit up all our
lives and she will be sorely missed. We will
leave this account open for one more week for
people to pay tribute. Thank you, from Letty's
family xoxoxo
```

Letty had no family; she was the product of his imagination. No one had access to that account but him. If his online persona was dead, where did that leave him?

Chapter 5

Dionysus stood on Curtain Road, splendid in its individualism. Ionic columns adorned the doorway and marked each end of the shop. Although calling it a shop diminished the enterprise. Adrian had taken his team to Shoreditch, right in the thick of things. After selling Harvey's Wine Emporium to a Turkish carpet importer, Adrian grabbed all the possibilities the new premises had to offer.

Firstly, he renewed the previous owner's victualler's licence, enabling him to operate as an upmarket bar as well as a purveyor of fine wines. A few half columns became tables, a selection of stools lined the bar and Catinca, his Romanian assistant, called on all her hip and trendy friends to staff the place. Dionysus became *the* place to go. And in Shoreditch, everywhere wanted to be the place to go. Secondly, he issued a free quarterly magazine, delivered to local addresses, with wine recommendations for the season. Its beautiful design, expert advice and entertaining tone had endeared itself to the neighbours, encouraging them to explore the new place on the block. Dionysus burst onto the scene like a diva.

Beatrice admired the building from across the street. Her friends had done a marvellous job, or perhaps she should give credit where it was due. The look and feel of the place had Catinca's stamp all over it. No faux grapes and plastic vines, but stylish signage and a wonderful trompe-l'oeil half window. The top half was clear, showing whoever was sitting at the window bar from the waist up. Below the counter was a mural on the glass: togas, sandaled feet, nubile legs, fallen amphorae, hairy thighs and hooves. Bacchanalian undertones to excite curiosity. She itched to get inside.

"Beatrice!" Adrian called over as soon as she entered the room. He handed some change back to his customer and strode over to embrace her. "I've been on tenterhooks, wondering when you would arrive. What do you think? You shall have the guided tour but first I need to hear how you are. Would you like a glass of wine?"

"Adrian, it is quite wonderful." She meant it. The distressed wooden floor, white columns, displays of wine bottles and glittering bar made her almost giddy on the atmosphere. The lunchtime crowd was just thinning out and she could see the space for what it was. Jed, or it might have been Ezra, delivered a platter of olives and cheese to a couple by the window. Behind the bar, a young black man Beatrice didn't recognize poured a glass of something pinkish into a flute. Over in the shop half of the room, a pretty young girl showed two different bottles to an elderly gent who craned his neck to read the label.

"Yes, please, a glass of wine and time to acclimatise. This is a whole different experience," she said, her admiration heartfelt.

All the staff wore white shirts, black ties, long green aprons and black trousers. Except Adrian, in a black suit and green tie. Beatrice scanned the shop for Catinca and spotted a short female with an ornate hairdo, dressed in a sober green dress with short sleeves. She had her back to Beatrice, indicating out of the window to a customer, but one look at her Converse trainers confirmed her identity.

Adrian guided Beatrice to the bar. "Theo, this is my special guest, Beatrice Stubbs. Could we get that bottle out now?"

Theo, an exceptionally handsome sort of chap, gave her a

wide smile and reached over to shake her hand. "Heard a lot about you. Great to put a face to the name." His eyes flicked up to her hair.

Before she could reply, Adrian continued.

"I thought we'd go Hungarian in honour of your trip. We're having a bottle of Tokaji."

"Tokaji? Isn't that sweet?"

"Not this one. It's as dry as they come. Theo, could we also have an extra glass and a nibbles platter? Thanks."

Theo poured three measures and as if summoned by the sound of a filling glass, Catinca arrived, arms spread wide for a hug. "Beatrice! Where you been? Not seen you for ages."

Beatrice embraced her warmly. "It has been a while since I last came to London. Your hair looks amazing. All those plaits!"

Catinca hopped up onto a stool beside her. "Celtic, innit. Took sodding ages, I can tell you. What do you think of this place, then?"

"Stunning. Whoever designed this must have an extraordinary eye."

Catinca gave her catlike smile and helped herself to an olive. "She's got two eyes and both of them extraordinary. Adrian let me handpick all staff for looks and personality. If I say so myself, I done a terrific job."

The barman had moved to serve customers at the other end, leaving Beatrice free to murmur, "Is he one of yours?"

"Gorgeous Theo? Yeah. Got a massive crush on him but business and pleasure, you know."

"Never stopped me," said Adrian.

Catinca laughed. "Nothing ever stopped you. Apart from Will." She pointed at the glasses, each wearing a mist of condensation. "Is one of them for me?"

"Yes, if you're off duty."

"I finished twenty minutes ago, mate. Jed and Tamsin got it covered. What we drinking?"

Adrian placed his hand over the label. "See if you can guess. Cheers, ladies!"

They toasted and Beatrice took a sip of the wheaty-coloured wine.

Catinca gave her glass a thoughtful sniff and then took a mouthful, rolling it around her tongue before swallowing. "Crisp structure, minerals, green apple, bone dry. I reckon it's German, Grüner Veltliner? Or maybe Riesling? It's not from the Alsace 'cos the bottle's the wrong shape, so probably Austrian."

"Not too far off. Next door. This is a Hungarian Furmint. I think it's rather special."

"Furmint? Nice."

"It really is. Very nice," said Beatrice. She put on her new glasses to read the label.

"Ooh, super specs! They suit you," said Adrian.

"Thank you. I think I'll pop into the Duty Free in Budapest airport and bring a bottle of this back for Matthew."

"What? You going to Hungary? When? What for?" Catinca demanded.

"I told you yesterday," said Adrian. "She's on a job." He spoke from the corner of his mouth. "The Body in the River."

Beatrice shook her head with a modest smile. "It's just for a couple of days, to see if there's anything the police have overlooked. His niece and nephew want some answers as to how their uncle died. My flight leaves at ten past five this afternoon."

"You have such a cool job! Always having adventures and going to gorgeous places," Catinca sighed.

"For the last month, I've been sitting in my car outside Tesco's, spying on some poor woman who was doing nothing more exciting than buying toilet roll. To be honest, I was getting well and truly fed up of the whole private investigation business till this came along. Talking of cool jobs, Adrian, is your handsome husband going to join us?"

Adrian grimaced. "He can't. Will had to go to Bromley to

investigate a suspected honour killing. Very nasty and definitely not cool. He sends his love and told me to invite you to dinner on Thursday, if you're not rushing straight back to Devon. You can stay over and break up the journey."

"Ooh, yes please! That would be much appreciated. Now, how about this guided tour?"

Adrian slid off his stool. "Let's go. You can bring your glass. Catinca, you coming?"

"Nah, mate. Seen it already. I'll stay here and flirt with Theo."

Beatrice followed her host back to the entrance so she could appreciate the full Dionysian experience. She hoped it would include something a bit more substantial than olives.

Chapter 6

Routine was your enemy. An agent had to be flexible, confounding expectations and slipping through the cracks. His awareness expanded in the assumption someone was watching. An expert agent, much like himself, but in all likelihood, younger, faster and better trained. He didn't look around for observers, but carried on pottering around the shops as if he were an unconcerned tourist on the hunt for souvenirs.

A designer dress shop caught his attention. One of those places which charge a month's salary for a wisp of something with a label. What interested him was that the shop was on the corner, which meant it must have more than one exit. He opened the door and expressed an interest in the summer kaftans. A whispered chat with the assistant resulted in an understanding nod. She brought him what seemed to be a patterned duvet cover with a hole for his head and pointed him in the direction of the changing rooms. Once he had changed, she looked him over with a critical eye and added a large floppy hat, some jewelled flip-flops, a silver bracelet and a woven beach bag for his clothes. In return, he counted out a blood-curdling amount of kuna, with a little extra for her help, and if necessary, silence. Ten minutes later, Davor emerged from the staff entrance onto the streets of Dubrovnik. Letty Louise lived again.

He used every element of his knowhow, ducking into doorways, hiding behind postcard carousels, doubling back and retreating to the rear of a dingy bar just to be sure no one was on his tail. Right next door, there was a bookshop. Davor slipped inside, browsing the racks until his heart rate decreased to normal. So few customers patronized the shop, he could observe every one. He made some rational calculations.

The only reason that social media account existed was as a point of contact for them or anyone else who wanted to employ him. Since he had worked exclusively for the company for years, no one else used it. Now the company no longer needed his services, why not just leave it alone? Why not leave him alone? No, he had been kidding himself they would allow him to retire in peace. With the information he had, he could bring down the whole organization. He was a loose end and they didn't like loose ends.

He had to think like them. If he were charged with eradicating an ex-agent, he would not attempt it on the tourist-thronged streets of Dubrovnik. A professional would wait till he was alone, perhaps walking through the woods of Mljet, cause a fall and job done. He couldn't go home. Davor had always been able to disappear when the need arose, hence his nickname: Le Fantôme. He had a range of identities to choose from and had certain safe places no one else knew about, not even them. The truly scary thing was, if they had hacked his social media accounts, where else had they accessed? His Croatian bank balance? The vault in the private bank? His secret account in Geneva?

If he wanted to stay alive, it was imperative to act fast. He left the bookshop and with great caution, moved along the street towards the bank. Navigating the cobbled streets in ladies' flip-flops was a challenge he had not previously encountered. He would not attempt to take any more money than he had withdrawn today from the PBZ local account. Instead, he reached the private bank without mishap and requested access to his vault. The employee who escorted him through the security procedure did not bat an eyelid at his client's attire, merely commenting on the weather.

The man left him alone in the room to open the vault. Davor kept his hands steady as he punched in his code, and the heavy steel door swung open. A huge exhalation escaped him when he saw it was all still there. The passports, the jewellery boxes, the gold ingots and the suitcase filled with dollar bills. Now he could afford to disappear, just like a phantom.

Chapter 7

The main reason Catinca loved hanging around Spitalfields Market was not the array of jewellery stalls, brightly coloured garments and fashion ideas, but the opportunity to feel local. She greeted the woman who made earrings out of feathers and stopped for a chat with the Rastafarian geezer selling top hats and bowlers. He fancied her, that much was obvious, but even such a boost to her ego failed to cheer her up.

It was time for a change. Her creative side was frustrated since she'd finished designing Dionysus. Yes, it was her idea to style the staff in uniforms, but that meant the assistant manager couldn't display her flair for fashion, limited as she was to boring green dresses. Her only outlet was her hair and make-up. She even had to wear black Converse trainers to meet her own dress code.

She ran her hand over some silk skirts with handkerchief hems, imagining how she could style the rest of the outfit. A turban or hair wrap, definitely, with some well-massive earrings. Chunky wooden bangles and statement necklace. Flat sandals would work best but not for someone her size. Otherwise she'd trip over the pool of fabric. It would need to be wedges to give her some height.

"We got that one in green, if you want to see?" said the punk who was managing the stall.

"Nah, mate. Sick to death of sodding green." She sauntered away to look at the vegan cosmetics and henna hand paint.

What was she doing with her life? When she'd arrived in London from Romania, her dreams of studying art and making a career had soon been smothered by the urgent need to get a job, eat and find somewhere to live. Now, she had her settled status to stay in Britain, so all those worries were in the past. She had a good job with responsibility and freedom to apply her design eye, with friendly colleagues in a cool part of town. She earned enough to afford a nice room in a shared house, had built herself a reputation as a fashion icon and enjoyed exploring London's cultural life with her mates. But ...

Was her future to be always Adrian's assistant in bigger and better shops? Become a sommelier at some flashy hotel? Find an internship at some interior design company? Or monetise her influencer status? She put back the cocoa bean butter she had no intention of buying and checked her watch. Ten past four.

Beatrice would be at the airport by now. Flying to Hungary, investigating an exciting case, doing something important and using her talents. Catinca was on her way back to work, a glorified waitress-cum-shop assistant whose talents were limited to wine displays.

She should eat something from one of the funky food stalls and get back for her evening shift. Instead, she pushed open the door of The English Restaurant, ordered a vegetable wrap and a beer, and sat down at a table to compose her resignation letter.

Adrian didn't take it well. "I don't understand. We're a team. We came up with this concept together, as partners. Why would you want to leave now, just when we're becoming a success? Is it the money? We can discuss that. Or if you're tired of the shop, you can deal with the bar instead. Catinca, you can't just hand in your notice. I feel like you're pulling the rug from under my feet."

His face showed shock, upset and desperation, she could see

that. He hadn't seen it coming. Nor had she till two hours ago.

"Mate, I am tired of shop. But also bored of bar. This is what notice is about. Not pulling rug but giving warning. I wanna move on is all. Wanna use my talents. You done me a massive favour and taught me everything about wine. Thing is, it's not what I want. You're flying, you don't need me no more."

"Of course I need you! Anyway, where would you go?"

Catinca's temper flared. "Already got an interview for new position. Will let you know Monday. Gotta get back to work now and sorry for being late this afternoon."

"Catinca!"

"What?"

"Is this something personal?"

She stopped and swallowed, trying to find the right words. "Personal? Yes, but in positive sense. You gave me a chance and now I'm brave enough to go further. You are best boss I ever had, Adrian, and also good mate. If I was lazy cow, I'd stay here forever, doing you nor me no favours. I'm not lazy cow. I got dreams. You know what that poet says?"

Adrian's voice was unsteady. "Tread softly because you tread on my dreams?"

"Nah. If you love somebody, set them free." She ran round the desk, hugged him fiercely and left the office before her tears gave her away.

Chapter 8

Lajos Bálint wore far too much aftershave.

When Beatrice's mother was alive, she had an expression for overly perfumed men: 'He smells like a pox-doctor's clerk!' An expression Beatrice had not heard used by anyone else, and which never failed to make people laugh.

The business associate of Gennaio Colacino, heavily scented as he was, had an affable manner and appeared perfectly happy to talk to a private investigator. Beatrice shook his hand and backed off to sit on the opposite side of his desk. Thankfully, the air conditioning pumped cool wafts onto the back of her neck, keeping Eau de Lajos at bay.

"So shocking! We did business for years, Mrs Stubbs." He pronounced it Stabbs. "A good man, hard negotiator, very good taste, I am sad for him and his family."

"Yes, his family are the ones who sent me to find out more. Can you tell me something about your business relationship? I understand he came here to buy spices, is that right?"

"Spices and herbs. All varieties of paprika, especially sweet and smoked. Also celery and caraway seeds. The dried peppers and thyme he liked very much and sold to his brother, the chef. He came back, every quarter. He knew quality product. Gennaio tested the samples and we drank a beer to seal the deal. He was a good man, I say again."

Beatrice pressed a knuckle to her nostrils, hoping it would come across as a thoughtful gesture. "The police seem to think he was in the wrong place at the wrong time. He went to a park where drug dealers operate and got killed in a fight."

"Rabbish! Why would a man whose nose and taste buds are the tools of his profession go looking for drags? I don't know why he went there that night, but Gennaio Colacino would never stick powders up his nose, smoke foul weeds and risk his livelihood. Tell me, Mrs Stabbs! The police? Pah! They know NATHING!"

The man's emphatic gestures puffed more of his aftershave in her direction, which mingled with the complex aromas of the spice factory. Her nose twitched with the peppery scent of paprika and a headache threatened to surface. In addition to it all, she could detect an intrusive odour of cat urine. When she got up to thank the man and make a break for fresh air, she noticed the litter tray in the corner. No wonder Mr Bálint needed a nosegay.

The police detective wasn't trying to be awkward, Beatrice could see that. There simply was nothing to tell. Gennaio Colacino had left his hotel on a Tuesday evening and taken a boat ride up the Danube. The boat company confirmed he had disembarked at *Kopasi gát*, a riverside park. On Wednesday morning, his body was spotted floating in the river. In addition to the knife wound to his throat, there was some facial bruising, damage to his hands and his neck was broken, presumably when he fell into the river. His wallet, phone and watch had all been taken. The area, family friendly and lively during the day, was less welcoming by night. The police were aware of at least one gang using the park to deal drugs and some individuals prowled the foliage looking for casual sex.

Considerable efforts had been made to find witnesses, without success. The detective understood the family's distress, of course, and was more than happy to share the report with Beatrice. That said, there wasn't much to share. He'd gone to an unsafe area at night, got into a fight and ended up dead.

She asked a few more questions, but learned little of value. She thanked the man for his patience and made her way to Keleti railway station in search of a cab. A queue of bright yellow taxis stood outside the terminal and she managed to convey her destination via a combination of badly pronounced Hungarian and pointing at her guidebook.

The driver, who was missing a finger, recognized the name. "*Igen, tudom.* I know. Is OK."

They drove along the busy shopping street of *Rákóczi út*, the driver humming along to something on the radio and Beatrice admiring the architecture. One of the things she loved about continental Europe was the way people live in the city centre. The ground floors of many of these five- and six-storey buildings were coffee shops, restaurants, chain stores and bars, but the upper floors were apartments. People leaning out of windows and sitting on balconies to hang out washing, water plants, drink a coffee or just watch the world go by made her feel warmly disposed towards the world.

Hotel Zenit was a good deal more plush and pricey than her own humble residence. She decided that if the staff were pleasant, she might have lunch there. This was her final meeting, and having got very little from Gennaio's business connection or the police, it was her last hope. Her flight was not until tomorrow afternoon, so she could still go and have a look at the park where he died. What good that would do, she had no idea.

The hotel manager, an elegant woman whose blonde hair was wound into the most fabulous forties-style roll, had been expecting her. With a firm handshake, she led Beatrice into the lounge area and ordered coffee for them both.

"I'm very grateful for your time, Ms Garas. To be honest, my enquiries so far have turned up very little to help further this investigation."

The woman's grey eyes were regretful. "Unfortunately, I am not able to add much either. Signor Colacino had stayed with us before, but other than the obvious contact details and food preferences, I can tell you nothing new. I printed all the information we have and the dates of his previous stays."

Beatrice tasted her coffee. It was outstanding. "That is extremely efficient of you. Was there anything unusual about this stay?"

The blonde head shook slowly. "Apart from the obvious, I don't think so. He always stayed two nights during the week. Every visit was for business meetings so he was only at the hotel to sleep and eat breakfast. He checked in on Tuesday morning and left shortly afterwards to see a supplier. He asked us to call him a taxi. That evening, he returned to the hotel to change and left again. The key card records show he did not return to his room after that. He was due to check out on Thursday morning but no one had seen him. It was fortunate that we did not need the room. Usually if a guest does not check out on time, we pack their things and put them in storage. When the police arrived on Thursday afternoon, I could assure them that his room had not been touched."

"When you order a taxi for someone, do you know their destination?" asked Beatrice.

"Not necessarily. But Signor Colacino was quite precise and gave us a business card with the address. He couldn't pronounce it, you see. He didn't know a single word of Hungarian." She slid a piece of paper from her plastic file and showed Beatrice the address.

It was exactly the same place Beatrice had visited that morning. The aromatic spice merchant who had told her nothing whatsoever.

Ms Garas could see her disappointment. "As I told the police, we cannot offer anything of value. I wish we could."

Beatrice wasn't listening. Her eyes had continued down the page until she noticed an entry which caught her interest. "Ms Garas, who is Charles?"

"I'm sorry?"

"This entry for the same day mentions the boat trip. 'Signor Colacino's motorboat will collect him from Dock 8 at 20.00. Arrangements made by (**charles**)' I just wondered if Charles was a hotel employee and if so, whether I could talk to him."

The manager turned the paper towards her, her puzzlement clearing as she read the entry. "Ah, I see. No, that's not an employee. Charles is an international concierge service."

Beatrice gave her a blank look.

"You haven't heard of international concierges? Wealthy individuals use this kind of company to get what they want when they want it, wherever they are in the world. You know how a concierge at a five-star hotel can usually help guests get tickets to a concert or an exhibition, secure a table at the best restaurants or source an evening gown at short notice? For example, our Zenit concierges have excellent local contacts, here in Budapest. Then there is another level: the international concierge service. These organisations have a far wider reach. They can get you tickets to a football game in Bogotá, fly your hairdresser from Milan to Los Angeles for an awards ceremony, source caterers, venue and top-level entertainers for a surprise party in Dubai, anything. Whatever you need, they deliver."

"Handy people to know," Beatrice observed. "I wouldn't imagine retaining such a company comes cheap."

Ms Garas smiled. "I couldn't say. All I know is the only time we communicate with such a VIP service is when big money is in residence."

Beatrice savoured the last mouthful, emptying her cup. "That was one of the best coffees I've ever drunk and I've tried plenty. Ms Garas, here's the thing. Gennaio Colacino was not short of cash. He had a thriving import business and drove a Ferrari. But is that what we would call 'big money' in terms of international concierges and so on?"

She leant forward, holding Beatrice's gaze. "No. Signor Colacino was not in that league. He didn't arrange for the pleasure boat. Someone else paid for that." She shook her head before Beatrice could articulate the question. "No, I don't know who and I never do. Charles sends the orders and we comply. Finding out who pays the bill is impossible."

"Thank you, Ms Garas. Did you share this information with the police?"

"Of course. They showed no interest. I'm sorry, Ms Stubbs, I must leave you now. Here is my card and you may contact me at any time. I will be happy to help and offer you more of our Hungarian coffee." She smiled and held out her hand.

Beatrice stood to thank her, a flicker of hope in her stomach for the first time since arriving in Budapest.

Chapter 9

Four hours out of Livorno and approaching the island of Corsica, Davor rose from his seat on the ferry. There was half an hour before they reached the port of Bastia. Travelling as Le Fantôme again, he wanted some insurance for a discreet border crossing. He looked around the deck to assess his options. The pickings were slim. Perhaps those two elderly ladies could be charmed into a conversation. Judging by their disapproving faces, it was unlikely to be worth the effort. He moved inside, avoiding the eyes of the Italian workmen when buying himself a beer. Small talk didn't interest him. He took his beer and returned to the outer deck, hoping for an innocent-looking group he could latch on to.

A shrill screech rent the afternoon air. A toddler having a tantrum. Perfect. That ruse had worked more times that he could remember. He softened his expression, gazing at the young French family with a kindly comprehension. A crying toddler could easily be distracted by magic tricks. For the exhausted father, an offer of water (paper cup filled with blonde beer) and a friendly wink. Sympathetic chit-chat with mama and nursing baby. His understanding treatment of the now tear-stained but silent child naturally led to enquiries about his own family.

His performance was rehearsed to perfection. "Twenty-three

years old, she was. Such a tragedy. I know I'm biased, but she was the most beautiful woman I've ever seen, apart from her mother. The train derailed and she was in the first carriage. She died with my grandchild in her arms." He blinked and creaked to his feet. "Treasure each moment with your beautiful family. I wish you luck and love."

"Stay!" called the young woman, her eyes watery. "Sit with us. Unless you are with friends?"

Davor turned, with a shake of his head. "No, I am alone. Thank you, madame, but I cannot intrude on your family's private time for longer." He gave a bow and reversed his step.

"Wait, please!" The father stood and reached out to catch his arm. "We are almost at Bastia. Sit with us. Good company is always a pleasure. Where do you stay in Corsica?"

Davor wavered for a second, and then sat with a grateful smile, caressing the toddler's sleepy face with his thumb. "I am a wanderer. Walking the trails, from village to town, staying wherever there is room."

They welcomed him into their small circle, offering recommendations and even an invitation to stay in their cottage. He demurred with great modesty, but allowed them to see his emotional reaction to such generosity. Latched on to this charming group and holding the hand of the chubby child, he attracted no attention and passed through immigration control as if he were a local. The affected sadness and bent posture remained until he bade his new friends farewell. Even then, he stayed in character, waiting for the bus, sitting quite still and watching every single person on the square. Outside, he was old, frail and unwell. Inside, he was smiling. Stage three of his journey was complete. He was now on French soil. Next stop Marseille and the hunt could begin.

Chapter 10

Business contact: nothing. Police: just the facts. Hotel: possible hint of a lead. Pleasure cruiser company: blank looks and downright rudeness. The night before, she'd spent four hours online (although twenty minutes of that was spent looking for her glasses) trying to find any mention of the international concierge company, and got no further than their website: a landing page with their lowercase name **(charles)** in black. The small print informed visitors the site could only be accessed by members and none of her devious techniques had dug up a contact address. Never had her lack of police authority been so frustrating.

After her complete failure at the boat rental place, she made up her mind to have a decent lunch before leaving for the airport. She deserved it after snacking on room service last night, meeting one dead end after another. This would not be added to expenses, but paid for herself. She would also write an honest report for Bruno and Chantal. There was the slimmest chance she could find who hired the boat which ferried Gennaio to his death, but she held out little hope. Her contract was for one week and then she'd be back to stalking housewives.

The friendly receptionist, who was just naturally helpful and would never describe herself as a concierge, recommended a local restaurant which served authentic Hungarian food. With an apologetic look, she warned Beatrice it had no frills. Good thing too. Beatrice loathed frills.

One classic goulash later, accompanied by a glass of Bull's Blood red, Beatrice took her leave of Budapest, intending to nap all the way back to London. Once checked in, she bought a bottle of Furmint for Matthew from the Duty Free shop and wandered through the press and souvenir stall, looking for something silly for Luke. A striking image on the front of a magazine caught her eye: yellow sails on blue water. The title of the publication was *The Cut Above* and it sat in a central position of the business section. The headlines advertising the contents told her all she needed to know about the consumer it was trying to attract.

NOTHING SAYS SUMMER LIKE VINTAGE CHAMPAGNE.

INSIDE THE RARE BOOK LIBRARY OF DESIGNER MERRYLINE O.

JETSET OR OFFSET? HOW TO SUPPORT THE PLANET *AND* YOUR LIFESTYLE.

MEET CRAD LLEWELLYN, LIFESTYLE MANAGEMENT GURU.

BACKSTAGE AT BASELWORLD: GEMS, TIMEPIECES AND THEIR CREATORS.

Merryline? Crad? What kind of names were those? Good job she didn't have to 'style' herself for today's market. *Bea S - P.I. Does what she says on the card.* She picked up the magazine in full knowledge it would trigger either envy or disgust.

Merryline O. had a collection of first printings and special editions in a purpose-built circular room. The glossy photographs showed off the books to best effect and Beatrice released an envious moan. Her own bookshelves were a well-thumbed but disorganised hotchpotch of paperbacks and research material. Posed and plastic as this designer woman seemed, her passion for the collection rang true. Each answer to the interviewer's questions revealed a little sparkle, engendering the same in her reader. Beatrice chose to pay the five Euros for this publication full of overpriced tat for people with too much money and very little taste, just to read the rest of the woman's opinions.

On the flight back to London, she finished the interview and made a note to look up this designer when she had a moment. Fashion held even less interest for her than rap music, but an intelligent mind should never be ignored. She flicked through the rest of the advertorials, her eyes drooping, and fell asleep. On landing, she took a taxi to her old address. It was always strange to come through her old front door and rather than trotting upstairs to home, let herself into her ex-neighbour's flat on the ground floor. Adrian and Will wouldn't be home for a few hours yet. They could enjoy a convivial dinner and she would stay overnight, before travelling home to Devon in the morning. She wished she had more to tell them. An uneventful business trip and only a tiniest sniff of a lead was nothing to celebrate. Whichever way she tried to spin it, the whole Budapest episode had been a damp squid.

That was the only trouble with Beatrice's Boudoir. Adrian and his husband Will kept their spare room so cosy and relaxing, she couldn't resist. She'd only lain down for a ten-minute rest after calling Matthew, but when she awoke to smells of cooking, two hours had passed. She sat up and checked herself in the mirror. A little puffy and crinkled after her nap, but perfectly presentable in front of her friends. The sleep had restored her to full strength and whatever they were cooking excited her appetite. She wriggled into her slippers and made for the kitchen.

Adrian was squeezing fresh limes and humming along to 'Some Enchanted Evening' when she came round the corner. As always, he looked fresh and fragrant in knee-length denim shorts and a short-sleeved white shirt.

"The traveller returns!" He washed his hands and came to kiss her on the cheek. "How was Budapest? Would you like a G&T?"

"Yes, please. What culinary creation are we having for dinner? If the smell is anything to go by, it's going to be heavenly."

"Aubergine and lemon tagine with almond couscous accompanied by mint yoghurt and grilled flatbreads. Will's running late but should be here by seven. I saw your door was closed so didn't disturb you." He poured a healthy measure of gin, added a slice of cucumber, two ice cubes and filled the rest of the glass with tonic. "Your aperitif, madame. Can we toast a successful trip to Hungary or not?"

"Not sure if it was successful, but I survived. Cheers!"

"Cheers! Have an olive or some grissini, you're bound to be starving. I'll just get this into the pot and we can chat."

Beatrice didn't need asking twice. She bit into a breadstick and hitched herself onto a stool, with a sense of homecoming. "Your new wine shop, or should I say wine bar, is a triumph, in my opinion. You and Catinca have done a fabulous job. The name Dionysus will be on everyone's lips as The Sensation of Shoreditch."

"Thank you. It's doing incredibly well, far better than I had expected. There's only one downside." He placed the lid on the pot and set it to simmer. "Catinca has resigned."

"No!" Beatrice refused to believe it. "What happened?"

He came to sit opposite her, his expression disconsolate. "I have no idea. She came back from lunch on Tuesday, the same day you were there, and handed in her notice. She said it was time to move on. Beatrice, I'm devastated. We built this business together. Even worse, she won't discuss her reasons for leaving or what her plans are. I know she has an interview in the morning, so I'll have to go in early to open the shop, but she won't say what job, which company, or why she wants to quit. It's been a horrible couple of days." He rubbed at his eye with a knuckle.

Beatrice caught his hand. "Don't do that. You've been chopping onions and that will really cause tears. When does she leave?"

"It's OK, I'm not crying. Not yet, anyway. She leaves at the end of the month and then I will be bawling my eyes out."

"Do you know anything about her job interview tomorrow?"

Adrian shrugged. "No idea at all. When I asked, she just said she would be back by lunchtime. I can't help asking myself where I went wrong. Why is she so unhappy she would want to leave?"

"Maybe she's not? It might be a case of wanting to strike out alone." Beatrice tried to stay positive.

"That's what Will says. He thinks she's planning on turning her influencer status into a career. She's certainly got a good basis for a platform, with over 5,000 Instagram followers."

Beatrice understood all the words but none of the content. They sipped their gins, both deep in thought until a key turned in the front door. For a second, Beatrice expected a volley of barks until she remembered Huggy Bear was 200 miles away.

No matter how tired, dishevelled or exhausted Will Quinn appeared, his good looks still struck a person like a Taser. He embraced her and kissed Adrian.

"Dinner smells like the dog's bollocks!" he said, sniffing the air.

"No canine testicles involved, I'm happy to say, it's all veggie," Adrian replied. "Beatrice and I are drinking G&Ts. Would you like one?"

"I'd love one. Just let me jump in the shower and change. Time to wash off the day. All well, Beatrice?"

"All very well, but I wouldn't mind knocking some ideas around, if you're up for it?"

"You know me, always up for it. Two minutes."

They watched him unbutton his shirt as he went to the

bathroom. Once the door closed, Beatrice looked at Adrian.

"You have an exceptionally handsome husband."

Adrian couldn't suppress a grin. "So does he. We know we're lucky buggers."

Unfortunately, Beatrice had just taken a swig of gin. The burst of laughter caused her to splutter all over the olives, grissini and chef.

The tagine was everything it promised to be and Beatrice devoured everything on her plate, accompanied by a boisterous Moroccan red. Will put all his energy and intelligence into Beatrice's situation, suggesting the Budapest force should pressure the concierge company to reveal the person or organisation behind the commission. As always, he played it by the book. Beatrice listened to his ideas with genuine attention, until she sensed Adrian becoming distracted.

"Adrian, you must be bored to tears of us talking cop. Let's change the subject. That tagine was one of the best meals I've enjoyed this week. Did I tell you about the goulash I had for lunch? I really think Hungarian cuisine has much to offer."

The conversation turned from murder to menus as they moved to the living room, ending as it always did, with the three of them designing their ideal imaginary restaurant. Observing their increasing efforts to stay awake, Beatrice thanked them for dinner and offered to wash up in the morning as both had an early start. She kissed them goodnight and retired to her room. Adrian placed a hand on her arm as she departed.

"Would you have a word with Catinca? She loves you and won't refuse you anything. All I want to know is why she wants to leave. Will and I can't get a word out of her, but you might."

"I promise to do my best." She meant it. She would call Catinca in the morning and ask if she would meet her for lunch.

The next morning, an odd flatness beset Beatrice. She lay in bed, trying to muster enough energy to shove off the duvet and clean up. There was only one thing to get her out of such inertia. Caffeine. She made herself a cappuccino at her hosts' whizzy machine and returned to bed for half an hour, listlessly flicking through the magazine she had bought in Budapest airport.

Bored, she skipped over the pages, until she came to a picture of a tanned, dark-haired man with flecks of grey at his temples surrounded by beautiful people in artificial poses. Very handsome and obviously airbrushed, his face nevertheless invited the reader's curiosity. What did he have to be so smug about?

"More than a concierge service. This is lifestyle management."

His company does not advertise, hides its presence and only accepts clients by personal invitation. Discretion makes (charles) highly desirable by those in the know.
Interview by Geneviève Baron-Heche. Photographs by Anton Verbier.

Crad Llewellyn relaxes on his Suffolk estate, surrounded by family, friends and partners invited from all over the world. International lifestyle management service **(charles)** *burst onto the luxe map three years ago and has snatched an impressive chunk of market share. Over a Long Island Iced Tea, Crad explains how one man with a network of contacts grew into a company of 2,000 partners and an annual turnover of $3bn.*

GBH: **You describe the 2,000 people who work for your company as partners. Why is that?**

CL: *I never use the word 'employee'. I call them partners. Multilingual, well-connected, agile, informed and adaptable,*

armed with local knowledge and an understanding of our clients'
needs, it's a partnership.
GBH: Presumably your partners can call on each other's
expertise?
CL: That's the beauty of it. Each client has a dedicated partner
who knows them so well; they can make suggestions and educated
guesses as to their preferences. I'll give you an example, imaginary
of course, as discretion is our USP. A New York property developer
has a particular interest in collecting Surrealist art. One of our
partners in Barcelona hears of an exclusive auction and puts out
the word on our network. The client partner in NYC alerts the
collector and she wants in. Invitation sourced, accommodation
arranged, transport and insurance for potential purchases
assessed. Everyone's happy.

"We give our clients the most precious thing in the world: Time."

GBH: Tell us a little about how one individual built such a
remarkable empire.
CL: I'm a networker. I'm a natural extrovert and cannot help
connecting people.

Beatrice had read enough. The sycophantic journalist whose
initials made her snort, the company's mission statement
regurgitated as answers and artificial photographs of the man
posing at his various properties turned her stomach. On the
other hand, she had found (**charles**). Time to pay Mr Llewellyn
and his partners a visit.

The excitement was like an electric shock. Twenty minutes
later, via Companies House, she had found the headquarters of
(**charles**) via the name of its CEO, complete with phone number,

email and London address. That was when she faltered. Sure, she could call and request an interview, but as what? She had no authority and no story to cover her. What possible reason on earth could persuade these people to tell her who had rented the Budapest boat? She was still thinking like a police officer, assuming she could apply her authority and insist on information. This kind of firm would only open the doors to an official request. She needed a copper. And as luck would have it, she knew a couple.

"London Metropolitan Police, DI Whittaker speaking?"

"Hello, Dawn, it's Beatrice. Can you talk?"

"Oh, hello! You back already?"

"Yes, and I have a lead. You know you said if I needed any official stuff, I could call on you? Well, I need a favour."

"What I said was, if you need any official stuff that I can swing *without losing my job*, you could call on me. What sort of favour?" Dawn sounded suspicious.

"Pay a visit to a company and try to get some information. It shouldn't take long. It's in Central London and I'd go myself but they won't tell an ordinary civilian anything."

"Where are you now?"

"At Adrian and Will's place. I'm heading back to Devon tonight."

"Why didn't you ask Will to do it? His ID is as solid as mine."

"For one thing, because he's only a DS and you're an inspector. And secondly, I nearly got him killed last time I asked him to use his police credentials to help in one of my private enquiries. Anyway, Will has strong principles and would probably refuse."

Dawn laughed. "Whereas I can be bought for a bottle of Chardonnay? All right. Give me the intel and tell me what you need."

"Two bottles, at the very least. Right, have you got a pen?"

Chapter 11

Catinca walked up and down Old Street, killing time before her nine o'clock appointment. She kept checking her reflection in shop windows. Tricky to know what to wear for an interview like this. She had to be smart, professional and look like she could handle herself. Wouldn't hurt to have a bit of style at the same time.

Although the M&S suit was well square and too hot in this weather, it did make her look like she had a proper job. At least she'd kept the Celtic braids and would never give up her Converse trainers. Her stomach grumbled. She hadn't eaten anything this morning, too nervous about what was to come and how hard she would have to work to get this job.

She checked the time on her phone. 08.50. Time to go. It wasn't a question of being late as she had assigned the hour herself. Nine am was not too early to wake a potential employer and not too late so as to miss her interviewer altogether. She paced up the road and turned into Boot Street, arriving at the squat block of flats on the stroke of nine. She rang the bell of the ground floor flat.

Several seconds went by and then the front door opened. There stood Beatrice Stubbs, wearing a pinny and holding a tea towel. Her face was a picture of surprise.

"Catinca?"

"Morning, Beatrice. I've come about a job. I want to work for you, as a private detective."

Beatrice stared at her for a second then stood aside. "You'd better come inside."

Catinca sat at the breakfast bar while Beatrice made two cups of coffee. She waited till Beatrice placed the cappuccino in front of her, noting the pretty pattern she had made in the foam, and sat on the opposite side. Then she began her speech.

"I know what you're gonna say. There is no job. You can't afford to employ an assistant. There's no way you can steal Adrian's staff. I have no experience as detective. Private investigation is not as sexy as it sounds. I know all of that. But listen."

Beatrice didn't get a chance to interrupt. Catinca steamrollered on, determined to flatten all objections.

"I'm leaving Dionysus anyway. Had enough and wanna try something different. If you don't give me a job, I'll find another one. Not selling wine, though."

Beatrice studied her face. "I didn't realise you were unhappy working for Adrian."

"I'm not, mate. Just gone as far as I can and wanna move on. I come to this country with big ideas, see, so it's time to do something about them. I told him that, but he don't believe me. He got Will to try and find out real reason I wanna leave." She shook her head in exasperation. "Real reason is simple. Time for a change."

Beatrice scooped some foam off her cappuccino. "Fair enough. The thing is, you're right. I can't afford an assistant, you don't have any experience and it really is the exact opposite of sexy. Not only that but you live in London and I live in Devon. How would any kind of assistance work?"

Catinca gave her a scornful look. "You ever heard of virtual teams? Is all about communication, mate. I could be in Guatemala and you in Devon and I could still be great asset. So here's proposal. Trial run. I got three weeks' notice to work at shop. On the side, I work as your assistant. Find out information, track people down, file paperwork, whatever you need. I'm good with technology. You don't need to pay me. After three weeks, if I been useful and earned us some money, you take me on. I learn fast, ask Adrian, and I already done my research. Read up all about the body in the river. Not that there's much to read, but I know what you're working on."

The silence stretched on as Beatrice pressed the bridge of her nose between forefinger and thumb.

"What do you say, mate? Give me a chance?"

"I'm sorry, Catinca." Beatrice shook her head. "It just wouldn't work. I can barely manage to organise myself. Finding work for you would be another whole task for me. So rather than an assistant taking some of the strain, I'd have more work. Not to mention the employment laws and legal status of the agency."

"I can do boring jobs. I do surveillance outside Tesco's, I organize own self. Legal status, you employ me like you employ cleaner. All official, all ..."

Beatrice's mobile buzzed into life. She grabbed it and looked at the screen. "Excuse me, I have to take this. Hello, Dawn? ... Have you? Well done! What time is that? ... Sorry, how do you mean? ... I see." Her eyes stopped their flicking around the room and rested on Catinca. "Can you hold a second? I might just have an idea." She muted the phone and asked, "Is Romanian anything like Hungarian?"

"No. Totally different languages. I should know. Mum was Romanian, Dad from Hungary."

"Can you speak any Hungarian? Because I might just have a job for you."

A thrill rushed through Catinca. "*Biztosan!*" She gave Beatrice a double thumbs-up.

"Dawn, can you meet Catinca and myself half an hour before your appointment and we can work something out? ... Excellent, see you there. And I owe you an entire case of

Chardonnay." She ended the call and held out her hand. "I must be out of my mind, but OK, let's give this a try. You are on trial as my assistant for the next three weeks. God knows what we're going to tell Adrian."

A black cab delivered them to Fitzrovia and Beatrice asked the driver for a receipt. A blonde woman in an even naffer suit than Catinca's was waiting outside The Hunter's Moon pub. The area was posh and clean – the London of the movies – and nothing like the East End areas Catinca knew.

Beatrice motioned them to sit at an outside table. The pub wasn't open yet, so no one would bother them for sitting down and having a chat.

"Dawn, this is Catinca. Catinca, Dawn." Catinca reached out a hand and Dawn took it with a friendly smile.

"All right, Catinca? You're the Hungarian, right?"

"No, Romanian, but I can speak and understand Hungarian. Learnt from Magyar father. Mostly swearing."

Dawn laughed. "First thing everyone learns in another language. Hello, how are you, another beer, piss off. Right, Beatrice, how are we playing this?"

"When you told me the concierge company have agreed to talk to the police but don't understand why the Met is involved, I had a thought. It's a good point and the last thing we want is for our questions to look fishy. Catinca is now Ms Radu from the Budapest CID or the equivalent. She speaks no English. You have to translate for her."

"What about her ID?"

"Do you happen to have your passport on you?" Beatrice asked Catinca.

Catinca lifted her shoulders to her ears. "Whatchoo think? Don't normally need it to get on the Northern line."

"Hmm. OK, Dawn, just flash yours and be impatient. Maybe they won't ask to see both. Catinca will say some things in

Hungarian and you ask the questions as if on her behalf. Let's try a rehearsal. Catinca, say something to Dawn."

"*Ez a szoknya kényelmetlen.*"

Dawn nodded with a slow blink and turned to Beatrice. "Detective Radu would like to discuss a recent case of murder."

"Sounds plausible to me," said Beatrice. "What did you actually say, Catinca?"

"This skirt is uncomfortable."

Dawn laughed and smacked her palms onto the wooden table. "That works. Unless whoever we're meeting speaks Hungarian. What if I need to say something to you?"

Catinca thought for a moment. "Say *Más valamit*. It means 'anything else'. Pronounced like Maash Walameet. You try."

"Maarsh walamit. Will that do?"

"Yeah, you sound like a Magyar-speaking Brit. What if they do speak Hungarian?"

"That's a risk we'll have to take. If they do, Catinca, you'll have to step up and play detective. We need to know who hired that boat for Gennaio Colacino. Pull the 'just eliminating people from our enquiries' and don't make it too heavy. Get me a name and get out."

"Got it. Where shall we meet for a debrief?" asked Dawn.

"The Sanctuary Bar, just off Grosvenor Square. Midday. Three executive ladies having lunch. Anyone following us would need to be smart and suited or they'll stand out like a toad in the bath. Right, off you go and good luck!"

Catinca followed Dawn through the traffic, her palms sweaty and her pulse causing a flicker at her collarbone. They arrived early and stood around the corner in the gateway to a pretty park, where Catinca took the chance to teach Dawn the words for yes and no in Hungarian. Somehow her senses were heightened. Everything seemed sharper, more detailed, louder and more colourful. At eleven o'clock exactly, they stood at the impressive-looking portico. Dawn scanned the shiny black door with lion's head knocker and pressed the bell to her right. The name badge beside it was brass and had one word engraved on it: **(charles)**.

"Good morning?" a female voice came from the speaker and Catinca looked up at the small black ball above their heads.

"Good morning. DI Whittaker and Ms Radu. We have an appointment to see Mr Llewellyn at eleven."

"Come in. Reception is on the right." A buzzer released the door and Dawn pushed her way in, Catinca on her heels.

The hall was carpeted with a dark grey weave which seemed to swallow all sound. Another glossy black door stood open to their right, giving them a view of a bright room with several curving desks. Dawn withdrew her ID and walked into the room, head held high.

A young woman rose to meet them, dressed entirely in black. Her face was smoothly contoured and she wore her long dark hair in a sleek plait.

"Good morning, officers." She gave Dawn's ID a brisk glance. "I'm afraid Mr Llewellyn has been called away, but I am Catherine Masters, a senior partner with the firm, and can answer any questions you might have. Come through to a meeting room. Can I get you some coffee?"

"We won't, thank you. We don't want to take up too much of your time. We just need some information to help us with a case in Budapest. Ms Radu has some questions which I'll have to translate. She doesn't speak English."

The woman smiled in a faintly patronising way at Catinca as they sat at a round table and Masters closed the door. "That's fine. How can I help?"

"OK. The situation my colleague is investigating is a murder enquiry. Our information is that your company made a boat reservation for Gennaio Colacino at 20.00 on the tenth of June this year. The company was Luxe Craft and the journey was from Hotel Zenit to ..." she checked her notes and shook her head. She showed the words to Catinca.

"*Kopasi gát,*" Catinca said. "Park."

"*Igen,*" Dawn replied. Catinca didn't react but acknowledged Beatrice's mate learned pretty damn quick.

"I see. I can find the relevant information on that service with the detail you have given me. Can you tell me precisely what you need to know?"

Catinca itched to speak up but stuck to her irritated expression of 'What the hell is she talking about?'

"Who employed you to make that booking?"

The Masters woman waggled her head in an apologetic precursor to a no.

Catinca broke into furious Hungarian, reciting one of the most familiar litanies of her childhood, with the same threatening tone he father had used. 'If you don't clear that room up in the next five minutes, I will take you outside and give you such a beating, you will be unable to sit down for a week.'

Dawn relayed the message to Ms Masters. "My colleague says this is a murder enquiry and anyone obstructing justice will feel the full force of European law. And yes, that does apply in this jurisdiction."

Masters opened her laptop with a dubious expression. "Even if I am able to find a name, it's likely to be a secretary or P.A. for a larger organisation. It is unlikely to help your investigation, DI Whittaker."

"Let us be the judge of that," Dawn replied, her eyes gentle.

No sounds intruded from outside so the only noises came from the keyboard and mouse as the senior partner tracked down the info they needed.

"As I said, no detail. The person who booked the pleasure cruiser goes by the name of Hugues and represents The MdM Foundation. A charitable concern. Sorry we couldn't be more helpful. Was there anything else?"

Catinca remembered to look blank as Dawn nodded her

thanks and turned to Catinca. "Maarsh walameet?"

"Email," said Catinca, with a beckoning gesture using the whole of her hand.

The woman looked from one to the other and in an almost unnoticeable movement, checked the mirror behind them. "I'll print it for you immediately. This way, the receptionist will have it ready on your way out."

Catinca scratched at her temple, shielding her face from the cameras or faces she realised must be behind the glass. They collected the document, thanked Catherine Masters and walked in the direction of Tottenham Court Road Tube station. Neither said a word, aware anyone could be watching or listening. Outside, Catinca looked grim as the grave. Inside, fireworks exploded in her mind. First day on the new job and she'd pulled a total blinder!

Chapter 12

It seemed more diplomatic to arrive at Dionysus separately. Catinca went first and by the time Beatrice arrived half an hour later to ask Adrian for a little chat, the lunchtime rush had thinned. Catinca and the handsome black chap whose name Beatrice had forgotten could manage the bar with ease, leaving Adrian free to join Beatrice in the office.

She stated it as simply as she could. "You asked me to find out why Catinca wants to leave and I have. Not the way I expected, but still. She isn't unhappy here. Quite the opposite. She simply needs the space to grow. This morning, she turned up at your flat for a 'job interview'. She applied for the role of my assistant. Before you open your mouth, there is no assistant's position and I certainly never even hinted there was."

Adrian did not open his mouth, looking around the room as if he had mislaid something.

"I told her it was impossible, but then she helped me get some information. With zero fuss or drama, she did so very efficiently. As a result, I have agreed to take her on for a three-week trial while she works out her notice. This will not affect her work here, as she can do the research I give her in her free time. She said that even if I didn't employ her, she would still be seeking another position. You gave her wings, Adrian, and now she wants to use them."

His eyes filled with tears and he covered his face with his

palms. She gave him a minute to compose himself, aware of the fact that to him, she'd changed sides.

He took out a handkerchief, blew his nose, patted his lashes and faced her, a swollen redness around his nose and beneath his eyes. "I feel the victim of double disloyalty. Why wouldn't she tell me that was her plan? Worse, couldn't you have consulted me before taking over my partner the very morning after I confided in you? I even asked you to talk to her to find out what was wrong! This is incredibly hurtful, Beatrice."

She leaned across the table. "I refused her, I promise. As luck would have it, she came at an opportune moment when I needed her language skills. That's why I agreed to this trial period. There is every possibility that I won't be able to keep her on. But she swears she will go somewhere else, do something else. She's determined to move on and I'd much prefer it was with me than lose her altogether. I'm sorry you feel I've been disloyal. That was not my intention."

He rotated his wedding ring, his gaze past her shoulder. "I don't suppose it was. But a brief phone call, just to ask permission, would have softened the blow."

"You're right. I'm sorry."

He sighed and met her eyes, his expression reproachful. "All right, apology accepted. At least she's staying in the family, I suppose."

"That's true. Don't worry, I'll take good care of her. Like one of my own."

Adrian gave her an arch look.

The thunderstorm hit the minute Beatrice's train pulled into Exeter St David's. Charcoal skies had been brooding since Bristol, flashing threats of lightning and ominous growls, like a monstrous black cat swishing its tail. After greeting her with a brief embrace, Matthew grabbed her bag and rushed through the downpour, his jacket turning from beige to dun in seconds.

Beatrice held a copy of *The Guardian* over her head and dodged puddles until she reached the car. They took their seats, mopping moisture from foreheads, spectacles and hair.

"You do like to make an entrance, don't you?" asked Matthew, turning the key in the ignition. Rain battered the windscreen. The wipers were barely up to the job at full speed.

"Thank you for coming to get me. Even in such horrendous conditions, there's something romantic about you, me and railway stations. How are the animals?"

"You old softy. The animals? One is peaceful and soothing, who fits perfectly with my desire for a quiet life. The other drives me to distraction twice daily. Why that wretched dog will not stay within the confines of our capacious and enticing garden, I do not understand. She tries everything in her power to escape and has eluded me three times since you've been gone. Worse still, she's started bringing friends home. Every day we have a gentleman visitor, if not two."

"Good gracious. That sounds suspiciously like she's in season. I must ask Gabriel if he had her spayed after rescuing her from the puppy farm. If not, it may mean a trip to the vets." She said no more until he had navigated his way out of the city and reached less crowded roads. "Now listen, I need to tell you a couple of things."

Matthew kept his eyes on the road, but released a long, creaking groan, like a felled tree. "Will I like either of these things?"

"With the right mindset, very likely."

"Oh dear."

"Firstly, I have taken on an assistant. Catinca is working for me on a three-week trial period. Secondly, I need to fly to Bordeaux on Thursday to pursue this case. Only for a couple of days. Will you be able to manage without me?"

Matthew was silent for a few moments, manoeuvring the car around a slow-moving council vehicle. Finally, he spoke.

"Leaving aside the assistant conversation, which will take a little longer than a twenty-minute drive, I'd like to know how a body in the Danube requires a trip to Bordeaux."

"In fact, the two things are not unconnected. Catinca, with the aid of Dawn, managed to track down some useful information. A charitable foundation commissioned a concierge company to organise that fatal boat trip. Based on the email address they were given, Catinca discovered the network known as MdM has a variety of concerns, the charitable foundation only one of many. Their businesses include a Paris fashion house, a perfumery, a vineyard, a property portfolio and interestingly, a stake in some of Europe's best-known restaurants. Their HQ is in Bordeaux, at the vineyard. I've secured an appointment with one of the managers and given Catinca the task of compiling a dossier on the MdM network while I'm away."

Matthew indicated and took the turn-off to Upton St Nicholas. Lightning threw the road into sharp relief as if someone had turned on a floodlight and the ensuing crack of thunder made them both tense.

"Heavens! I fear Mahler is no match for this weather," said Matthew, changing down a gear to avoid some huge puddles on the country lane.

"Mahler?" asked Beatrice, her self-possession jarred by the unnerving conditions.

"The forecast said thunderstorms and I was unsure of how the animals might react. So I put them in the cellar with a Mahler CD for company. Dumpling is in his carrier with some milk and kibble and I left water and a chew for Huggy Bear. I just hope the Symphony No. 8 has sufficient drama to outdo this beastly weather."

"Nearly home now," said Beatrice, more to herself than Matthew.

By the time Matthew pulled onto their tiny forecourt, the time between lightning flash and thunderclaps had expanded to seven seconds. The storm had passed. Beatrice wished someone would mention that to the rain. Huge raindrops pelted her as she ran for the door, yelling at Matthew to leave her case till the morning.

She shook herself off in the hallway while the stubborn old devil insisted on bringing the suitcase with him, shucked off her jacket and trotted down the stairs to check on the creatures. Huggy Bear, obviously just awoken, leapt up to do her little dance of glee, bouncing on her back legs. Beatrice caressed her ears and checked on Dumpling. Still curled into a furry ball, he opened one green eye and closed it again. She turned off Mahler, unlocked the kitty carrier and placed it on the floor, then followed the excitable terrier up the stairs.

Matthew was on the phone. "... not in the mood to drive anywhere tonight, but you're always welcome round here. I can get something out of the freezer or ... oh, yes, I think Beatrice would enjoy that!" He placed his hand over the mouthpiece. "Tanya and Gabriel suggest an Indian takeaway from the new place in Crediton. Marianne can collect and we can enjoy a family dinner without having to go out. What do you say?"

Beatrice spotted the advantages in an instant. With Matthew's two adult daughters at the table, she could whip up enough enthusiasm and positivity to win Matthew over. On top of that, Indian food, little Luke and gorgeous Gabriel, without leaving the house. She gave him a double thumbs-up, pointed to the dog and went upstairs for a shower. Home sweet home.

She was sitting at her desk composing emails when a kerfuffle in the hallway announced the arrival of dinner. Beatrice finished writing her reply and closed down her machine. In the kitchen, Matthew's daughters were bossing each other about as they placed takeaway cartons on plates and arranged poppadums, naan breads and chutneys on a tray.

"Hello, you two. Ooh, look at this! It smells delicious."

Tanya came over to give her a kiss on the cheek. "Gabe and I tried this restaurant last week, eating in, not a takeaway, and it really was delicious. We got you Butter Chicken. Dad said it was your favourite."

"Your father is a wonderful man." She waited until Marianne had finished washing her hands and gave her a kiss too. "Your hair looks super!"

Marianne gave Tanya a triumphant smile. "Thank you, Beatrice. I'm glad someone appreciates it. *Certain* people say that hair straightening is passé but then again, they're country dwellers with no sense of fashion. How was Budapest?"

Beatrice broke off a piece of poppadum and crunched it between her teeth. "Not ground-breaking, but I do have a lead. Where are the menfolk?"

"In the cellar. Dad wants Gabe's opinion on the right wine. Luke's playing with Huggy Bear in the living-room. Marianne, bring those plates and I'll carry this tray. Can you give her a hand, Beatrice? We wouldn't want her to mess up her hair, after all."

Gabriel and Matthew emerged from the cellar at the same time and the whole party sat down to enjoy their food. After some confusion over who'd ordered what and Luke's insistence on sitting next to Beatrice, they raised their glasses and tucked in.

Conversation was lively and ranged over subjects as diverse as the afternoon's storm, Huggy Bear's season, the dangers of Internet dating (Marianne was experimenting), and the quality of the food. Luke declared himself satisfied with his Prawn Korma, while Tanya and Gabriel praised the range and preparation of the vegetarian dishes.

Matthew agreed. "I must say, this is rather a revelation. Since cutting back on meat, I've made all kinds of discoveries. This spinach and chick pea combination works beautifully. Did I tell you we tried jackfruit last week? Extraordinary texture, just like shredded pork. We ate it Cajun style with rice, peas and beans. Healthy eating has been quite the adventure."

Watching him mop up his sauce with a handful of naan bread, Beatrice chose not to comment.

Gabriel caught her eye with a grin. "Talking of adventures, how is your PI agency going?"

"Better and better. My trip to Hungary brought up a new lead I'll have to investigate in France. One bit of good news, I've taken on an assistant for a three-week trial run. If it works out, it could be permanent."

"Wow!" Tanya put down her wine glass. "So the agency is taking off?"

Beatrice sensed Matthew's gaze. "Perhaps. This Budapest job may turn out to be quite interesting. In addition, that fretful female in Salzburg has now finally decided to press the green button, so I now have two cases to work. This is a disputed will type of affair, where a gold-digging stepmother is refusing to accept her late husband's wishes and wants to fight his children for their inheritance. So it seemed the right time to take on Catinca."

Marianne's eyes boggled, Gabriel stopped eating and Tanya, once again, did not manage to take a sip of wine. Matthew laced his hands together and waited for her explanation, while the other four fired questions at her.

"One thing at a time. No, Luke, she is not coming to live here. She can work from London. I haven't 'stolen' her from Adrian at all. She had already resigned. She wants to try something new. Adrian isn't thrilled, but actually pleased Catinca is 'staying in the family' as he put it. No, I'm not sure I can afford an assistant either, unless we get some higher-paying jobs than I've hitherto managed. I honestly don't know if she'll be any good at it, but early signs are positive. I wouldn't have found the Bordeaux connection without her. One thing I will say is that she is immensely hard-working, keen to learn and take instruction, and I happen to like her. Very much."

In the ensuing enthusiasm, she met Matthew's eyes. He lifted one eyebrow, clearly aware of her persuasion-in-public technique and gave her a look which said 'We'll see.'

Tanya, one of Catinca's greatest fans, proposed a toast. Even Marianne raised her glass of water to celebrate Beatrice's new partner and the next phase of PI Beatrice Stubbs.

Chapter 13

After two days at home, during which Gabriel had arranged an appointment for Huggy Bear with the vet to be spayed, Marianne had met a man with 'real potential' and Beatrice had sent a formal contract to Salzburg, she was back in Gatwick Airport, waiting for her flight to Bordeaux.

She paid extra to access one of the lounges, logged on to the Internet and read Catinca's latest email. This detail would be added to the file of notes already printed and stashed in Beatrice's laptop case.

From: Catinca_Radu71@hotmail.co.uk
To: admin@beatricestubbs.com
Subject: More on MdM

Beatrice, couple more bits before you go. MdM got fingers in plenty more pies than Chateau Agathe. Vineyard is HQ and where Madame de Marsault lives. She's well old and don't do much - recluse, innit?

Her son Yves de Marsault runs wine biz - ask your Naples lot if they stock them wines. Second son, Xander d.M. controls perfume line. Factory in Bordeaux and office in Paris.

Another business in Paris is fashion house

```
Papillon - check this link! What kind of idiot
wears that sort of shit? This line of business
run by another family member, ex-model
Anastasia K. - says she's Ukrainian. They like
to keep it in family, innit?
Still digging. More to this bunch than the
pics in Paris Match. Good luck.
```

The screen to her left announced her flight to Bordeaux was boarding. She closed down her machine and headed for the gate, listening to the charming sounds of her fellow passengers' conversations and wishing she'd paid more attention to her French lessons at school.

Château Agathe's claim to be a castle was no pretence. This was a classic country house, with grounds, ramparts, turrets and a vista across the valley. Wisteria climbed at least half of the building, lending it a soft lilac festoon. Black shutters framed each window on all three floors, mascara for the house's eyes. A small lawn-mowing machine trundled over the lawns like a turtle, and ankle-height signs directed visitors to their desired locations. Beatrice paid her taxi driver and wished him a *bonne journée*. She was early for her appointment with Mr Hugues, so followed the garden trail signs around neatly kept shrubberies until the heat became too much.

She moved into the shade cast by the side of the main house and saw the office entrance, outside which were parked a Porsche Cayenne, an F-Type Jaguar and a Smart car. She stood back into the sunshine and faked a selfie, but trained the camera on the vehicles. Every detail is important.

One last check of her watch and she returned to the main door, fanning herself with her hand, and rang the large bell. Ideally, Mr Hugues would invite her to sit under an umbrella on the terrace, offer her a Mint Julep and tell her all she needed to know.

That was not the reception she got. A snotty-looking man in his twenties with foppish blond hair opened the door and gave her an unsmiling once-over. "Yes?"

"Beatrice Stubbs. I have an appointment with Dennis Hughes." She showed him her card.

"It's not Dennis Hughes, it's Denis Hugues, pronounced De-nee Ugues. I am Monsieur Hugues. How can I help?" He didn't move, his body blocking the door. The name might be French but his accent was educated upper-class Home Counties.

"Well, you could start by inviting me in out of this heat. I've travelled a long way to talk to you and I find this weather quite oppressive."

He pushed back his floppy fringe with a flamboyant gesture. "I can give you a few minutes. Come this way and please don't touch anything."

Beatrice stared at his retreating back, stunned by his rudeness. He led the way to a small drawing-room, filled with beautiful antiques, and gestured to a chair. He offered her nothing to drink but stood with his arms folded, radiating attitude.

Beatrice sat and took out her notebook. "Mr Hugues, as I explained in my email …"

"Your email said you were making enquiries on behalf of the Metropolitan Police. That is why I agreed to a meeting. But my research tells me you are not a police officer, but a private investigator. I really don't understand why you are here." He pronounced the words as 'rarely' and 'hyar'.

"Better let me explain, in that case." She chose her words carefully, avoiding outright lies but allowing him to make assumptions. "I have been asked to assist in an enquiry. The police force in Budapest are investigating a murder. Met officers in London offered support. My role is to eliminate one particular aspect of the case, so the UK element can be closed down and the responsibility handed back to the Hungarians."

"I repeat. You are not a police officer. You have no right to question me."

"Do you know anything about how the British police work, Mr Hugues? Because I do. I served with them for my entire working life. We often make use of private detectives, journalists, even members of the public to help us find the information we required. As an ex-Detective Chief Inspector, my knowledge and skills are very much appreciated." All true, but with no relevance whatsoever to this case. He didn't know that, so her conscience was clear. "Some organisations would prefer not to deal directly with the police but through a third party, especially when it's simply a matter of helping with enquiries and eliminating involvement. However, if you feel more comfortable dealing with a law enforcement official ..." She left the sentence hanging, otherwise the next words out of her mouth would be crossing the line between implication and deceit.

He exhaled loudly through his nose, like a horse. That was a good sign. Expression of frustration disguised as impatience. Beatrice knew it well. He looked at his watch with as much exaggeration as if he were centre stage in an am-dram panto.

His arrogance tempted her to go further. She replaced her notebook and stood up to leave.

"Another thing I learned from my years as a detective is when someone has something to hide. Innocent people will readily answer questions. Those who won't usually need to be placed under arrest before we can get results. I can see I'm wasting my time here. Would you mind calling me a taxi, please?"

"We have nothing to hide! It is presumptuous and impolite of you to say so. Why should we answer questions from some private detective of whom we know nothing?"

"Because you want to co-operate in finding out who killed Gennaio Colacino?" Beatrice watched his face intently. The kid was good; she had to give him credit. But she was better.

Throwing a grenade into the conversation worked best when the witness was being observed by experts behind mirrored glass. Beatrice had interviewed enough liars, shysters and bull-shitters to observe the signs all on her own. Minute facial movements told her he knew exactly what she was talking about: flare of nostrils, dilation of pupils and momentary hesitation while he prepared his 'What are you talking about?' face.

"I have no idea ..."

She held up a hand. "Save it, Dennis. We both know why I'm here, so please spare me the moral indignation. Your organisation had a concierge company arrange a boat trip for Colacino. When he arrived at his destination, he ended up dead. You see why we're asking questions? Now, why did MdM want to send Signor Colacino on a boat trip?"

His complexion wasn't built for lying. "Perhaps if you can give me the dates and details, I'll see if there are any records." He opened a roll-top desk and withdrew a laptop.

Beatrice remained standing. "June the tenth, eight pm, boat from Hotel Zenit to *Kopasi gát*. Why did you offer him a boat ride, Mr Hughes?"

"My name is Denis Hugues, if you don't mind. As for the man you mention, I have no idea. We offer hospitality to so many of our stakeholders, it makes sense to outsource the arrangements to a third party. Just let me check. 10 June, Budapest, depends which of our ... ah! Here it is. A World of Wine reception in which Château Agathe was one of several participants demonstrating our newest vintages. Mr Colacino was an importer of some significance. Naturally, our company invited him to a tasting at the park. A networking event on a pleasure boat berthed at *Kopasi gát*. Fifty guests were invited and transport provided for each person. According to our records, Mr Colacino accepted the invitation but didn't show up. The event was a great success, written about most favourably in two magazines. I'll email you the links."

Very slick, thought Beatrice. *Not answering any questions, hostile attitude and then suddenly it's all there on a plate with a cherry on top.*

"As I understand it, your company made two separate requests regarding the transport for Mr Colacino. Why would that be?"

"No idea, sorry. Timing change, minor adjustment to location? We would expect the travel operator to handle granular detail." He snapped the laptop shut and replaced it in the desk. "I'm afraid that's the extent of my knowledge of the incident."

"Thank you. I appreciate your co-operation. Should I have any further questions ...?"

Brideshead Revisited brushed back his fringe and faked a tight smile. "Here's my card. But you won't need it. All the information I have is right there. Taxi for the airport, I assume?"

While he phoned for a cab, Beatrice became aware of a strange pulsing sound, getting increasing louder. Denis heard it too and she registered the alarm on his face at exactly the same instant she recognised the sound as the blades of a helicopter. He ended his call.

"The taxi is on its way. I am terribly sorry, but I must ask you to wait outside. We are expecting ... guests, you see." He waved her to the door with considerable impatience. Beatrice looked over her shoulder. The machine was touching down at the end of the long lawn, awaited by two men in suits.

"I understand and of course I can wait outside. May I just use the bathroom before I go?"

Muscles in the young man's jaw clenched but his upbringing overrode his irritation. He opened the door with a worried glance past her at the garden. "Certainly. The cloakroom is this way."

The spacious cloakroom or downstairs loo as Beatrice would have described it was wallpapered with peacock-feather design, with turquoise floor tiles and blue ceramic fixtures. The overall effect was tasteful but with only a subtle pair of sunken spotlights, rather gloomy. She had no need of the facilities, so simply reorganised her handbag for a few minutes, ears alert for any sounds outside. Once she heard voices, she flushed the toilet, washed her hands, unclipped the strap of her handbag and emerged.

In the hallway stood a group of four men and a woman. Denis Hugues spotted Beatrice and broke away, his arm outstretched to guide her to the front door. She gave the party a polite smile and followed her escort until she was two steps from the exit. Only then did she release her grip on her bag. It fell to the floor, spilling phone, purse, deodorant, hairbrush, a packet of tissues, a bundle of insignificant bits of paper and a paperback onto the mat.

"Oh no! I'm so sorry. Something tells me I need a new handbag." Beatrice knelt, collecting her things with clumsy hands until a pair of shoes entered her sightline.

"Can I help?" a rich voice enquired in barely accented English.

She looked up into an aristocratic face, with concerned brown eyes and a friendly smile. The guest was handsome, polished and smelt quite lovely. Like a crate of freshly picked lemons.

"That's all right, thank you. Sorry for the disturbance," she said, stuffing items haphazardly into her bag. It didn't matter. All the documents, notes and laptop were zipped safely into the interior compartment.

"Madame Stubbs, your taxi is here!" called Denis. He caught her arm and practically dragged her to the door.

"*Attends*, Denis!" The aristocrat walked towards her, his hand outstretched. He held her business card between forefinger and thumb. "This is you? Beatrice Stubbs, Private Investigator?"

"Yes, that's me. I do apologise for the interruption. You'll probably be finding my dry-cleaning receipts for weeks to come. Thank you for your help and *au revoir*." She didn't attempt to take the card and turned to Denis, who was almost hopping from foot to foot.

His voice stopped her in her tracks. "Just a moment, madame."

"Her taxi is here!" shrieked Denis. "She must go!"

"Tell the driver to wait, Denis, and put the bill on our account, please. Ms Stubbs, my name is Yves de Marsault. I am the owner of this property. Do you have time for a drink before you leave? I've never met a private investigator before."

"Do you know, that would be very nice. I admit I am terribly thirsty." She didn't look round but called over her shoulder. "Shan't be long, Dennis!"

Always better to talk to the organ-grinder than the monkey. In a larger reception room decorated in eggshell white with notes of primrose and violet, Yves de Marsault suggested she join him in a glass of sauvignon blanc from the family vineyard. She accepted eagerly and explained the reason for her visit, but kept it sketchy. Working in association with Metropolitan Police and Budapest force to eliminate the innocent from further enquiry. He listened with attention and asked if his staff had given her what she required.

"Absolutely. Mr Hugues has been very helpful. My opinion is that we can hand over this line of the investigation to the police and let them do the rest."

He handed her a glass. "*Santé!*"

"*Santé!*" she replied and took a sip. Fresh, cool and layered, this was a wine to savour and more than likely, save up for. "This is excellent, Monsieur de Marsault, which I'm sure you already know. Is this the signature wine of Château Agathe?"

He nodded once, a smile spreading. "It is. One of our best vintages, reserved for special guests. Tell me, do you prefer whites or reds?"

"Truthfully? Whatever is on offer. I'm not an expert, but I happen to know a couple of people who are. They've introduced me to some extraordinary adventures in a bottle."

He laughed, showing expensive dentistry. "I don't think I've ever heard such an honest answer from any guest at the château. But I'm curious, what does a private detective do? It sounds, how can I say? A combination of glamorous and sleazy."

Now it was Beatrice's turn to laugh and her amusement was genuine. "Perfectly put! You hit the nail on the nutshell. It's mostly sleazy, but one does get the odd moment of glamour. Such as visiting a beautiful château and drinking divine wine with the host." She remained on guard. He seemed charming, accommodating and welcoming, but it was only a matter of time before he returned to the reason for her visit. And she'd just handed him an invitation.

He didn't bite. "What interests me is how one finds such a profession. What kind of career path leads you to set up a detective agency? Am I being rude? If so, I apologise. As a child, I grew up on Georges Simenon and dreamed of becoming a junior Maigret. Sometimes, I wonder if it's not too late." He revolved the stem of his glass and gazed at the contents.

Either he was an exceptional actor, or this man was telling the truth. Why wasn't he drilling her as to the reason for his visit? Was it possible he had nothing to hide? In which case, who was that foppish fool outside trying to protect if not Yves de Marsault?

Beatrice played along. "I remember Simenon from when I studied French. There's one in particular that sticks in my mind. It was called *On ne tue pas les pauvres types*. I apologise for my dreadful accent."

"I loved that one too! I must have read it over twenty times. After I learned English, I discovered the British Golden Age of Crime. You have a rich literary heritage. Was it that which lured you into the detection profession?"

Beatrice studied this man with a cynical eye because she was beginning to like him. A terrible way to start with a suspect.

"Like many people, I have an urge to right wrongs. That's why I joined the police force. By the time I retired, I was Acting Detective Chief Inspector, which was not a bad place to end one's career. A private investigation agency seemed the next logical step. Although, up to now, it's not been terribly exciting."

"Up to now? Are you investigating us?" His eyes shone and he looked practically gleeful. "What a thrill!"

"No, I'm not investigating you. Just following up on a lead, as I said. Your company ordered a boat for someone who ended up dead. But Mr Hugues has given me all the detail and I see nothing to connect MdM to the deceased. He was merely a client the company wished to flatter, I understand."

He leaned forward. "Did you say a boat? Was this in Paris?"

"No, Budapest."

His manner changed, his eager enthusiasm dissipating as he looked pensively into his glass.

"Why would you think it was Paris?" asked Beatrice.

He focused on her once more. "When you said a body in the river, I assumed it was the Seine. That's where we do a lot of our business, on cruises up the river. We throw the best parties. Boats along the Seine, at the Centre Pompidou, in *Les Jardins des Tuileries*. If you ever find yourself in Paris, you should come along. Let me give you my card. May I keep yours?" He got up to reach for his wallet.

She took her cue. "By all means. Thank you for the wine, it was awfully good. I should toddle off to the airport and let you get on. I'm sure you're very busy. Nice meeting you."

He held out his hand, shook hers and handed her a monogrammed card. "The pleasure was all mine. Have a safe trip home."

Beatrice crunched across the gravel to the taxi and thanked

the driver for waiting. Denis Hugues was nowhere to be seen, but she'd bet her last Euro that he was watching from one of the château's many windows.

Yves de Marsault occupied her thoughts as the taxi sped through the Bordeaux countryside, billowing fields of sunflowers and lavender on either side of the road. His guileless manner was the exact opposite of the Hugues chap. As if he had nothing to hide. If MdM had something to do with Gennaio's death, she wasn't sure Yves knew about it.

The fact remained, all she had was a feeling and vague suspicion. No proof, no leads and the trip, whilst interesting, had proved a dead end. She would have loved to pursue this further, but her conscience would not allow her to take these people's money with every expectation of coming up empty-handed. She would have to tell Bruno and Chantal that she'd failed in her task and reached the same conclusion as the police. She was no closer to finding out who killed Gennaio Colacino.

Chapter 14

Davor waited till the plane had emptied before leaving his seat. That way, the likelihood of anyone recognising him from the flight was reduced. He was in no hurry. Bordeaux Airport was packed with holidaymakers. A group of women all wearing the same hen party T-shirts laughed and squealed their way through Baggage Reclaim. Several families tried to hang on to their over-excited offspring, but soon gave up and allowed the children to hurtle around the irresistibly wide space to stretch their legs. Business travellers without hold luggage strode past, many already on their phones. Davor withdrew the passport he was currently using, just in case he was stopped going through Customs. It was rare on an internal flight, but he knew from experience never to make presumptions.

He breezed though and made for the taxi rank, until he saw the queue. Without breaking stride, he walked past the motley assortment of tired, hot, uncomfortable tourists and into the airport building through the next set of doors. He took the escalator upstairs to the Departures section and exited onto the higher level. Cars pulled up to set down their passengers for mere minutes as traffic police prowled the area. As Davor expected, taxis came in regularly and looped around to collect the people at the head of the queue outside Arrivals.

He timed it carefully. The police were at the other end when a cab pulled up to deposit an older woman with eccentric hair. She didn't have luggage, just a capacious handbag, and paid the driver through his window. Obviously a Brit. He moved past her as the driver handed over a receipt. In one fluid movement, Davor got into the back seat and closed the door behind him.

Before the driver could protest, he spoke in rapid French, suggesting the cabbie would earn himself double the fare and the passenger's eternal gratitude if he bent the rules a little and just drove. He reached forward to give the man a 'friendly' squeeze of the shoulder. The guy wasn't stupid and sensed the threat.

"Where to, chief?"

The Hotel Ibis was large and anonymous enough for him to blend in. Plenty of other single male travellers were checking in, drinking alone in the bar or eating in the café area. No paid him any attention. He gave the least possible attention to the desk clerk, tapping away at his phone and answering questions as briefly as courtesy would allow.

Yes, he had a reservation. No, he hadn't stayed there before. Business, not pleasure. Yes, his passport was right here. No alarm calls, thank you. Yes, a newspaper would be good. *Le Monde*, if possible. No, he had no need of the tourist brochures, because he'd done his research online. Just the Wi-Fi password as he needed to get some work done in preparation for tomorrow.

He took his key and retreated to his room. After a thorough check of the room, he began to unpack. Tonight he would scope the local area, checking what supplies he might need. Perhaps stop at a restaurant and sample a local dish. Then he intended to return to his room, run through his visualisation techniques and get an early night.

In the morning, he had to be at the top of his form to enter the spider's web.

Chapter 15

Catinca finished work at Dionysus by four o'clock and hurried straight home, updating her Instagram story on the bus. She couldn't be faffing about on social media tonight. She had stuff to do and was more driven than ever.

Beatrice had shelved the Budapest/Bordeaux job, and in some ways, Catinca could see why. After all, since the Italian relatives had responded with a thanks-for-trying email, there'd be no more cash to pay them to investigate or fly off to European cities to ask questions.

But delving deep into what the Internet had to offer cost nothing at all. There was no way Catinca was giving up yet, so while Beatrice was spying on some greedy will-contesting grabber in Austria, her assistant was still working the case. After a quick sandwich of peanut butter and Branston pickle washed down with a Red Bull, she sat down in her room to work. Catinca was methodical in her research, like an archaeologist, dusting off whatever she could find in the small print of each website, cross-checking and recording every discovery. Strikingly, a certain Luxembourg law firm represented not only the fashion house and the perfumery, but had acted for the vineyard, the restaurant chain and the matriarch personally in various lawsuits on public record. She dragged out a piece of paper from her design file and made a map of all these connections. At the heart of it all sat Madame Agathe de

Marsault.

Time to find out more about this old bird who didn't get out much. Catinca began with her favourites – gossip and fashion sites – which proved to be a trove of information. How much of that was hyperbole, she have to double check. But one particular fact was incontrovertible. Madame had lost her husband, Gerard, two days after his fiftieth birthday. At the celebratory party, the man suffered a heart attack while on the dance floor. His wife had gone into mourning for several years. Their three sons had taken over the business. The vineyard with her home, the eponymous Château Agathe in Bordeaux, a perfumery in Paris, plus a large number of hotels in France and restaurants across Europe. Three sons?

Catinca checked the Wikipedia page. Three sons. Zane, who was killed in a car-racing accident in 1996; Yves, the bloke Beatrice had met in Bordeaux; and the youngest, Xander, a right ugly git with a jaw like an anvil, managed the Paris perfumery. Seemed like the loss of husband and eldest son made the old girl retreat from public life permanently. Rarely seen in public, refused interviews, although she was not averse to a bit of litigation. Fourteen court cases brought against former employees, competitors, journalists for defamation and three different suppliers. Wouldn't want to get on the wrong side of that lady.

She made notes on her map and starting researching the bloke who died. Zane de Marsault, twenty-five years old, married to ex-model Daria Kravets, a member of the aristocratic Kravets family of Odessa in the Ukraine. Zane was a looker and a playboy who messed about with boats, motorbikes and fast cars. Crashed in Paris-Dakar rally and died of his injuries in 1996. No children. Widow never remarried and operates chain of restaurants via daughter company of MdM.

The restaurants were interesting. Top-level chic places in most European capitals where you had to join a waiting list for a table. Perhaps here was the connection to Ecco and the dead importer floating in the Danube. Weirdly, the Subito chain was the culinary opposite of five-star fine dining. A franchise of snack bars right across the Baltic region sold junk food on street corners. So, she had Yves for wine, Xander for perfume and the widow Daria for restaurants. As for the hotels, maybe they were Madame's territory.

Catinca lifted her gaze to the ceiling and thought. The widow was going to be minted after handsome young husband popped his clogs. Aristo family background and wealthy in-laws with more than one luxe brand to their name and her ambition is to flog slices of pizza and limp sausages? No way. Obvious conclusion had to be money-laundering. Which meant they'd got some other kind of business going on they wouldn't want anyone to know about. No wonder they didn't like people turning up and asking questions.

The sound of the cistern drew her attention to the present. She listened, narrowing her eyes. Sure enough, there was the faint sound of scrubbing then the taps in the sink began to run. She allowed herself a smile. Last week's bollocking had taken effect. She didn't enjoy screaming blue murder at her flatmates, but neither did she like entering a bathroom that stank of piss and a toilet bowl splattered with stains. Steve and Micky were twice her size, but she'd forced them both into the bathroom, locked the door and read the riot act. For the past few days, they had religiously cleaned up after themselves and she had made a point of checking. If they kept this up till Sunday, she would reward them by baking a batch of cookies. This nocturnal pair of weirdoes wouldn't be up for a celebratory dinner as both were awkward and uncomfortable in social situations. So leaving them a tin of bickies and a little note saying thanks would do the job. She had no idea what they did for a living or why they slept all day and worked all night. The only thing she cared about was they paid the rent and maintained the basic standards of hygiene. Even if it meant a gentle kick up the arse when necessary.

She returned her attention to the map of connections. None of this connected the family in any concrete way to the death of Colacino. Catinca pulled up the notes Beatrice had sent on her trip to Budapest. Lajos Balínt – Colacino's business associate gave them nothing. The police – just the facts, although they'd not exactly strained themselves. The hotel had led them to the water taxi company, but Beatrice had found the owners rude and uncooperative. Catinca considered it from the Luxe Craft perspective. Police asking questions, company involved in murder enquiry, another woman turning up with more questions when they thought the publicity had died down and Beatrice would have asked her questions in English. Of course she'd got nothing. If someone were able to get these guys on side, starting by speaking their language, perhaps they might be a bit more generous with information.

She found the number for the management, checked the time and called Luxe Craft.

A male voice answered in Hungarian. "Luxe Craft Water Taxis, how can I help?"

Catinca, enjoying a chat in her father-tongue, played it straight. "Am I speaking to the manager? I need to speak to someone senior, please."

There was a pause. "You can talk to me. Gergely Roth."

"Thank you. My name is Catinca Radu and I work for a private investigation agency. We believe your agency has been unfairly implicated in a situation involving the police. I'm pretty sure you know which one I'm talking about."

He took several seconds to reply. "Maybe."

"Our objective is to find the real culprit and prove your company had no connection to the death of this man. I know you've already spoken to the cops and have probably been fighting off reporters, but I want to promise you, we have no other goal than identifying who killed the Italian. And before you ask, we know it wasn't you."

"How do you know?"

"Because this is a much bigger operation than a taxi service, Gergely. What can you tell me about that job? I'm guessing that as the boss you didn't handle it yourself."

"I did. That was a VIP call and I deal with those just to be sure they don't screw it up. All it takes these days is one sullen look from a deckhand or a rich bitch breaking a heel on the boardwalk and they'll find someone else. I pilot all commissions from concierge companies personally."

Adrenalin started to electrify Catinca's system. "Really? Looks like I got lucky finding you. Is there anything you can tell me about the pickup, the drop off, the trip itself? Any detail you can remember?"

"I told the police all I know. Picked the guy up, he sat at the back and talked on his phone the entire time. Handed him over at the other end and next thing I know, he's dead."

"Hang on, Gergely. My understanding is that you dropped him off at the park, where he was to join a party boat, right?"

"Yeah. I dropped him off at the bottom of the park, as instructed. There was someone there to meet him to take him to the party. That boat was at the top. No idea why they wanted him left at the bottom when I could have berthed beside the pleasure cruiser and saved him a walk."

"Your instructions came from charles, the concierge service, right?"

"It was a concierge service, yes, but whether it was charles … can you wait while I check?"

Catinca scribbled notes on her pad while she waited for the man to return.

"You still there?"

"Yes, I am. What did you find?"

"Water taxi booked by charles under the name of Briony.

Later request from Debbie at same company asking to deliver passenger to guide. Both email addresses are first name at cctravel dot com."

"That is really helpful, thank you. One last thing, when you deposited your passenger, did you see which way he went or recall anything about the guide?"

The pause lasted so long Catinca was worried she'd lost him.

"I turned my boat around as soon as he got off, so no, saw nothing more. Guide was big, classic security guard. Suit, bald head, sunglasses at that time of night. He was either ignorant or didn't speak Hungarian because I said 'Good evening' to him but got no response. So I wished my client a pleasant evening and he said 'Same to you' and gave me a tip. That's all I have."

"Well, it's a lot more than I had before. Thank you so much and I wish you a wonderful evening."

"Are you here? In Budapest?"

"No, I'm currently in London. Why?"

"Shame. We could have had a drink. Next time, huh?"

Catinca laughed. "Definitely. I'll keep your number. Thanks again!"

She replaced the receiver and could not repress a grin. She was born for this kind of thing.

Chapter 16

If Beatrice were a city, she'd choose to be Salzburg. The high fortress, a gift from an archbishop to his illicit lover, spoke of romance and beauty and art. The buildings in the centre seemed blessed with an abundance of windows and the clean waters of the river bore swans, coots and moorhens. Every other park or church she passed seemed to have choirs or classical musicians performing, filling the air with sound and serenity. The green mountains in the distance promised healthy air, pine forests and white flowers. The mediaeval city wore its age with pride and dignity, kept itself clean and everywhere you looked, there was cake.

When one had to spy on a woman buying toilet paper, it was far nicer to do it on Griesgasse by the banks of the Salzach than in Waitrose on Gladstone Road in Exeter. But at the end of the day, it amounted to the same thing. Hours and hours hanging about, trying to be inconspicuous, trying to catch the ruddy female in the act. This was not a question of snapping some shots of her in flagrante with her lover, but more proving the woman was lying about her impoverished status.

Hana Maximilian had hired her to follow Patricia Eis, a thirty-eight-year-old widow who was contesting the will of Hana's recently deceased sister, Inga. One might expect an older lady with an only son to leave her substantial fortune to him, but he had died of cancer over a decade ago. So Inga divided her bequest three ways. One third went to her sister, Hana. The other two thirds were left to her grandchildren, Tobias and Romy, who were both at Salzburg University. Her daughter-in-law, the children's stepmother, got nothing. In Inga and Hana's eyes, she didn't need it as she had inherited her husband's fortune and property.

Patricia was calling foul, saying death duties for her late husband and his considerable debts had left her with nothing but the house. She insisted she had some claim to the money as she had raised the children after their father's death. Hana, as executor, refused and things moved fast from hostile to outright nasty.

At her initial meeting with Hana and her great-niece and nephew yesterday lunchtime, Beatrice was surprised by the level of vitriol from these polite young people.

"How dare she say she raised us? We were sent to boarding school in England after Papi died! In the holidays, she would have parties and friends here all the time."

"We weren't welcome. She made that clear. So we spent all our time with Tante Hana and Oma Inga. We lived there in name only!"

"They are telling the truth, Mrs Stubbs. It is possibly true that Patricia has no money left. But it certainly had nothing to do with death duties or debts. My nephew left his affairs in order. He knew he was dying and as a practical man, arranged everything for the children's education."

The girl's face reddened. "She spent everything! And when there was nothing left to spend, she sold our father's art collection and spent that on facelifts, hoping to hook another man she can bleed dry."

"Romy, don't upset yourself, my dear. Let's simply tell Mrs Stubbs the facts."

Tobias caught hold of his sister's hand. "The facts, Mrs Stubbs, are that she is a vain, silly woman who squandered everything my father left her and now is trying to grasp some of my grandmother's legacy. Thank God we have Tante Hana to fight her or Romy and I couldn't manage."

"Thank you, Tobias. You see, Mrs Stubbs, we need proof. We know she uses designer handbags, wears expensive jewellery, drives a Mercedes Cabriolet and takes her friends to five-star restaurants. But without evidence of her spending, it's our word against theirs."

Beatrice listened, put on her glasses and took notes, wishing with all her heart this wasn't happening to this lovely family. How many people in the world were consumed with bitterness and rage over money, bequests, a sense of injustice and the most ferocious hatred for family members? Was it worth spending years of their lives fighting in courtrooms where the only profiteers in the long run would be the lawyers? She said none of this and simply assured the family she would do her best.

It wasn't going at all well. Either Patricia Eis knew she was being followed, or since her legal team had stated their intention of contesting the will, she was on her best behaviour. She left home at ten, visited the post office, went to a perfectly ordinary supermarket and bought, amongst other everyday items, toilet rolls. Lunch was not lobster and Bollinger at the Opera House, but a sandwich and a Coke at an Imbiss. She sat outside and made at least three calls on her phone. No point in getting too close, as Beatrice wouldn't have understood the German conversations anyway. Using her nondescript appearance as a disguise, forcing her unruly hair into a ponytail, Beatrice took pictures of everything. But none of it showed anything other than a housewife doing her errands.

"Do something, you horrible sow," she muttered. "I can't fail at two jobs in succession."

As if she had heard, the woman dropped her litter into the bin and walked away from the river. Beatrice followed her past the birthplace of Mozart, weaving in and out of the crowds of shoppers and along to Alter Markt. This was the place. Louis Vuitton, Hermès, Prada, Cartier and stores advertising names Beatrice recognised but couldn't imagine how to pronounce: Balenciaga, Schiaparelli, Ermenegildo Zegna, and Christian Louboutin. Didn't matter, she was hardly likely to buy anything in any of those intimidating looking boutiques. But Patricia Eis might. Her mark entered a shop called Welt der Mode and Beatrice spotted a café on the opposite side of the street. Gratefully, she sat at a table, ordering coffee and a slice of Sachertorte.

Playing the tourist, she took photographs of the metal signs which protruded from the shop fronts, hanging from chains out into the street. This one depicted a cup of coffee, complete with wisps of steam, all wrought from iron. The picture was charming, like the city itself, but she had other reasons for taking pictures.

The cake and coffee arrived and Beatrice made the executive decision to have a break. She kept an eye on the shop, while tucking into the most delicious slab of light chocolate sponge with a jammy layer in the middle, all covered with chocolate icing. It was the most deliciously decadent treat which she damn well deserved after all this haring about Europe. If she got what she needed, she could go home tomorrow and spend some quiet time at home with Matthew and the animals. She missed them and was bored with hotels, airports and lurking about waiting for something to happen.

The door of the shop opened and the target emerged, empty-handed unless whatever she'd just bought was in her handbag. So no incriminating shots of huge purchases and Beatrice couldn't even finish her cake. She took one more mouthful, left the correct change on the table and set off in pursuit of that sour-faced wretch in her floaty blue dress and high-heeled, red-soled shoes. She needn't have bothered. The woman stopped at a taxi rank and got into the first cab. Beatrice took several more shots, although whether taking a taxi home counted as outrageous decadence, she wasn't sure. Oh well, at least she could finish her cake now the woman had gone.

Sadly, when she got back to the café, so had her cake. The table was cleared and reset for the next customer. She released a heartfelt expletive and retraced her steps. It wasn't only young glamour pusses who could hop into a taxi. Fractious, hot and irritable private detectives on expenses had every right to ride in comfort too.

She uploaded all the photographs to her work files and put off calling Hana Maximilian with a progress report. Mainly because there was none. Instead she called Matthew for a general update on what had happened since she'd last seen him on Monday.

"At last! It's very good to hear your voice, Old Thing."

"You too. Sorry it's taken a while to call, but all this dashing about has left me with precious little time or privacy, to be honest. If I can just get this job done tomorrow, I might be able to come home."

"Gracious, that was quick. After all those months of emailing the client, you can wrap it up in a couple of days? You are improving with age, I'll say that."

"I said 'if', not 'when'. Today's progress has been dismal. I'll follow the wretched creature for the next few days and hope to come up with something by Monday latest. Tell me about the animals."

"Both in fine fettle. Other than that, nothing to report. Have you spoken to Catinca?"

"She's next on my list. Why do you ask?"

"I happened to call Adrian this afternoon. Got stuck on a crossword clue about Californian wine regions and thought he could help. He solved it instantly and we had a bit of a chat. Apparently Catinca has asked to take next week off and complete the rest of her notice after that. He wondered what was going on and I had to confess to being quite clueless."

"A week off? What on earth for? I've charged her with a little administrative work, that's all. If this surveillance work comes to nothing, my reputation as a PI will be shot. Meaning she's out of a job."

"Hmm, curious. Oh well, it'll all come out in the wash, I'm sure. Have you had any Viennese pastries yet?"

Beatrice launched into a gushing review of her Sachertorte, only distracted by a message from Catinca flashing onto her laptop screen.

`Call me. C.`

She chatted to Matthew for another few minutes, with another reminder not to feed the animals from the table, and ended the call. She looked out of the hotel bedroom at the wonderful layered views across the city. She would call Catinca, go for a walk and seek out a nice restaurant to sample some Austrian cuisine. It was a beautiful evening and if she was lucky, she might stumble across one of those open-air concerts where students of classical music demonstrated their skills.

Her phone rang.

"Hello, Catinca, sorry. I was just about to call you."

"All right? How you getting on?"

"Not well, I'm afraid. I've not got anything on this mark and I covered half of Salzburg following her around."

Catinca exhaled, a sound which could have been a laugh or a snort of disgust. "Thing is, I need you back here. Got some stuff to show you."

"What stuff? And why have you asked Adrian for a week off?"

Another exhale, which was clearly exasperation. "That man is massive bigmouth. I need a week off *because* of the stuff. Got a few ideas and I reckon we need to go to Paris."

Beatrice took her phone from her ear and stared at it.

Catinca continued. "Too much to tell over phone and anyway, too risky. Can't you finish up and get back tomorrow?"

"I don't know if I can finish up by tomorrow. One way or another, I have to get proof this woman is living the life of luxury while claiming poverty and trying to grab some of her stepchildren's inheritance. But all she's done today is buy groceries and window shop. Not a single shot incriminates her and I doubt tomorrow will be any better. The problem is, this is the only paying job I've got at the moment. I have no choice but to keep trying. Actually, come to think of it ... you are a fashion specialist. Are you versed in models and prices? Maybe I don't just need to look at *new* stuff she buys, but what she's already got. Fancy a bit of research into the rich and sour?"

"Where's the photos?"

"In the client folder. I uploaded them earlier and added a file of images with today's date."

"Let me have a look. You had dinner yet?"

"No, but I was planning to head out to try a local restaurant after talking to you."

"Do that and give me a couple of hours to work this. Call you back before ten, OK?"

Beatrice thought about it. "Thank you. But, Catinca, even if we do solve this, I'd need to have some kind of financial incentive to pursue any other case. If I work for free, I'll never be able to afford an assistant."

"Yeah, yeah, I know. My recommendation is Wiener Schnitzel with fries and Wachau Riesling. Talk to you later."

Chapter 17

The effects of the Red Bull had worn off and her advice to Beatrice on Austrian menus reminded Catinca of her own hollow stomach. The fridge was almost empty and her cupboard held a shabby selection of tinned meatballs, ravioli, packets of noodle soup and pasta. She needed something fresh and healthy to charge her brain, because she would be working late into the night.

She grabbed her bag and jacket, because London weather was an unpredictable thing, then ran down the stairs and up the street to their Sainsbury's Local. With a nod to the security guard who never spoke more than two words, but expressed his opinion on her various transformations with a wide-eyed wow or mock fear, she buzzed through the aisles, grabbing a superfood salad and a vitamin drink, plus some bread for breakfast. There was only one baguette left in the basket and Catinca spotted the name: Parisette. That would do. It was all about getting into character.

When she got back to the flat, she met Micky in the hallway, lugging a large holdall and looking surprisingly clean, scrubbed and smart.

"All right, Mick? You off out?"

He flushed. "Yeah. Away for ten days. Gaming conference."

"Sounds …right up your street. Have a great time."

"Yeah. You too." He stood there, looking at the carpet.

"Is that the one in Gravesend? One of my mates from work is going in costume."

"No." He gave a self-conscious laugh. "This one's for developers, not players. Silicon Valley. Got a flight to San Francisco at half ten tonight."

"Wow!" Catinca had never seen either of her flatmates outside their own street so the thought of Micky in America left her speechless.

"Better get on," he said, flushing once more.

"Course. I'll get out your way. Oh, just to say, thank you. Bathroom is perfect."

"No worries." Micky shuffled past and down the stairs to the street. Catinca took her food into the kitchen to find a plate and a fork when another voice made her start.

"Umm ..." Steve stood in the hallway with a wheelie case, stooped as always and with a sheepish smile. "See you in a couple of weeks."

"You going an' all?"

He nodded. "First time for me. Micky's been before."

Catinca grinned at him. "Hope you have a fantastic time. And don't worry, I'll keep the bathroom clean while you're gone." She winked at him and he gave an embarrassed laugh, before bumping his case down the stairs.

Right, so with the boys away, she had the place to herself. Starting tonight. She tipped her salad into a bowl, grabbed a fork and took her dinner back to her bedroom to decode her favourite subject: fashion. It took around an hour to research all the items Beatrice had photographed. Then she turned her attention to finding some social media links and a way of connecting to Patricia Eis. That took around twenty minutes.

Catinca sought out one of the rich lady's higher profile friends and followed. Then all the dominoes started to fall. Catinca's own influencer status was well established so she received an enthusiastic welcome. She reciprocated, commenting on several pictures. Next, she found a photo which included the Eis woman and enthused about her style. Obvious step was to follow Patricia Eis. Got accepted, thanked her, liked every photo in 10 and typed in some bland approval every one in 20. Gotcha.

From: Catinca_Radu71@hotmail.co.uk
To: admin@beatricestubbs.com
Subject: Your photos

How was Schnitzel? I had sodding Sainsberry salad.
Listen, you already got everything they need. I been thru all images and her Instagram account. We got shitloads to show this is one Big Spender. Pay attention to dates. Some of the stuff came out in the last few months *S/S 2019 (That's Spring/Summer collection coz I know you don't do fashion.)

IMG 201907272: (Outside house) Patricia Eis in Balmain jacket* (S/S 2019) priced about £3.5K and Aläia dress at £4,570.
IMG 201907277: (Close-up on body) Handbag is Tom Ford alligator in pink. Retails at £14,750. Can't source shoes but wish Converse did pink sequins – WANT!
IMG 201907279: (Close-up on face) Earrings are Chopard rose gold hearts, £5,390. Piaget rose gold watch with alligator strap just short of 15K.
IMG 201907283: (Eating sandwich) Prada dress* (S/S 2019), currently on sale at £2,750. Louboutin patent pumps sell for £475.
IMG 2019072815: (Getting in cab) Earrings Vintage Dior – upwards of £6K. Necklace and bracelets all Dior Mimirose Collection* – £3.5K in total. Shopping bag is Chanel, obvs. Priced at around £4K+.

Attached doc contains all retail links and
current pricing. Is possible she bought some
stuff earlier/cheaper, but in two days, you
captured her toting over 50K in kit. Plus
that's quids, not Euros.

Just hand Instagram account direct to lawyers.
It's all there, mate, everything you need to
know. Job done.

Now come home. Cx

PS: Going to bed. Nackered.

Catinca logged off with a sense of satisfaction. While washing
up her dinner things, her thoughts returned to the female she'd
just cyber-stalked. All that cash and she wants to look like a
clone of every other wealthy woman. What's the point? No sense
of style or originality. If Catinca had the money, she would
combine the most wonderful, eclectic items with flea market
finds and create 1,000 fabulous looks and show people how edgy
pink can be. She left the crockery to drain and marched into her
bedroom. No more green. Tomorrow, she would be going rosé.
Adrian was hardly likely to sack her for improvising on her own
dress code.

Fifteen minutes later, she was all prepared for the following
day. A strappy pink gingham dress with green sprigs hung
outside the wardrobe, her unplaited hair had all the right
textures for a wild pair of bunches and she'd unwrapped a brand-
new candy-striped pair of Converse trainers. Once she
assembled the right jewellery for the morning, she washed her
face, cleaned her teeth and got into bed. Before she slept, she
planned her shots and captions for the next day. 'A Rose by any
other name #retrostyle', 'Back to Pink #gingham', 'Fashion
ambassador #citychick #london #paris'.

She opened her eyes wide.

Paris.

Why not? They needed a way in and her credentials were impeccable. If they had any sense, they'd jump at the chance. She threw off her blanket and opened her laptop, waiting impatiently for it to come to life, composing her email in her mind. What a way to enter Paris! Her eyes shone in the blue light of the computer screen.

Chapter 18

He shaved, dressed in his funeral suit, polished his brown rubber-soled shoes and practised his accent. If at all possible, he would avoid talking to anyone, but casual questions must be answered in character. Today, Davor was an Italian-speaking Swiss compliance consultant visiting France for meetings with clients. His half-day off was a tour around a château to relax. He was timid, uncertain when speaking French or English and anti-social if an Italian latched on.

Two days ago, he had taken the same tour, wearing old clothes in faded colours, a broken pair of sunglasses stuck together with sticky tape, scuffed worn-down shoes and two days of growth on his face. He spoke gruff French and did not encourage conversation. It differentiated him entirely from the quiet, well-dressed and self-effacing tourist of today. Neither was memorable, which was exactly as it should be.

He wore sunglasses again today, but this time, with no hidden camera. He had all the detail necessary to access the house and had planned the mission to the last detail. As always. He'd even sourced the right flowers. The only variables would be timing and his fellow tourists.

As the taxi crunched to a halt on the gravel forecourt, a smile tugged at his lips. A bus was disgorging its passengers, a voluble group of schoolchildren, whose teachers were trying to herd them into some kind of assembly. Wonderful. Teenagers were as wilful and unpredictable as cats, thus causing the most innocent of diversions. Other guests were a British family comprising three generations, two young backpackers from New Zealand and himself.

The tour was exactly the same as before, even down to the same jokes from the guide. This one was older than last time and the obviously scripted 'funnies' weren't funny at all. He looked sour and resentful, especially when one of the teachers asked a question. Davor loitered at the rear of the party, ostensibly making notes, and waited till they entered the long rose-covered bower which led to the vineyards before slipping away. He stopped for a second, phone to ear, just in case anyone checked to see where he was. No one looked around and he ducked along the outside of the bower, keeping tall fir trees between himself and the security cameras.

He moved fast and with purpose, as if he had every right to be there. The route, seared into his memory, unfolded exactly as predicted. Bower – fir trees – greenhouses – summer house – lawn – low stone wall – *et voilà* – you have reached your destination. He strode confidently past the greenhouses, scanning left to right when he almost collided with a man coming out of the summer house, carrying a tray.

Without hesitation, Davor went on the attack in his unaccented French. "What are you doing here?" He glanced at his watch. "At this time of day?"

The man's forehead corrugated into a frown and he hissed his reply. "Keep your voice down, *putain*! She's asleep in there." He jerked his head behind him at the hexagonal summer house. "Today she wanted *goûter* in the garden and look how much she ate." He showed Davor an untouched tray of pastries and rolled his eyes. "Make yourself useful and tell Maurice to keep the tour away from this side of the house. Screaming kids will put her in an even fouler mood." With a glance over his shoulder, he stalked off over the lawn.

"*D'accord.*" Davor pulled out his phone and mimed speaking into it while returning in the direction he had come. Thoughts fizzed around his brain as he circled behind the greenhouses and crept up through the shrubbery towards the summer house. Could it really be this easy? He squatted behind a bush sprouting lurid purple blooms and surveyed the scene. Between him and the house lay a perfectly kept lawn with a sprinkler waving back and forth in a broad circle. Beyond that were the low wall and veranda delineating Madame's quarters.

He sat. He watched. He timed his move. Creeping up to the back of the summer house, he peered through the slats. He could see the doors, the back of a chaise longue and the table which presumably, a tea tray had recently occupied. With all the sounds of birdsong, insects and summer breezes caressing leaves, he could hear no breathing. When the lawn sprinkler created a veil of droplets between him and the château, he slipped around the structure and in through the summer house doors.

He stood just inside, allowing his eyes to adjust to the shady interior. The chaise longue was striped by light from the slatted walls and partially open door. The old lady slept like a child, on her side with her face pillowed on her hands. In the hollow between her bony elbows and silk-covered knees, a small ginger Pomeranian stared at him with belligerent eyes as black as beetles.

Davor understood dogs. He took off his sunglasses, lowered his eyes, crouched and bowed his head. The dog did not growl but kept its eyes on him. Still in a deferential position, Davor shuffled forward and placed his gift on the table beside the sleeping woman's head. He reversed to the doorway, took his eyes off the animal to check the sprinkler and ducked away through the shrubs when the moment was right. He moved with purpose, slipped off his jacket in the warmth of the sun, replaced his sunglasses and without anyone noticing, rejoined the tour.

It didn't matter that he wouldn't see the moment of realisation. The second they understood the message, frosted fingers of fear would splinter and crack throughout the family. While the Black Widow slept, vulnerable as a newborn, Le Fantôme had left his mark. A sweet posy of lavender, a watercolour card and a message.

'Greetings from the other side. *Grosses bises*, Letty Louise."

Chapter 19

"Leather. No, wait a minute, that's tobacco."

"Final answer?"

Beatrice wafted the tiny vial under her nose once again. "Yes. That is essence of tobacco."

Matthew shook his head. "Sandalwood. I'm really not sure perfumery is your forte, Old Thing. Out of ten, you've only got three right."

"For a novice perfumier, that's pretty good. Don't put me off with all your doom and bloom. Let's try one more and then stop for afternoon tea. Where's Huggy Bear? You didn't leave her in the garden after walks, did you?"

"No, she's under your chair. That's probably the reason you can't detect smells accurately. Your nostrils have been infiltrated with the pong of recently-caught-in-summer-shower dog. What do you want to try next? More base notes, fruits and florals, or perhaps given the circumstances, we should tackle the aquatic section?"

"Don't even give me a hint. Just pass me an essence and let me guess."

Matthew ran his eyes over the rows of brown glass samples and with a smug smile, selected one. "I'd say this should ring a few bells."

The aroma was instantly familiar. Beatrice closed her eyes, concentrating on the happy signals the scent had evoked. Words crossed her mind: blossom, candyfloss, summer breeze, pink carnations and pedal-pushers. She opened her eyes, firmly convinced she was right. "Bubble-gum!" she said, with a victorious smile.

"Cherry. Which might be a flavour of bubble-gum, I couldn't possibly say."

With a frown, she handed back the bottle. "Frankly, perfume testing is a pain in the rear. Why anyone would devote one's life to differentiating any whiffs other than nice and nasty escapes me. Shall we have some tea and a flapjack?"

He packed away the samples kit in his usual meticulous manner and she went into the kitchen, followed by the always optimistic Huggy Bear. Her dismissal of the skill involved in professional scent-making was in inverse proportion to the fear dogging her. Her ability to fake the most fundamental expertise was lacking in any conviction. Even Matthew could see it.

"The thing is," he said, entering the kitchen and setting the tea tray, "you don't have to do this. Why not have Catinca pose as the expert? I truly can't imagine how you expect to pass yourself off as an artisan perfume-maker with three days to learn the basics."

As always, his comprehension of her limitations both soothed and irritated her. "I cannot let Catinca go to Paris on her own. She's inexperienced and naïve when it comes to detection. My guidance is essential. We have a clear goal: find out if these companies are façades to launder money. For this, we need to try to find out as much as possible about their legal structure, but also attempt to see what is going on behind the curtain. Hence the entire masquerade. Plus we are talking about two different enterprises: one being the fashion house, which is Catinca's speciality and the second is the perfumier, which ought to be mine. Catinca has managed to wangle an invitation for both of us – she as fashion influencer and me as potential bespoke perfume creator. I have to go, Matthew."

She filled the teapot and placed it on the tray, along with two flapjacks on a single plate. There were more in the biscuit tin, but if she put them out, he would eat them.

He took the tray into the conservatory, where the late afternoon sunshine threw golden light onto the lawn, hydrangea and potted geraniums. Foliage still glistened and dripped after the surprise shower, and the open door permitted a breeze to flow past them into the house. Beatrice relaxed into one of the rattan chairs, wondering why she would ever wish to leave such a blissful environment.

"If you have to go, then go you must. I am just not sure how you want to establish this view behind the curtain...what do you expect they will show to new business interests?" Matthew placed the tray on the table, paced across to the ottoman to give Dumpling's grey fur a stroke and settled in his own garden chair.

"First step is to get close to those who run these companies. I will have to trust my instinct when it comes to the criminal potential of these individuals – if I get close enough. Once I am convinced they have blood on their hands, I have the dexterity to lift a bit of that curtain, or at least put an ear to it."

"Oh dear, please don't tell me what that means. Are you staying on the right side of the law, Old Thing?"

Beatrice fixed him with a fierce stare. "I gave up a lot of privileges when leaving the force, so it's only natural to take a liberty here and there."

"I see. I trust your judgement and hope you two will be careful. My remaining confusions circle around who exactly the client might be. That is, who is paying for your trip, time and expenses? Secondly, I still fail to comprehend the perfume angle. After a consultation with my daughters, I think I understand the meaning of 'influencers' in the world of fashion. But I'm struggling to see where you fit in. Shall I pour?"

"Please do, I'm parched. Right, I'll tell you again and if there's any part of this you don't understand, say so. But just because

I'm talking, that doesn't mean I'm in any way distracted. I'm watching my flapjack. One each and that's your lot."

Huggy Bear rested her chin on Matthew's foot and Beatrice could swear she batted her eyelashes.

"As if I would dream of stealing yours! You have a very low opinion of me."

"I have a very realistic picture of you. Which reminds me, I saw Susie from The Angel while I was at the shop this morning and she happened to ask if we enjoyed her blackberry and apple pie. I told her I hadn't got a chance to try it yet. However, after a full inspection of the fridge and freezer, there is not a trace of a fruit pie."

"Oh yes, Susie's pie. The family demolished most of that when they came round the other day and I finished the leftovers. Now then, as far as I understand it, influencers are people on social media with a huge following. If they recommend a product or post photographs of themselves wearing a particular item, its success is guaranteed. Apparently, Catinca's fashion sense has elevated her to such a position. Her status is such that the Parisian fashion house extended an invitation in response to her email. She is a VIP in the world of silly money for ridiculous items. But where do you fit in?"

"You are an arch-distracter, Matthew Bailey, and I've known you too long to fall for it. When I get back from Paris, you and I are going to the doctor to check your cholesterol levels. You'd better hope they have decreased since last time, otherwise afternoon tea will be a slice of cucumber and tea with lemon. The reason I have to go to Paris is to play the role of Catinca's perfumier. What you need to understand is that many of these influencers use their reach quite cynically, requesting free samples and demanding access to events just for the kudos of their endorsement. Catinca has never done that. In fact, she makes a feature of her independence and non-slavish attitude to designer labels. Her most popular ensembles come from charity shops and end of line sale items. She's never even tried to get a free pair of Converse trainers, despite the fact she is their greatest fan."

Matthew sipped his tea with a fond smile. "True. Try as I might, I cannot imagine seeing anything else on her feet. Yes, I'm with you so far. Independent, ethical influencer in the world of fashion requests a visit to a designer, who rolls out the red carpet. The step I'm missing is the perfume."

Huggy Bear let out a deep sigh and rolled onto her back for a tummy tickle. Matthew obliged.

Beatrice continued. "Catinca's ruse is that she is setting up her own high-end, self-curated boutique somewhere near Spitalfields Market. She wants to talk to key companies as potential suppliers. In addition, she intends to launch her own perfume line under the name of the shop – Radu. To that end, she has sourced a small scale perfumier who can create the scent to her own specifications. She asked the people at Papillon for an audience and if she might bring her local expert to learn more about the craft at professional level from the gurus at Parfums Parfaits. Apparently, they all but bit her hand off. Hence my having to learn the basics of perfumery in three days." She let out a sigh to rival the dog's and tucked into her flapjack.

Matthew relaxed into this chair and lifted his face to the sunshine, a pose well known to his partner. He was thinking. Not just a moment of distraction, but analytical study of a problem with an academic's brain. Beatrice chewed on the sticky oats, waiting for the outcome. When he was good, he was very, very good. But when he was great, he was brilliant.

Finally, he was ready to speak. "Ego. That's the way to play it. Put yourself in this posh Parisian's shoes. He or she will expect adoration and fawning, plus plenty of intelligent questions. You must be humble, starry-eyed and appear overwhelmed. If you make a faux pas, that's entirely natural. This is a beetle touring the dragon's lair and certain clumsy stumbles are to be expected.

Let's practise now. I am the snooty *parfumier* from the 5th *arrondisement*. You are the British amateur I am supposed to host. Focus on what you need to know and find a way to ask your questions, while flattering my ego. *Allons-y*!"

Beatrice took her cue from Huggy Bear and batted her eyelashes. "Monsieur, I cannot tell you how happy I am to be here today. This is an experience I will never forget."

His nostrils flared. "Why the Alabama accent? You're supposed to be a West Country scent specialist, not a debutante from the Deep South."

"Good point. Just drawing on my inner Scarlett O'Hara for inspiration." She tried again. "One is quite overcome by your kindness. I must express my most sincere gratitude for such gracious hospitality. Pray tell me, how did you rise to the impressive rank of High *Perfumier* in such an exalted institution?" More eyelashes.

"Neither are you Princess Margaret. Can you not just be yourself, with a touch of plausible mendacity? It's not that difficult."

"Oh really? You bloody do it then! I'm the Monsieur Le Parfum and you are a private detective passing herself off as an expert in a subject she knows as well as pocket science. *Bonjour, madame, je suis Jean-Michel le Nez*."

Matthew didn't hesitate. "Monsieur le Nez, I cannot thank you enough for giving me your time today. It is an honour and a privilege. I have admired your expertise and reputation over my entire career in the world of scent, so to be here with you today is one of the highlights of my life."

Despite herself, Beatrice was flattered. "That's very kind of you. What do you need to know?"

"My interest as Ms Radu's creator of scent regards scale. As you may know, I am at the opposite end, devising bespoke signature perfumes for specialist commissions. Could you treat me as a complete novice in the world of professional *parfumerie* and walk me through the steps?"

Beatrice stared at him, wondering if she could get away with sending Matthew to Paris in a convincing wig. "How did you get to be so good at this?" she asked.

He poured them another cup of tea with a contented smile. "Put yourself in their shoes. Humble but not fawning, respectful, astute and curious. Ask questions, don't assume expertise, shrug off any curiosity with modesty and respect their education. The French love that. Now, I'm going to do the crossword and rest my eyes for an hour. I'd recommend you do your research on their real products and your imaginary ones. Did we already decide on what we're having for dinner?"

"Vegetable soup with a wholemeal bun?"

He stared at her in horror. "On Saturday night, all we're having is vegetable soup?"

His heartbroken expression made Beatrice laugh. "Oh all right. I'll make mackerel with gooseberries and a side of paella. We can even crack open a bottle of Spanish red."

Matthew's eyes gleamed. "I know just the thing. That Priorat Marianne's new chap gave me. Best go and fetch it now to ensure we consume it at room temperature."

"When did he give you a bottle of wine?"

"Wednesday or Thursday, I think it was. When you were in Salzburg. They all came round here because I was babysitting Luke while they went out as a foursome."

"I didn't realise you'd met him. Well?"

"Well what?"

"Matthew, don't be so obtuse. Tell me about the new boyfriend."

"Seemed perfectly pleasant. Polite and well mannered. Not to mention the bottle of Priorat."

"Oh it's hopeless trying to get an impression out of you. I'll call in to see Tanya tomorrow and get some proper gossip. Did you at least get his name?"

Matthew scratched his chin. "Jason, I believe. Or was it Gareth?"

Beatrice rolled her eyes. "As I say, hopeless. But one last thing, you asked about the money. Expenses are paid by MdM – and they're going the full Monty, if you'll excuse the expression. Five-star hotel, limos from the airport, restaurant reservations, the works. As for the client, if I find anything to connect this lot to Gennaio Colacino's demise, his family will pay the bill." This last was merely supposition, but she conveyed confidence. "Weren't you going to get the wine?"

Matthew studied her for a moment then shook his head. "I have to say, one of the things I love about our relationship is that both of us hold the consistent belief that the other is lying. Keeps us on our toes, no?"

Huggy Bear got to her feet and trotted after him as he left the room.

Beatrice looked over at Dumpling. "He ate that whole pie himself, didn't he?"

Dumpling blinked his golden eyes, inscrutable as a sphinx.

It took three calls and several messages, but finally Russell Lane got in touch.

"Hello, Beatrice. I hear you were looking for me. How's tricks?"

"Russell! Thank you so much for calling me back. Is all well in Naples?" She scanned the study for her glasses. As usual, they were nowhere to be seen.

"Last thing I heard, yes. I live in Ischia now, so don't see as much of the restaurant gang as I used to. Although I did hear you went to Budapest to follow up on what happened to Gennaio."

"Yes, that's actually why I wanted to talk to you. I want to pick your brains as a personal security expert because I have a lead regarding the Gennaio situation."

"Brilliant! What can I do to help?" His enthusiasm made Beatrice smile.

"Technology. I'm rather out of the loop, I'm afraid. You see, I'm heading to Paris next week to talk to some people. The thing is, if I wanted to plant a bug on someone in order to record our conversation and crucially, what might be said afterwards, how would you advise me to do it?"

Russell's professionalism swung into play. "I assume you won't have a chance of removing the listening device?"

"No, that's the problem. I have an audience with someone rather important and I'll only get one shot."

"Hmm. You could get a device that sends a signal to a receiver when it's connected to a mobile network. Then it sends whatever it picks up. All you have to do is call a number and retrieve the recording. It's not the most reliable method, but in a city like Paris, you'll probably have pretty good 5G coverage."

Beatrice squinted and made notes. "And how long would something like that last?"

"Depends. If you plant it in an office, it could transmit for around forty-eight hours. If you plant it on a person, it will only last till they take off whatever item of clothing it's attached to."

"Yes, I'd want to attach it to a person. Where could I buy such a thing?"

Russell gave her the name of two shops in London and one in Paris she could try. Then he pointed out a snag. "Is this conversation going to be in English?"

"Yes, he'll speak to me in English. Oh hellfire. The rest of it will be in French, of course. I'm going to need a translator. A discreet translator."

"What about Bruno? You couldn't ask for someone more discreet as he's the one paying you to investigate this. His French is fluent because he studied at the Sorbonne."

"Brilliant idea! Thank you, Russell, you are a godsend."

"Not a problem. Good luck, Beatrice and if there's anything

else, give me a shout. I'll do anything to nail the people who killed Gennaio."

Chapter 20

Every detail merited 100% attention. Three days in Paris would require no fewer than eighteen different outfits and enough accoutrements to fill a second suitcase. Fortunately, since MdM were offering first-class flights, Catinca was able to fit her clothes, trainers and toiletries into her hold luggage, keeping her sketchpads, handbags and jewellery in her carry-on bag. Style had never been more important. She'd spent the entire weekend planning her looks, photographing each from every angle.

The only issue was Beatrice. Catinca had sent her detailed instructions which she knew perfectly well her new boss would skim read and turn up in M&S slacks regardless. Accessories were the only way to brand the stubborn sodding woman as An Artist. Catinca selected scarves, shawls and statement jewellery, all in shades of herbs and spices: cinnamon, turmeric, sage, ginger and saffron. At least she didn't need to worry about Beatrice's hair. That already marked her out as an eccentric who stood out from the crowd.

On arrival at London City Airport, before they even checked in, Catinca herded her straight into the toilets. Thankfully, Beatrice had got the message regarding neutrals. A cream blouse, beige slacks (M&S with an elasticated waist, natch) and simple white deck shoes gave Catinca a blank canvas. Ignoring all the moaning and complaints, she added a dip-dyed green shawl across Beatrice's shoulders, a green wood bangle with brass inlay on her wrist and put her tatty handbag into a straw tote printed with images of exotic herbs.

From there, they dropped off their suitcases, navigated security and made a bee-line for the Duty Free. Beatrice browsed the wine shelves while Catinca focused on finding the right perfume product. She asked the staff for newest releases and managed to snag a couple of samples, one Hermès: *Ange des Neiges* and one Jo Malone: Hemlock and Bergamot. Maybe best not to tell Beatrice the names. After bagging their goodies, they repaired to the lounge and indulged in a glass of champagne. After all, what else would an influencer do?

"You really do look the part," said Beatrice, with a chuckle. "Those sunglasses, the hat and that lipstick. If I didn't know you, I'd be intimidated."

Catinca sipped at her champagne and glanced at her reflection in the mirrors behind the bar. The white suit, black Fendi shades and retro Biba bag as an ensemble was well sodding impressive, but the hat? She might be a short-arse but with Converse high-top wedges and a brilliant white fedora, she turned every single head in the room.

"That's the point, mate. Ignore all the staring as if it happens all the time. Drink champagne, leave half the glass and stalk off as if we got better things to do. When we get to Paris, give it massive attitude. Flap scarf, wait for people to open doors, play A-list and people gonna believe it."

Beatrice looked doubtful but took the plunge. She flapped her shawl in front of her face and over her shoulder, her bangle catching the light. "Darling, is there nothing else to read than newspapers? Not a copy of *Harper's Bazaar* or *A Cut Above*? And they call this First Class!" She swigged half a glass of her champagne and in a loud voice, announced, "That's flat and I shan't drink it. Would you be a poppet and order me a Bloody Mary while I tootle off to the powder room?"

Catinca watched her sashay across the lounge and couldn't

help but grin. Then she straightened her face into a stroppy pout and signalled to the waiter. "Could we have two Bloody Marys over here? Oh, and make it Stolly, would you?" Even if they couldn't pull this gig off, they'd have a whole lotta fun trying.

The limo driver, at Catinca's request, took the scenic route to their hotel. First, L'Arc de Triomphe, followed by Jardins du Trocadéro to look across the river at the Eiffel Tower. Along the Seine, up to the Champs Élysées, past the Louvre and the little island which was home to the fire-damaged Notre-Dame cathedral. Then as far as Place de la Bastille before turning back along Rue de Rivoli to Place Vendôme. The driver, an attractive woman in chauffeur's uniform, directed their attention to the key sights, but did not try to encourage small talk. The sunglasses were an essential part of Catinca's armour. If anyone saw her eyes shining at all these famous locations she'd only ever seen on screen, the game would be up. The persona of a city sophisticate betrayed by her inner excited schoolgirl.

Hotel de Marsault was the poshest building Catinca had ever entered. It had doormen to greet you and usher you inside, wearing top hats and tailcoats. Bellboys with those little caps scampered to the boot to fetch their cases. The foyer, glimpsed through the revolving doors, whispered of luxury, fresh flowers and chandeliers. Keeping in character, she asked the chauffeuse her name.

"Delphine, *mademoiselle*. I will be your driver during your stay."

"Thank you, Delphine, and I'm so pleased you're going to look after us. I don't deal in cash – too dirty – but I would like to give you this. It's my own design." She placed a velvet bag in the woman's hand.

"That's very kind. I will return at two-fifteen to take you both to your appointments."

"Perfect. See you soon."

The moment Catinca dismissed the bellboy with a charming smile and a small gift – "Save it for later" – she closed the door of the suite and faced Beatrice, who was staring at her open-mouthed.

Catinca burst into howls of glee, incredulous herself. Beatrice joined in, shaking her head in disbelief. Pent-up tension evaporated into belly laughs and Catinca finally took off her hat. "Right, mate, let's explore. First stop, bathroom. I wanna check out the toiletries selection."

"First stop for me is the mini-bar. I want to assess the champagne selection."

In order to do some last-minute cramming, they ordered room service when Beatrice had finally stopped dithering over the menu.

"It's just impossible to choose. I want everything."

"Be practical, PI Stubbs. Nothing fishy or with onions. You gonna be up close with some posh noses so you don't wanna belch. Have a salad or an omelette. I'm having Croque Monsieur."

As they ate, Beatrice gave her a frank look of admiration. "You really are quite brilliant at this. I have more questions than I can articulate."

"Like what?" asked Catinca, chewing on the best slice of cheese and ham on toast she'd ever eaten. They should offer this dish at Dionysus. She checked herself. Adrian should offer this dish at Dionysus.

"How do you blend in so easily? I mean, I can see you look amazingly stylish because you always do. But the way you step into first class like you belong? How you deal with staff? And what did you give to the chauffeur?"

Catinca's eyes strayed to the white fedora on the sideboard as she considered her answer. "Three things. One, know your shit.

Research, read, study photos of current fashions as if you got a test on Monday. Two, dress the part. I know you think I make a fuss but I'm telling you they check what you wear as if it's your passport. You're wearing an Alice Temperley scarf I got at a car boot sale, a pre-owned Kenzo tote and one of my own designs on your wrist. They judge, Beatrice, that is what they do. Attention to the detail."

"And the bell boy? How did you tip him?"

"One of them little trio of whiskies I bought at the airport. Always think ahead, see. Number three, fake it. Watch how the rich and famous behave and act the part. I gave the nice chauffeur lady a bracelet I found in an Oxfam shop. Changed the stones and polished the silver and added one of my seals. It looks vintage. Sort of thing a lovely woman can wear on her wrist to add a flash of class to her uniform. She'll tell her friends it's a limited edition. S'pose it is, in a way. Ha!" She cackled at the thought of herself in a five-star hotel in Paris, eating posh food, and wished she could send a photo to her mother. Her smile disappeared.

"Right, let's get this down our necks and practise attaching these bugs. We're on stage, mate, so we can't put a foot wrong. You ready?"

Beatrice flicked a hand into the air as if she were holding a cigarette. "I am if you are. Oh dear. Did that sound a bit *Thelma and Louise*?"

"I sodding hope not. You know what happened to them two. Come on, Coco, we got work to do. You wanna try planting one on me first?"

Delphine pulled up at the doors of Papillon at one minute past three. Catinca wished Beatrice a good afternoon in the breeziest of goodbyes, despite her nerves, and stepped out of the car. An assistant waited in the air-conditioned lobby to furnish her with a security pass hanging from a lanyard.

Catinca eyed it as if the man had handed her a strip of rotting fish skin. She took it between finger and thumb and dropped it into her handbag. Nothing would persuade her to ruin her outfit with such an ugly thing.

He coughed and with an apologetic smile, said, "You need that to get through the security gates, but you don't need to wear it all the time."

"Thank God," Catinca replied, thickening her accent. This was her moment in the spotlight and she had prepared an entrance such as this for years.

The lackey guided her through the security section and explained that she would meet Anastasia Kravets in an hour. First, she would have a private fashion show of the pieces Ms Kravets had personally selected. He ushered her into the inner sanctum.

A second assistant took over with a bright welcoming smile. "This way, Ms Radu. Can I get you any refreshment?"

"Thank you, no," Catinca replied, with the faintest upward twitch of her lips.

The woman took her into a long carpeted room with cream walls and half a dozen seats. She motioned for Catinca to sit and launched into her spiel.

"We are very happy to welcome you to Papillon today. Ms Kravets has chosen a selection of pieces from the current season, some from this year's Autumn/Winter collection and a few vintage items from previous seasons as her personal favourites to display for you in a private showing. The show will last around twenty minutes and I will be on hand to answer any questions you might have. Then I will take you on a tour of our design studios and tailoring workshops, where you can see how our experts collaborate in the process of creation. Finally, at four, you have an audience with our artistic director herself. During the show, you are welcome to take photographs. If you would like a model to stop so you can see more detail, just say so. If you would like something to eat or drink while you watch, I will arrange it. During the tour, for reasons of privacy, photographs are not permitted and no food or drink is allowed into the workshops. Thank you. Are you ready to begin?"

Catinca gave a curt nod and trained her eyes on the catwalk. The lights changed, just a touch. Audience chairs darkened while the catwalk glowed brighter. Excitement buzzed in Catinca's stomach, the same feeling she had at the start of any performance, but she maintained her poker face. Which got harder and harder over the next ten minutes.

The Spring/Summer Collection she already knew and disliked. Sodding 1980s come back to life in pastels. Ruffles and bows, velvet and buckles, all in shades she wouldn't even choose for toilet paper. She watched in silence, stifling a yawn, hoping Autumn/Winter would bring something to keep her awake. It didn't. Asymmetric cuts in neon colours, slashed necklines, coloured sunglasses, stupid mini handbags only big enough to take a credit card and a lipstick. And of all the horrors, acid plaid! This was the worst of the 90s all over again. She clenched her fists, enraged by the blatant recycling of trends and worst of all, trends that were shitty in the first place. This woman had zero imagination.

"It's bold, isn't it," whispered the assistant, who sat one seat away.

Catinca made a noncommittal grunt which turned into a groan when a model came out in a pink plaid trouser suit and a bucket hat.

The music changed from some well sad rock anthem she didn't recognise to a classical piece she did. *Carmina Burana*. Seriously? Was this some kind of a joke? She rotated her head slowly enough to be zombie-style and shot a WTF look at the assistant. The woman didn't even notice, gazing at the entrance of the first retro piece. Catinca focused on the model sashaying towards her in the most divine duster coat she had even seen. It was beyond beautiful. It was art.

The swishing ankle-length hem was the colour of sand, with printed shells rippling as the girl moved. Silky golden fabric faded to bubbly white and blue from the knee, deepening to a Grecian blue as the observer's eyes moved up the body. Impossibly lovely! How on earth had they made that? You couldn't dip-dye with enough detail to create surf, waves and the natural shades of the sea. She was just about to shout 'Stop!' when the model reached the end of the catwalk, swept her arms into a T shape and turned her back. Catinca saw it and gasped.

A photograph, printed directly onto the lightest, most fluid material, gave the impression the wearer was wrapped in the ocean. On the arms were distant yachts blending into the horizon. She took out her phone, the first time in this show, and took a video as the model twirled and retreated. The next was already emerging, her long foal-like legs in gladiator sandals emerging from a sleeveless shift dress. The neckline was sunset pink, descending to a stark black city skyline around her torso, melting into the reflection of the skyline in the silvery sea. Again, a photograph printed on silk? Chiffon with an under-layer of something soft to caress your curves? It was inspired and heart-achingly lovely, a perfect moment not in an album or online, but on your own body. This was the marriage of vision and texture and emotional impact. She stopped filming. She would ask for details of which year this stuff came out later. Now, she had to concentrate on the moment and all the sensations cascading around her like a memory she'd forgotten.

Once it was over, the assistant handed her three brochures so she could check the detail of what she had seen. Catinca knew her English had faults, but the trying-too-hard-to-be-cool tone of the descriptions made her toes curl. She shoved them into her Fendi tote and signalled she was ready to see the rest of the workshop. Much like the show, the tour fell into two distinct halves. The artistic visionaries were anything but, in Catinca's eyes. Phonies, the lot of them. They dressed the part, groomed, arty, *outré* but not one of them wore anything with real imagination. As for their closely guarded designs, all watered-down copies, slavishly following the main brands. This didn't make sense. How could a design house with no innovation or imagination command such status and top-level real estate? And who designed the vintage stuff?

The workshops were a different matter. Catinca fluttered from one table to another, admiring the tailors' cutting skills, adoring the seamstresses' understanding of fabric. Folds, ruching, symmetry, embellishment, structure and sheen, Catinca was in her element. Any question the French speakers didn't get was translated by the assistant lady, who had proved quite helpful, despite Catinca's misgivings. What luxury to have such fabrics, such talent at your disposal! With this array of seasoned talent and raw material, why wouldn't you create something original, fabulous and lovely to make folk catch their breath?

At four o'clock and with much fanfare and reverence, the assistant escorted her to the studio-cum-office of Anastasia Kravets. The woman herself was on the phone but pointed to a chair with a brief nod of her ash-blonde head. Catinca did not sit. Instead, she stalked around the room, looking at each print in turn. This was her world. Imagination, design, beauty, ideas. She gazed at a print of a model in a black cat-suit, admiring the proportions, then allowed her focus to take in the reflection in the glass. The trip to the bathroom for a touch-up was a good idea. Her make-up was immaculate and her suit perfection. All she needed to add was the attitude.

Anastasia Kravets spoke rapid French into the phone, punctuating her speech with frequent gestures. Backlit as she was by the floor-to-ceiling glass walls, Catinca could not observe details, but itched to study the woman up close. After over a minute of increasingly irritated discussion, the hostess put down the phone and stood to welcome her guest.

"So sorry about that. Last minute panic at a show in Tokyo." She rolled her eyes and with a brilliant smile, held out a hand. "I'm very pleased to meet you. I've followed you for a long time. I love your style." Her dark vowels marked her accent as Eastern European, as did the impressive bone structure and heavy brows. "Please call me Anastasia."

"Thank you. And you can call me Catinca. Tell you what, so happy to be here. Papillon is brand I been watching for ages. Today is like birthday and Christmas all at once."

Anastasia's face warmed. "How lovely! Come, let's have some refreshment and conversation. Shall we sit?" She waved at the sofa and the gorgeous coffee table piled with art books and magazines. "I don't have much time because I need to leave for a meeting. How was the tour? I hope Claudette answered all your questions."

"That lady was well helpful. I didn't wanna do anything before asking you, but is it OK to give her small gift? Just a token, my own design."

"Of course you can. She's my right hand, you know, I would be lost without her. Listen, I want to drink a glass of wine. Will you join me? Red or white?"

"Ooh, lovely! White, please. I had champagne at lunch so best not mix it."

"In that case, we'll have champagne! *Fin*, we're celebrating!" She pressed a button on her phone and before she and Catinca had even settled on the cream cracked-leather sofa with gilt legs and armrests, a side door opened and a handsome young bloke stood awaiting instructions.

Again, Catinca understood little of the conversation although she did catch the word Roederer. Ordering a genuine French champagne, not some cheap knock-off, was a good sign.

They began, as they must, by exchanging compliments. The

office was so elegant! This sofa, this table are both to die for! Restored pieces? How charming! Where did those earrings come from? Your own design! What an eye you have! Papillon's Lautrec range was inspiring – such fabulous vintage colours. How does a woman as busy as Anastasia design everything herself?

The geezer was back with a silver tray, an ice bucket and two tulip glasses. Another point to Anastasia. No coupes, no flutes but long-stemmed tulips. Catinca approved and started to like this woman. He poured, they toasted a great working relationship and continued their mutual admiration.

"I'm excited about your proposed boutique, Catinca. Your imagination and courage will devise something head and shoulders above the crowd. Perhaps at our lunch meeting tomorrow, we can get down to business and how we can help each other."

"Yes, that'd be best. Today, I am sponge. Absorb everything. Also, you in hurry and I still little starry-eyed after this afternoon." She played up her accent, knowing it would always result in people underestimating her.

The woman laughed. "I was starry-eyed when I first got here. I couldn't believe they would let me and my imagination loose on a designer label!"

Catinca took a sip of champagne and set herself in listening mode.

Anastasia took the floor. "As a model, I spent a lot of time getting in and out of designer clothes. I appreciated the craftsmanship and learned a lot about how to put together a look. My aunt Daria was also a model, but more for magazines than catwalks. Daria and I have always loved fashion and where better to study classic haute couture than Paris?"

"You're so lucky," breathed Catinca. "From what I read, your aunt was a real beauty who married Zane de Marsault. That's such a tragic story."

Anastasia stiffened.

"Two beautiful people with the whole world at their feet. Too sad," said Catinca, playing up the gossip-mag style drama of the story and staring into her champagne glass.

Her companion softened. "A terrible accident, yes. It broke my aunt's heart. I was too young to remember him, sadly. When I got too old to continue as a model, I joined her in France. She had her own business and I wanted to study fashion."

"Too old to model? But you're beautiful! I'm serious. Most women would kill for face like yours."

"You're very sweet." Anastasia mimed blowing a kiss and then her face hardened. "Fashion is a brutal business, you know, and when you have an endless stream of fourteen-year-olds with pubescent pouts and nothing more than two quails' eggs for a chest, bones and balance count for nothing." She refilled their glasses, her gaze distant.

"Thank you. So from ex-model to fashion student, I get it so far. Beauty and brains. Then to head the most exciting brand in the industry? I'm missing something and I wanna know exactly what it is so I can follow in footsteps."

Anastasia threw back her head and laughed, her delight hypnotically lovely. White teeth flashed and her subtly blended face creased in amusement. "Contacts, darling girl. My widowed aunt had married into an important family. When they were looking for someone to head their fashion house, I had not only a reputation on the scene but the skills to match."

Catinca allowed her body to deflate and her gaze fell to the floor. It wasn't all an act. Disappointment was a near cousin of disgust and dissatisfaction. These people, hogging power, promoting their incompetent relatives, just like this woman. Beautiful, yes, but what did she know about fabric, texture, cutting, vision? People like her had no business accepting prize posts on no other merit than their relatives.

Mirth left Anastasia's green eyes and she focused on Catinca.

"You could follow in my footsteps, you smart, stylish young woman. How would you like to be an intern, here at Papillon? With me as your personal mentor? You and I might make a great team, not to mention fun friends."

Catinca's stomach flipped. All she had ever wanted was a job in fashion. She'd dreamed, fantasised and longed for such an opportunity. Now here it was, handed to her on a plate, with an accompanying glass of Roederer. Thing is, she was assistant to PI Stubbs.

She pressed her hand to her mouth, squeezing her eyes shut, her emotions not entirely fake.

Anastasia placed a hand on her forearm. "You and I are alike, Catinca. We work hard and take our chances. I offer one to you. You could be an asset at Papillon because you have a sharp eye. Think about it and let me know. I must leave you now, but we will meet at Les Deux Magots at midday tomorrow. One last thing – what did you think of the show?"

Crunch time. "Want the truth? The vintage line blew me away. The rest of stuff was edgy, contemporary, well-done, but the beachscape prints on dresses, coats and shirts. Honest, mate, most beautiful I seen in long time."

"Really? The Naïade line? Did you honestly like them?"

"Best of lot. Fresh, light, lovely stuff I wanna wear myself. Nearly tackled that model for duster coat. Who designed that line?"

Anastasia swallowed, almost tearful. "Me. All the images were photographs I took on my aunt's boat. Inspired by the sea and the fabrics I love against my skin. But Madame de Marsault thought that concept was too simple for Papillon and my aunt agreed. She said it was too personal. That's why they brought in the creative team. Do you think the idea is ...?"

With a knock, the door opened and the assistant entered with an apologetic smile.

Anastasia shrugged. "To be continued. Until tomorrow!" She

blew another kiss, picked up her phone and left the room.

Catinca was horrified. It was all very well leaving a glass of champagne half drunk, but a whole bottle? She refilled her glass, hoping they'd let her finish it before kicking her out.

Chapter 21

"First, the muse. Perfume begins with the imagination. What do we want this scent to inspire? Is it a sensation, such as enveloping oneself in a velvet cloak on a winter's night in St Petersburg? Is it an aspiration, perhaps bestowing the heights of glamour on the wearer as she places her foot onto the red carpet? Perhaps our muse is an individual. A woman whose identity is a story in itself, let us say Paloma Picasso or Edith Piaf. Or maybe a mood? Outside is a thunderstorm, skies are the colour of slate and rain sluices down the windowpane. The scent you select must lift you, transporting you to a golden beach and cerulean sea, where seductive ocean breezes persuade you to offer your body to the rays of the sun god. This is where we begin."

Xander de Marsault didn't half like the sound of his own voice. All Beatrice's concerns about making herself plausible as a perfumier were unfounded. All she needed to do, as Matthew had predicted, was flatter the man's ego and listen. Her contributions were limited to 'quite', 'yes', 'I see' and 'mmm'. He led her from his office to the workshop, or *atelier* as he called it, pontificating in the most pretentious prose Beatrice had ever heard.

He opened a door for her. "Here is where the alchemy is created! Can you imagine, madame, that in this humble laboratory magic is made? Each man and woman in this room is an expert in the field, wielding immense power simply by inspired choices and expert blends. These people spend every day trying to make the world a more beautiful place. Come, this is where the idea takes shape and becomes a sensual truth."

Beatrice took in the workshop which didn't quite meet her idea of a modern laboratory. The first thing that struck her was the lack of natural light. The entire room had spotlights and angled lamps, creating curious pools of activity and corners of shadow. Like Santa's grotto. High wooden desks like those from the biology classes of her youth divided the room, each bearing demi-johns and glass casks filled with intensely coloured liquid. These vessels were connected by tubes, measured by dials and observed by individuals in white coats and hairnets. Magicians they might be, but from where she was standing, the perfumiers looked more like dinner ladies.

For the first time since asking her if she wanted a coffee, Xander de Marsault asked her a question. "Your concept, madame? Tell me your vision and I will suggest the notes. Our experts on the floor may add their own ideas, *non, tout le monde?*"

The netted heads nodded, smiled or simply gave her the once-over, returning their attention to their work.

Beatrice was ready for this. She'd repeated and rehearsed until the whole bloody mantra invaded her sleep. She slowed her voice and upped the Mary Poppins clipped tones.

"Thank you. You're awfully generous to share your secrets. We want to create a signature scent for our flagship store in Central London. Like I said, Catinca Radu …"

He closed his eyes, lifting chin and palms as if to ward her off. "Concept, *s'il vous plaît.* No background, no explanation, nothing more than the essence of an idea. Please, let us rise above the mundane and talk on a higher plane. What is the meaning of your perfume? Whose dreams does it fulfil? Why is it magical?"

Catinca's words rang in her ear. *Number three: fake it.*

Beatrice flung her shawl around her neck and commenced her performance.

"The meaning of this perfume is adventure and glamour, the old-school style. This is the essence of travel by train and boat, with leather luggage covered in labels. This is the Orient Express. This is St Moritz in winter, Biarritz in summer. Classic restaurants, vintage posters, darling carpets from Turkey, antique French dressers, Portuguese pottery and hand-fired Italian tiles. It fulfils the dreams of people who dress for dinner, who love *Casablanca*, *La Dolce Vita* and *Manon des Sources,* who seek out charming little bistros off the beaten track, each longing for the ancient patina of authenticity, the illusion of becoming a local, even only for a day. The magic lies in the mysteries, secrets and romance of Old Europe. That is the essence of Radu."

She held her pose, hand outstretched as if she were Maria Callas ending an aria. Activity in the lab behind Xander de Marsault had ceased, each face focused on her performance.

Monsieur de Marsault's expression was sardonic, one eyebrow raised. "*Quelle surprise*! A British company wants to celebrate its love of Europe. *Bon*, if that is your aim, let us create the basic structure of such a scent."

He guided her to the nearest wooden desk and introduced her to Elodie, a hawk-like woman in her white coat and hairnet. They drew up stools and sat opposite the woman whose unblinking amber-coloured eyes reminded Beatrice of Dumpling. "What thoughts did you have regarding top, heart and base notes? Elodie can advise you on the compatibility of the blend."

This was where Beatrice was on shaky ground. The only way to go was to pretend with conviction, or convince with pretension. "Top, or head note, should be led by bergamot. There needs to be citrus, perhaps orange and something herbal. Basil, rosemary? I cannot decide. As for the heart, sweet spices, cinnamon, cardamom, nutmeg. I believe here we need floral and

I wonder if orange blossom or tuberose would balance the head. Now base should be woody, so sandalwood, leather and something else. Chocolate or vanilla, I suggest, to express indulgence."

Elodie's warm gaze rested on her with a focus that spoke of concentration. "Yes, that is an interesting combination. I think we could try changing some elements to less dominant notes, so that the scent is not at war with itself, but complemented by each layer."

"*Chapeau*, Elodie. I agree with you," said Xander. "*Les mouillettes, s'il te plaît.*"

Elodie handed him a swathe of little paper strips which he took over to a bank of bottles against the far wall, muttering to himself in French. They watched as he selected a dab each from around a dozen bottles and brought them back to the table.

"Top note. This is what you suggested. Orange, bergamot and basil." He waved three strips of paper beneath their noses. To Beatrice, it was a lovely blend but she sensed Elodie shaking her head.

"Basil is wrong. Too brash and impudent. I suggest thyme."

Xander flared his nostrils. "Thyme? Try this first." Again he wafted three *mouillettes* just under their noses. To Beatrice, it smelt exactly the same as the one before. She breathed in, adopting a pensive expression until Elodie had given her verdict.

"No, I don't think Sage works either. That hints at English Sunday lunch, not French country garden. But I do agree with using clementine instead of orange. It makes it feel younger."

"Aha! Again she catches me. I cannot hope to fool this nose, Madame Stubbs. The Olfactory Princess! You think thyme? *Attends*." He returned to the sample shelves and pressed another droplet onto one of the blotting papers.

"This time, Elodie, let our guest have the last word. Madame Stubbs, this is the first aroma your potential client receives. Close your eyes, inhale and tell me what story it tells."

Suppressing a sigh at all this absurdity, Beatrice did as she was told and breathed in. The muted sounds of the *atelier* faded and she was sitting on a picnic blanket in an orange grove, a wicker hamper open beside her, butterflies performing a ballet over the wildflowers to a choir of cicadas as a warm breeze carried notes of the Mediterranean, whispering 'You're not in England anymore'. It wasn't what she'd asked for, but it was exquisite.

She opened her eyes to see two wide smiles. "That is it. That's exactly what I wanted." She jumped up, hugged Xander and gave him a kiss on the cheek. He looked at her as if she had just smacked him with a wet fish. Beatrice didn't think it possible, but his entire posture stiffened up a few notches.

Xander stepped away from Beatrice and bowed to Elodie. "La Princesse."

She shook her head without modesty, more a touch of impatience at a premature celebration. "It may still require changes. Now to the heart note. My sense is that you are right to say spice and floral should be centre stage after the delicate introduction of the top note, but must not drag the wearer too far from the initial sensation. May I ask a question?"

Xander's phone rang and he turned away to answer the call.

"Of course," Beatrice smiled, masking her terror of how quickly the woman could expose her as a fraud.

"The top note painted a picture for you. It did the same for me. The chances of those two pictures being the same are a billion to one. Scent has individual associations for every one of us. Let us take in the top note once more and in one minute, share all the associations that occur. Concentrate on the scent and nothing else. If closing your eyes helps, do so."

She drew a figure of eight with the *mouillettes* and closed her own eyes. They breathed in for several seconds, concentrating on their own imagery.

"*Putain!*"

Beatrice's eyes flew open at the sound of Xander's furious voice. The reactions on all the faces in the workshop confirmed what she had surmised. The word was a curse which shocked everyone in the room.

He wrenched open the door, taking the phone from his mouth and resting it against his chest as he called over to them. "*Désolé, Elodie, je dois partir immediatement.* Madame Stubbs, family emergency, I have to leave. So sorry."

With that, he was gone. A murmur susurrated around the room, accompanied by shrugs and downward tugs of several mouths.

Elodie stared after him, blinking several times in succession. "I apologise, Madame Stubbs. Where were we? Heart notes, and I think …"

Beatrice saw an opportunity and grabbed it with both hands. "Elodie, may I interrupt? I didn't like to say so, but I think Monsieur de Marsault misunderstood the reason for my visit. I am actually an artisan perfumier myself. I know perfectly well how to create a scent. My colleague's request was simply in terms of comparison of business model, not a lesson in perfume-making. That's the one aspect I do understand," she lied, hoping the woman had not seen through her weak performance. She plastered a sugary smile onto her face. "What I had hoped for was an insight into the company, its marketing, distribution arrangements, financial structure and details such as confidentiality agreements. I really am here to learn. I respect the fact you are an expert at a level to which I can only aspire in the olfactory field, but the perfume I create will be my own, not a copy of yours. Would you have a few minutes for a coffee and a chat regarding how Parfums Parfaits operates?"

The whisky-coloured eyes blinked and Elodie slid off her stool with a fluid dancer's grace. "I don't drink coffee, Madame Stubbs, but I find a peppermint tea refreshes my nose around this time of the afternoon. Shall we go up to the gardens?"

Chapter 22

A weekend at the beach had done him good. Swimming against the pounding surf, relaxing under the sun, working out all his tensions by running along the promenade, eating, resting and swimming once again. His skin turned the colour of cognac and he slept ten hours at a time, waking only to splat a mosquito or take a leak.

On Monday, he'd checked the society news in the trashy mags at the kiosk and browsed gossip sites at the Internet café. He didn't log in to social media or anything else which might volunteer his location. Nothing about an intruder at Château Agathe was reported in the press. He would have been shocked if there had been a whiff of vulnerability from the family. *Les Impénétrables*. He bought some Brie, grapes and a half bottle of Chablis and strolled back to the beach.

Tuesday morning found Davor at a street café, drinking a Ricard, an hour before his train was due to depart, considering his next move. The gift he left in the summer house could not have gone unnoticed. Now the family, the company, knew how close Le Fantôme had come to its black heart – their precious *Maman*. Close enough to break her aristocratic swanlike neck. His complete absence since his visit would act as the opposite of reassurance. He was a snake in the grass, hidden from sight, ready to attack at any time, blending in as he'd done so many times before. But this time he was not acting on their orders.

Nerves would be stretched, security increased and the flames of paranoia fanned. Davor smiled to himself, imagining the hysteria.

A waiter brushed past and Davor caught his eye, lifting his glass.

"*Oui, m'sieur.*"

A return visit to Château Agathe was out of the question. His face was recorded twice on their cameras, albeit in different disguises. Going back was madness. He might as well deliver his own head on a plate. The stakes had reached their peak. One player against all their cards. No compromise, no truce, just a single winner. His life or their company.

He tuned out the sounds of children's laughter from a nearby table and returned to the insoluble conundrum that faced him. He knew too much. They had to erase him as they had erased so many others. Even if he were to kill every last member of the family, they still had agents out there with instructions for vengeance. He could not win.

His nostrils exhaled a snort of annoyance. Of course he could win. All he needed was a cool head and a plan. So far, everything had gone as smoothly as a Swiss watch. Strike once and at the heart of the operation. Let them panic while you disappear. Then you come back and strike harder. Three times in total until they called off their dogs.

He smiled with a bitter shake of the head. Wasn't he one of their dogs? How many times had he been called off, leashed and restrained, until the time was right? There was only one way to end this. Scare them so badly they'd leave him alone. When they recovered themselves, he'd be gone. Not in Croatia, not in France, but adrift for a time. Perhaps work as a martial arts instructor in Jakarta for a couple of seasons, grow vegetables in Haiti, play chess in Kyrgyzstan, just until he could see how the land lay.

Priority number one: leave footprints in the inner sanctum.

The summer house had been a stroke of luck, or so he thought. Now he regretted abandoning Plan A. He should have entered her bedroom. He'd taken the lazy option, like the slow, fat dope he'd become. Time to sharpen up. Next time, he'd get it right.

He looked at the advertising hoarding across the street, showing an elderly couple laughing on a sunlit meadow. Pensions, insurance, whatever, he couldn't be bothered to read the text. What it was selling was security. Something Davor had never known. Never would.

But neither would his ex-employers. He would haunt them like every sin they had ever committed until he drove them mad.

Concentrate on the practical side, he decided. How to get in? How to let them know Le Fantôme could pass through walls? No men with guns, no dogs, no movement-sensitive cameras could catch him. The family were defenceless against such a phantom. And they knew it.

The waiter returned with his pastis and placed the glass on a clean paper coaster, brushing a fly from the tablecloth. The insect glided lazily away to reappear in the same spot three seconds later. Davor watched the thing; grey-black wings, bluish body, domed eyes, unhurried movements until the instinct for self-preservation triggered a brief diversion into the air.

A thought took shape in the assassin's mind. It had been a while since he'd relied on technology but one had to move with the times. It didn't matter if he was physically present or not. All he needed to do was take a photograph, something precious or sentimental to her, and post it online. But what?

He tilted his face to the sun, closing his eyes and inhaling the sea spray, the mouth-watering aroma of grilled sausages from the restaurant and that hint of aniseed from his glass.

No need to worry. He would know it when he saw it. *Trust your instincts, old man, they've never let you down.*

He downed the pastis, left some coins on the table and picked up his newspaper. It crossed his mind to use his copy of *Le Monde* to squash the fly, still perched on the edge of the table like a spy. But the nasty little creature had given him the idea. He chose to let it live and strode off in the direction of the station.

The fly remained.

Chapter 23

Charming Elodie of Parfums Parfaits had revealed some potential leads, all of which needed following up. Still, all those fragrances and tones blended into nothing more than a headache for Beatrice Stubbs. And the bug she had placed on Xander's collar when she hugged him would start sending the first audio recordings in the next hour. Her immediate urge was to return to the hotel, close the curtains and have a restorative nap. Yet Paris fluttered its shutters, a cool breeze luring her towards the river. A walk in the fresh air might clear the confusion and her head.

She stood for a moment to get her bearings then turned left along Rue Etienne Marcel towards the statue of Louis XIV. The famous king on his rearing horse did not absorb too much of her attention, focused as she was on what she'd gleaned at the perfumery. Distracted by a handsome man emerging from a polished doorway, she admired the uniform classic façades around the square, wishing one of those balconies was hers. Wherever in the world she went, she always wanted to belong.

Heading in the direction of the river, she had a vague plan to wander Les Jardins des Tuileries and mingle with the tourists. The immense gardens with wide boulevards and green lawns provided enough space for everyone. Roses added random bursts of colour, the Seine flowed alongside, sculptures, fountains and extravagant green spaces told stories of aristocracy, money, power and privilege.

Her mind returned to the de Marsault family as she found an empty bench and tilted her face to the sun. The vineyard, perfumery, fashion business, high-end restaurants, low-rent fast food outlets and inter-connections had an equal claim to aristocracy, money, power and privilege. There was a link between these glamorous society folk and the death of Gennaio Colacino; she could sense it in her bones. She knew the family's sophisticated façade hid an ugly underbelly, just as the beauty of Paris – a dignified old dowager – hid a bloody history of brutality and injustice.

Yet she had to acknowledge who she was dealing with, which meant gaining proof would be complex and dangerous. Inhabiting the higher echelons of the social structure, this family company must have someone else to do their dirty work, with no trace leading to them. Whatever connected the murder of Gennaio to Château d'Agathe would be buried under several layers of obfuscation and nigh on impossible to reveal. At least she made the most out of her freedom as a PI, even if it meant a dangerous dance with fire. Beatrice didn't want to think what would happen if they found the bugging device and linked it back to her or Catinca. But that was unlikely, as it would probably end up in a laundry basket by the end of the day.

A flapping disturbed her hair, startling her back to the moment. A pigeon landed on the arm of her bench, gave her a sideways look with its orange eye and bounced to the ground. It paraded up and down the length of the bench on its lobster-hued toes, pecking at croissant crumbs, all the while cocking its head to watch her. Its pompous gait, silvery plumage and sense of entitlement made Beatrice think of generals and train conductors. Her study of the bird was interrupted by the buzz of her phone.

"Catinca? Hello. Where are you?"

"Just got back to hotel. You?"

"Oh, I'm sitting in the park, watching pigeons."

"Pigeons? This ain't no holiday, mate! We got work to do!"

"I'll be there in twenty minutes. Why don't you order afternoon tea?"

"OK, but room service, yeah? Lots to talk about and don't want no ear droppers."

"I'm on my way." Beatrice stood up, scaring off the pigeon, and headed for Place Vendôme, with a smile at Catinca's choice of phrase. That could have been one of her very own Bea-lines.

On arrival at the suite, she saw that Catinca was typing on her laptop at the window table. A trolley beside her bore a gilded cake tier, complete with pot of tea with a hot water flask for top-ups. A sight to gladden the heart.

Beatrice kicked off her shoes and padded across the deep carpet to her colleague, deciding that she actually enjoyed luxury and should do it more often. She opened her mouth to greet Catinca until her attention was distracted by the half birdcage divided into three trays of delicate sandwiches, classic scones and exquisite confectionery. On the bottom level: blini with caviar and trimmings, lobster rolls, salmon canapés and triangular cucumber sandwiches with tuna. In the middle, four puffed scones with tiny bowls of jam, cream and butter. Beatrice adored scones and often told Matthew that the fact he lived in Devon was the only reason she'd fallen in love with him. On the top, the prettiest selection of *petit fours*, macaroons, *tarte tatins* and tea-infused jellies. Beatrice closed her eyes and released a sigh of anticipatory bliss.

Catinca looked up. "I ordered the fishy one 'cos I just given up meat and knew you'd sniff at the vegetarian. Want to talk or eat or both?"

"Eat, of course! These creations are freshly prepared so must be consumed *tout de suite*. Balcony table or indoors? I'm starving after eating practically nothing for lunch and only an espresso all afternoon. But I'm perfectly capable of talking at the same time. Come on then, tell me what you found."

Catinca's fingers fluttered over the keys, a tap dance on the keyboard. "Be there in thirty seconds, just got to send ... this." She thumped her middle finger onto the return key and stretched her arms out to her sides. "All done. Time for sarnies. Better eat in here, right? Least we know no one can hear us. And it's sodding hot. Had to have a shower after walking from Papillon. Right then, you ready?"

Beatrice gave her a thumbs-up, her attention largely on the tea tray. The practice of allowing the junior member to go first was excellent management practice on several levels. Not least because it allowed Beatrice to eat and listen.

"Most important, that fashion brand is failing. No artistic vision, see. There could be, if they'd let Anastasia do her thing, but they won't. She's just figurehead, don't really run the company at all."

"Who's they?" asked Beatrice as she bit into a lobster roll.

"Her aunt Daria and Madame de Marsault. They call the shots. Poked around in the fashion press and the word on the street is the company is running at a loss. Second thing, this fast food chain, also run by the aunt. The woman is ex-model and well minted after death of husband. Why would she wanna flog pizza? Fashion house I understand – the world she knows – but fast food? Points to one thing in my mind."

"Money laundering," said Beatrice, eyeing the blinis. "Perhaps the fashion line is also a cover for dodgy income. To be honest, I don't think the perfumery is wildly successful either. Yet they are in a prime location on an incredibly expensive Parisian street. Do you want a sandwich?"

"Yeah." Catinca took a triangle of bread, inspected it with a frown and put it on her plate. "They are rolling in cash. Anastasia opened a bottle of top fizz for us and only drank half a glass."

"Isn't that what you told me to do?" asked Beatrice, pouring the tea.

"Leave half a glass, yeah, but not sodding whole bottle of Roederer! And she drives a BMW Z4 convertible. Saw a photo of her posing in it. I'm telling you, she is loaded but how come when business is bad?"

Beatrice nodded, thinking it over. "Right, I see. Did you find out anything to connect the family to Gennaio Colacino?"

Catinca took a tentative bite of her sandwich. It seemed to please her and she popped the rest of it into her mouth. "Not to Colacino, but I found another connection. On confidentiality agreement I had to sign, I saw name of law firm. Same Luxembourg company used by Madame de M. so I chased them. Just sent them email as prospective client, asking a few questions and dropping a few names. Let's see what that throws up. Whassat?" she asked, pointing at a scone.

"It's a scone. Quintessentially English. After all the years you've been in London, you've never encountered a scone?"

"Nope, and I tried everything: Turkish baklava, Scottish eggs, Portuguese natas, Polish bagel, Irish coffee, Belgian waffles, Cornish pasty, English muffins and Welsh rare bits. Never seen a scone before. Is it a cake?"

"It is and hugely controversial. First, whether you pronounce it to rhyme with 'phone' or 'gone'. Second, the regional debate about which goes on first, jam or cream. It's at the heart of the British cream tea. Next time you're in Devon, I'll take you to the best teashop in the world. Why don't you try one? Just to warn you, they're very filling, especially with clotted cream. Don't you want any more sandwiches before moving on to cakes? Why not try some caviar?"

Catinca wrinkled her nose. "Don't like caviar."

"What do you mean? This is the height of luxury."

"Growing up in Romania, you can get sick of fish eggs. I'm having lobster roll instead."

Beatrice waited for the verdict as Catinca chewed. "Well, what do you think?"

"Yeah. 'S'nice. Creamy. One's enough, though. Think I'll try a scone now," she grinned. "What did you sniff out at Parfums Parfait?"

Beatrice groaned. "The law firm is another connection. Because I asked one of the olfactory experts ..."

"What experts?" Catinca interrupted, slathering jam onto half a scone.

"Olfactory. It means the sense of smell. She told me about how the company operates, as a subsidiary of MdM and I managed to find out the name of the law firm by asking how they dealt with plagiarists. She showed me a sample Cease and Desist order, written by their lawyers. It's the same company you've just written to in Luxembourg. Xander de Marsault has practically nothing to do with the running of the company because they have a management team. He's rarely there, according to Elodie. He has what she described as 'other interests' in Eastern Europe. I'd very much like to know what those interests might be."

Catinca, her mouth full, nodded with enthusiasm.

"What worries me now," Beatrice continued, polishing off the salmon canapés, "is how big this is. If they find out what we just did ..." She put her hand behind her ear.

Catinca's eyes widened and she put the tea back on the table. "Oh shit, the bug! Totally forgot that bit. So sorry, boss! I was just so focused on the entire act."

Beatrice waved aside her apologies. "Don't worry. You got out a lot of that one meeting. Let's work with what we have."

Catinca took a sip of tea and studied Beatrice. . "Yeah, let's focus on our job. Find who killed Gennaio Colacino or enough evidence to make Budapest police interested."

"Exactly, focus on Colacino. We are not investigating this entire family and damn good thing too, or we'd be at it for years.

But we have nothing, other than the concierge link, to connect them to our original case – yet. As far as I know, all the litigation involving this family was instigated by them and there is nothing on record to show any criminal activity. Although ..."

"What?"

"After tea," said Beatrice, spreading cream on her scone before adding jam in traditional Devonshire style, "I'll give Dawn a ring. See if she'll have a quick look at the Europol database for me. If there's anything fishy about this company or any of its subsidiaries, I want to know."

"Top plan. Say hello to Dawn from me. In meantime, I'm gonna make a map of all them and how they hang together. Whew, I'm done here. If I eat any more, I won't be hungry at dinner. What time we going to Rool and Roger?"

"Catinca! You've had one tiny tuna sandwich and a scone. What about all these delicious little French fancies? At least try a jelly."

"Nah, I'm stuffed, mate. Shove a couple in the fridge for later. When we got to be ready?"

With a disappointed sigh, Beatrice said, "The restaurant is called *Raoul et Roger*, pronounced Roget. Our reservation is for eight, so a car will collect us at seven-thirty. I suppose we have to dress up for this, don't we?" She couldn't hide the reluctance in her voice.

"Course we got to dress up. But you got your own personal stylist. Get showered by half six and put on that silk pyjama combo. Then I'll do the rest." She gathered up her laptop and disappeared into her bedroom.

Two French fancies later, Beatrice knew she had to stop. She wrapped the remainder into a napkin and placed it in the mini bar fridge. Averting her eyes from the leftover scones and savouries, she wheeled the trolley out into the corridor, out of temptation's reach.

If she went into her sumptuous bedroom, she would fall

asleep, waking crumpled and cranky before the evening's much anticipated dinner. So she reclined on the sofa, picked up her phone and called Dawn, looking forward to a friendly chat.

"DI Whittaker?"

"Dawn, it's Beatrice, checking in from Paris. Can you talk?"

"Hold on." There was a moment of silence then Dawn's voice returned. "Right, I'm in the ladies. No one else around. You all right?"

Beatrice pictured the ladies' toilet, the place where she and Dawn had ranted, cursed, cried and bonded during her time at the Met. "Yes, I'm fine. Being spoilt rotten in a five-star hotel by the very people we're investigating. We've uncovered quite a lot of detail and I wanted to ask you for a favour."

Dawn did not respond.

"Oh, don't worry, this is nothing onerous, more a question of checking a database ... Dawn, are you still there?"

"I'm still here. Thing is, Beatrice, that concierge gig blew up in my face. Crad Llewellyn called Ranga and demanded to know which investigation I was working, the incident number, the Budapest contact and why his company had lost one of their most valuable clients as a result. Ranga calmed him down but immediately sussed what was going on. I've had a verbal warning and he's sending a strongly worded email to your inbox any day now. If I lift a finger to help you in the future, my career goes down in flames."

Beatrice sat upright, yanked out of her relaxed, post-prandial mood into mortification. "Oh, Dawn, that's awful. I don't know what to say. I'm so sorry. How could I get you into trouble for my own selfish ends after everything you've done for me? Unreserved apologies and I will tell Ranga this was all my idea. Which it was! Honestly, I'd rather give up this whole private investigation idea than make your life difficult."

"Ranga already knows it was your idea. He guessed and told me not to lie on your behalf. So I didn't. Just don't mention

Catinca, whatever you do. He thinks the 'Budapest officer' was you in disguise. If he suspects we had a civilian posing as a copper, you and I are both facing a court case."

"Oh hell and damnation." Beatrice squeezed her eyes shut. "You are such a loyal friend. It hurts me to know I sent a torpedo into your work life. I promise never to ask you to compromise your position again. From now on, we're drinking mates who shared a past. No more favours."

Dawn stayed silent for several seconds. "Yeah, let's stick to our roles. Don't beat yourself up. I'm just as much to blame. How many years have I been with the Met? Why the hell would I think I can blag intel from a well-connected geezer with no backlash? Oh well, I learned a lesson. When are you back?"

"Not sure yet. Listen, I feel so guilty about all this. Can I call you when I get back for a proper apology?"

"Course. You got a Chardonnay debt you'd better start paying off ASAP." Something beeped in the background. "Oh, shit, here we go. Beatrice, gotta run. Sorry I can't help. Have fun!"

Incandescent with shame, Beatrice ended the call and stared at the cream carpet.

Chapter 24

Thunderclaps and lightning flashes shattered the sky, penetrating velvet drapes, walls, ceiling and triple-glazed windows. Madame reached for her earplugs and silk sleep mask, but the reverberations shook the room so that even her bed seemed to shake.

She sat up in bed, furious on two counts. Her sleep was disturbed and there was no one to blame. The bedside clock, hands illuminated by her night light, showed the time as ten past four. Outside, the storm threatened and exploded like a tantrum of the gods while the house cowered under the covers. She rang the bell for the maid. If she was awake, she would not be alone.

It took over five minutes before there was a timid knock at the door of her boudoir.

"Madame?"

"*Enfin*! I thought you had run off with all the other mice. Bring me a hot chocolate and some toasted brioche with honey. Please don't make me wait as long this time."

"*Oui, madame.*" The girl, still in her robe, ducked out of the door.

Madame snorted. Attending the mistress of the house in a robe? Standards were slipping and it was up to her to crack the whip. When the maid brought her drink, she would not send her back to dress, as she had done in previous years. Instead, she would deliver a lecture on grace, dignity, comportment and an appreciation of the honour conferred upon such a position. If there was no change in her behaviour in the next week, she would be sacked and the whole training regime must begin again. Madame grew weary of this endless cycle.

With a shove of the heavy eiderdown, she eased herself out of bed and into her shearling slippers. She wrapped herself in a cashmere throw and shuffled across to the floor-length windows, pulling a cord to open the curtains. All she could see was a wind-lashed landscape of darkness, trees whipping like wheat stalks and sluices of water tumbling across the grounds. Her poor vines. She switched on an Art Deco lamp and checked Pierrot was undisturbed. The little apricot Pomeranian snored in his raised bed, so relaxed in his sleep she became envious. A magnesium flash of white lit the room and Madame looked up to see jagged lightning forking its way to the ground near the city of Bordeaux.

Another enormous thunderclap, so close it seemed above her head, made her catch her throat and whimper.

"The storm has passed, madame." The maid had returned, giving the matriarch almost as much of a scare as the thunder. "Three seconds between flash and clap this time. By the time you have finished your chocolate, we'll hardly be able to hear it. *Bonne nuit.*"

Madame let her go, all thoughts of a lecture forgotten. She stared out at the sky, waiting. Nothing but the wildest wind, the most vicious rain. Then came the flash. She couldn't see where it landed, but the landscape was illuminated as if in a spotlight for a mere second. She counted. *Un, deux, trois, quatre ...* Crash!

Yes, the storm was moving away. She sat at her table, positioned to watch the weather, and stirred her chocolate. The brioche smelt good but she really didn't want the bother of putting her teeth in. She would feed it to Pierrot in the morning. The hot chocolate was thick and sweet, made with dark *Cremánt* chocolate as she liked it.

Yves had told her not to check her tablet in the bedroom. Unhealthy. Sleep-disruptive. Wait till morning, he said. But she was wide awake, the storm had lost her interest and what else was she to do while drinking her chocolate?

She brought the thing to life, checked for emails and browsed a few social media sites, scoffing at the pathetic ways people feigned significance. Then she saw it. Seven items down in her feed.

Perfume follows you:
It chases you and lingers behind you.
It's a reference mark.
Perfume makes silence talk. – Sonia Rykiel

The quote was accompanied by a photograph. A bottle of perfume. The same bottle of perfume now sitting on her dresser. *La Reine*, a bespoke scent from Parfums Parfaits created for her birthday. It was the only one in existence. She knew before she even checked who had posted the picture and the quote. Letty Louise.

Her hands shook as she reached for her phone.

The woman at the other end sounded groggy. "*Allo?*"

"Daria, *ma chère*, I need you. It's Le Fantôme."

Chapter 25

It was all very well agreeing not to talk about the investigation at dinner, but Catinca didn't want to eat in total silence. Since her phone call with her mate at Scotland Yard, Beatrice had been withdrawn and quiet. She had submitted to Catinca's styling without even a roll of the eyes, which meant something was definitely off. Even so, she really did look the part, with a sweeping leopard-print chiffon cape over her silk pyjamas, a ton of jewellery and her make-up artfully blended in tones of bronze and gold.

The waitress poured a glass of sparkling water for each of them, then stood poised to take their orders. Catinca looked up at her. "I'd like the truffle risotto to start, followed by the six-cheese ravioli. Thing is, do you think that's too heavy? We had a big afternoon tea, see."

The waitress pursed her lips. "The portions are not huge, but both those dishes are very filling. Can I suggest the Caesar salad to start, with shavings of black summer truffle? That way, you can enjoy the taste while leaving you with an appetite for the ravioli."

"Great idea! I'll do that. Beatrice, what you having?"

"Umm, yes, I'd better go for something light to start. I'll have gazpacho as an entrée and carpaccio of beef as my main course. Are we going to order wine?"

"Of course," said Catinca. "Tricky to find a bottle which goes with both, though. I'd have gone for a Sancerre, but you're going to want something robust and full-bodied with yours."

"You can have both," said the waitress. "You don't need to order a whole bottle. We have a delightful Sancerre which will complement the truffle and the cheese I would strongly recommend. For *madame*, I suggest a light Bordeaux with the gazpacho, and maybe to bring out all the flavours of the beef, a rich Burgundy."

Catinca gave her a huge grin. "You really know your stuff. That sounds bang on." She folded her menu and handed it to the woman. "Thank you very much."

Once she had gone, Catinca fixed Beatrice with a hard stare. "Right, Misery-Guts, cough it up. We're in a posh restaurant, paid for by the Marsaults, having some lovely nosh and nice wine. We both look fabulous, thanks to me, and you're sitting there like a black hole, radiating negativity."

"Black holes don't radiate anything. They suck everything and everyone into destruction. There is no escape."

"You're a sodding bundle of joy, you are. What is the matter? Look out, here's the bread."

Beatrice pressed her fingers to the bridge of her nose. Catinca watched to see if that gesture was to stem tears. But as soon as the waitress placed the bread basket on the tablecloth, a dry-eyed PI Stubbs reached for a pumpkin-seed roll. "I already told you what the matter is. Because of me, Dawn got a verbal warning which will jeopardise any kind of promotion prospects she might have. This woman could rise to the top. She has all the right qualifications and experience, apart from her choice of friends."

The bread was so warm and soft, butter melted the second it was spread on the fluffy inside. Catinca chewed on her mini Parisette and closed her eyes in bliss. When she opened them, she pointed a finger at her new boss. "Tell me honest truth. Are you having one of your turns? You can tell me and I won't judge, promise. If this is to do with your condition, fair enough. All I wanna know if this behaviour is depressive episode or moody dramatics because I dunno much about dealing with depression. But I work for Adrian, so I'm world expert on moody dramatics."

To her surprise, Beatrice stopped short of sinking her teeth into her roll and started to laugh. Her face creased, her shoulders shook and the sound of her belly laughter drew smiles from adjoining tables. She put down the roll and wiped her eyes, still chuckling.

"Oh dear. You really do have a way with words. Catinca Tonic, that's how I think of you."

The waitress brought two bottles to their table, each neatly dressed in a napkin tie. She offered them a taste of their respective wines and poured a glass each.

"Cheers, mate!" Catinca tinked her glass to Beatrice's and then tilted it to her own nose. "Phooar, I'm gonna enjoy this, I can tell."

"*Santé!*" Beatrice sipped at her glass, a smile still playing over her face. "Delicious. We must leave this waitress a tip. She is a genuine expert."

"Too right. Must ask her the name of this wine. Pretty sure we don't stock it. Anyway, you didn't answer my question. What's going on?"

At last Beatrice tackled her bread roll. "You're right to ask and I think you're the first person ever to put it so bluntly. No, this is not a down cycle. At least not yet. As for moody dramatics, I wouldn't call it that either. It's a bloody great wake-up call, making me realise that if I can't do this alone, I shouldn't do it at all. I'm no longer a police officer and cannot think in those resource and support terms. I have to stand on my own two feet. Or retire and forget the whole silly enterprise."

The job offer at the fashion house flashed across Catinca's conscience, but she pushed it away and focused on the task in hand. "Four feet. You got me now. As a team, I reckon we are doing great. Toast? To The Stubbs Agency! May we kick arses wherever we go!"

Beatrice was laughing again. "To The Stubbs Agency!"

They raised their glasses once more then made way for their starters. Even after that lardy great scone, Catinca was looking forward to her meal.

Two hours later, the waitress approached to clear away their plates.

"Did you enjoy your meal, *mesdames*?"

"It was exactly right," said Beatrice. "Beautifully balanced. Thank you."

"Gorgeous. Everything worked perfect together. Good advice."

"That's very nice of you to say so. Can I interest you in a dessert?"

Beatrice got to her feet. "Cheeseboard for me, with a glass of ruby port. Please excuse me, I must visit the bathroom." She picked up her bag and swanned off in the direction of the ladies.

Catinca was pleased to see she stayed in role. "I don't fancy cheese after that ravioli. I'll give it a miss. Maybe just an espresso?"

"We have a selection of sorbets and lighter desserts, if you would like to see. We have a special this month called *Le Jardin Anglais*: lavender ice-cream with a Prosecco jelly and a ginger tuile. It's a huge hit."

"Prosecco jelly? OK, you persuaded me. One of them and an espresso. Thank you."

She stretched her chin towards the ceiling, releasing stiff muscles and tension, catching sight of herself in the mirrored tiles. Short she might be, but who else could pull off Moulin Rouge with such élan? Apart from the actual dancers, of course. Lace-up boots, ruched red skirt, pink petticoats and a scarlet riding-jacket she had found in a children's bring-and-buy sale, she rocked that look. Her feathers had gone a bit droopy. Next time, she might try a head-dress.

"Those toilets are the most glamorous I've ever seen," Beatrice breathed, flouncing into her seat in a cloud of animal-print chiffon.

"It's a tasty place, all right. See that bloke over there by the window? He was in that film, wasn't he? You know, he's an assassin and he takes in a kid ... wow, that was quick!"

The waitress placed a large tray in front of Beatrice, with half a dozen slices of cheese, some biscuits and a tiny fruit basket. "And one glass of ruby port."

"That looks divine," said Beatrice, her face relaxed and a little flushed.

"And here is *Le Jardin Anglais* with an espresso. Enjoy, ladies!"

Catinca sniffed at the two-toned glass, half lilac, half golden, with a wonderful wing-like biscuit poking out of the centre. She looked up at Beatrice with a sense of triumph, only to see her companion's face had gone pale as the cheese on her plate. She stared at Catinca's dessert as if it was a severed head.

"What?" hissed Catinca.

Beatrice took a hefty swig of her port, her eyes never leaving Catinca's pretty pudding. "That is my dessert," she whispered.

"Mate, you ordered cheeseboard."

"No!" Beatrice spoke through clenched teeth. "I didn't order it, I designed it." She finally lifted her gaze from the glass. "You know we couldn't find a connection between the Danube incident to our hosts? It's right there on your plate. The English Garden."

Chapter 26

Parisian church bells struck three am. Still in their glad rags, Catinca and Beatrice sat at the coffee-table, poring over their respective laptops in semi-darkness, filling in the gaps.

The fact the family owned *Raoul et Roger* was not news. MdM staff had booked the table, arranged the car and picked up the tab. Beatrice accessed the financial structure via the MdM website, with its classic corporate neutrality. There was no mention of the Nonna chain anywhere on their site and precious little on the rest of the net. So how this dessert, specifically designed last year by Beatrice to leave a trap for the fraudulent Nonna chain in the Naples case, made it to an upmarket restaurant in Paris, could only mean one of two things: it was a damn good recipe or MdM was somehow involved with the original Colacino case. Each line of business was overseen by a family member. Yves and the vineyard, Xander and the perfumery, niece Anastasia and the fashion brand. Madame Agathe herself appeared to be distanced from daily business, but hawkish when it came to reputation. Hence the law firm in Luxembourg. Her bereaved daughter-in-law, Daria de Marsault, was not part of the company. Not on the board, or shareholder, subsidiary, affiliate or supporter.

So if Daria's involvement was the restaurant and fast food line, was she behind the Nonna chain? Was she the person financing *Raoul et Roger* and the very hotel they sat in right now? If not, how else had they replicated Beatrice's own dessert?

"Nothing," Catinca spat, as if listening to her thoughts. "Someone is pulling strings and no way to find out who. But connection is bloody obvious!"

Fresh air would sharpen Beatrice's mind. And seeing as hours had passed since her cheeseboard, a pastry might help. She opened the fridge, took out a tiny *tarte tatin* and a bottle of water and opened the windows onto the balcony. The lights of Place Vendôme, muted in the wee hours, still suggested elegance and a rarefied atmosphere. Classic Paris. This sector was luxury hotels, that street was perfume, another art, and *haute couture* claimed its own *quartier*. Each with its own identity. A thought snapped across Beatrice's mind.

"Catinca?" She parted the gauzy curtains and returned inside.

"What?" Catinca did not look up from her screen.

"Sectors. These people don't multitask. Each family member has his or her own area of expertise. The company delineates specialist fields – Yves in wine, Anastasia in fashion, Xander in perfume, Daria in food, although Madame Agathe has an influence over them all. The only one we know for sure works in catering is Daria de Marsault."

"Nah. You told me Xander has other interests apart from perfume business. Daria is well influential in fashion house. Madame is big boss, that's clear, but I reckon they all interfere in each other's business. Too many cooks, innit? Can't find nothing to link Daria to defunct Nonna franchise or *Raoul et Roger*."

"What's her influence on the fashion house?" asked Beatrice.

Catinca let out an expansive yawn. "She and Madame put kybosh on only decent line they got. Rest of it derivative and dull. Anastasia's line, printing marine photos on quality cuts was not edgy enough. She ain't a designer, she's a rep. Nothing more than pretty face of the brand. Sodding shame as Naïade collection was best thing they had."

"Hang on. The Naïade collection?" she asked.

"Yeah. Inspired by photos she took off her auntie's boat."

Beatrice froze. "Do you have any pictures?"

Catinca pulled out a brochure from her handbag and handed it over.

Beatrice sat on the arm of the chair, studying every item until she saw it. A lifebuoy imprinted with the Naïade livery. A flurry of memories tumbled through Beatrice's mind. Locked cabin. Muddled head. Urgent thirst. Lumped over a deckhand's shoulder. Black, confusing water. Defeat.

Even if legally nebulous, it was clear that Beatrice had been dealing with Daria's arm of the operation back then. This was the second link between Gennaio Colacino's death and the Marsault imperium. "Your designer friend may well take pretty pictures, but those images implicate her aunt. Been there, done that, got thrown overboard."

Catinca's eyes widened and she sat up straight, like a fox scenting its prey. "You mean we've got them?"

"Yes. Albeit on wafer-thin evidence, I do believe we have."

In her king-size bed, eyes itching, mind racing, Beatrice stared at the ceiling. She and her innocent assistant were at a crossroads. She had no resources to investigate this family and its criminal activities. It was enormous, powerful and carried an influence she could not imagine. A private detective with an inexperienced hothead trying to tackle such a network would be like kittens wandering into the lions' den.

Did they have enough evidence to trigger a major enquiry? Would this be a way to redeem Dawn? No, it had nothing to do with Scotland Yard. Interpol? Perhaps one of her former colleagues would give her his attention. Or she could go to the top and call Fisher. She squeezed her eyes shut. It was only too easy to envisage that patronising pillock saying 'Well done and I applaud your techniques, Miss Marple, but I really don't think there's anything to worry about'.

She ground her teeth and winced as her fingernails dug into her palm. She could not do this alone. Painful as she found Fisher, she needed the weight of Interpol to bring this poisonous network out of the shadows. She curled onto her side. One more day. If she and Catinca could prove the web of connections within this family, she would hand it all over to law enforcement. No glory, no gain, no bloody fee, but they would be doing the right thing.

If only the right thing paid the bills. Her mind flittered back to Château Agathe; the grounds, the windows, the antiques, the helicopter and the wine. If one had to be a recluse, Madame Agathe de Marsault could have chosen worse places.

Beatrice's eyes closed, a parade of images dancing across her mind: *petits fours*, Catinca's feathers, geometric slices of cheese, Paris at night, gossamer tendrils and at the centre of the web, a patient black spider, waiting for her prey to fly into her trap.

Chapter 27

By the time Catinca awoke, it was gone ten and she had missed breakfast. She wrapped herself in a fluffy hotel robe, made a coffee in the posh machine and selected a couple of yesterday's cakes from the mini bar. There was no sound or movement from Beatrice's room, so Catinca took her breakfast and laptop out onto the balcony to check her emails.

Sunshine glittered across the square and several shops had already lowered their white awnings. The vast column in the centre cast a long shadow across the grey stone, where pigeons fluttered from lamp-post to railing, searching for crumbs of *pain au chocolat*. The scale and uniform beauty of the place seemed unreal. She drank it in, trying to store up all that elegance to fortify her when she next struggled past stinking bin bags and that constantly cluttered stairway up to their tiny flat above Costcutters in Bethnal Green.

She nibbled on a cake as she opened her email folder and spotted the one she'd been waiting for – the Luxembourg law firm. She skimmed it and got the message. In the most deliberately confusing English she could imagine, they said she wasn't welcome. Reputation for discretion, loyalty to established clientele, unfortunately new business only by personal recommendation, blah, blah, bloody blah. In other words, piss off.

A grin spread across Catinca's face. She'd had more rebuffs

than she'd had custard pastries and never let them bring her down. If lunch went the way she hoped, a personal recommendation would arrive in their inbox by teatime. *Try refusing me then, you crusty old gits.* Now to dress. It was twenty past ten and she hadn't even begun her toilette.

Les Deux Magots sat on a corner of Place Saint-Germain-des-Prés, with green-trimmed awnings, wicker cane chairs and waiters wearing long pinnies. Classic and discreet, exactly the sort of atmosphere Catinca had coveted when designing Dionysus. The taxi dropped her on the opposite side of the road and she stood beside another column, this stumpy one covered with advertisements. She didn't even check her phone, just gazed at the café. This was her moment.

Before crossing the road, she assessed her appearance in a nearby shop front. There were times when being an expert at cramming four weeks' worth of looks into one suitcase came in very handy. High-waisted palazzo pants, the colour of Riviera sand, with off-white Chuck Taylor All Stars on her feet. Pale blue Bardot top with gold button fastening. Hair in pineapple topknot with blue-enamelled shell earrings, gold rope necklace and charm bracelet Adrian gave her for being bridesmaid. One message: seaside, style and echoes of Anastasia's own Naïade range. Close as she could get to wearing one of the designer's own creations.

She approached the café with catwalk nonchalance and announced herself at the door.

"My name is Catinca Radu. I have appointment to meet Anastasia Kravets. Table for two at midday, please."

The waiter pressed his screen, a frown creasing his forehead. "I am sorry, Ms Radu, but the booking is cancelled. An assistant of Ms Kravets called us this morning. Perhaps you did not receive the message? If you would like to dine, I can arrange a table for one?"

Heat rose in Catinca's cheeks. *How sodding rude just to cancel and not inform guest!*

"No, thank you. Please call me a taxi. I wish to return to my hotel."

The man signalled to one of the outdoor waiters, who raised a hand and a cab pulled up to the wide pavement.

Once in the back seat, she gave the driver her address, but then changed her mind. "No, not Hotel de Marsault. Take me to Rue du Faubourg Saint-Honoré, *s'il vous plaît.*"

If Mohammed won't come to the mountain ...

At the desk, she saw the same assistant who had met her in the lobby the day before.

"Excuse me! My name is Catinca Radu. I was here yesterday, remember? I'd like to speak to Anastasia Kravets, please."

He shook his head. "I am sorry, madame, but Ms Kravets has left for a lunch appointment."

"I know! Her appointment was with me. But the restaurant says the booking has been cancelled. I wanna know why."

His face showed confusion. "One moment, please. I will call her assistant."

He spoke into the phone, listened for a moment and then came around the desk to speak in a low voice. "Madame, I am sorry, but I have instructions to ask you to leave the building. Please, would you come this way?"

"Leave the building? I was invited here as guest! What's going on?"

"Please, madame, I know nothing of the circumstances. My orders are to see that you leave."

The other receptionist was openly staring. Catinca stared from her to the security man.

"Shitty way to treat a client. I am leaving now and I won't be back." She walked out with as much dignity as she could fake and strode down the street, for once unimpressed by the designer shops and stylish shoppers. She was fuming. And not a little worried.

On her return to Hotel de Marsault, she stalked up to the reception desk. "Any messages for me? Catinca Radu, Suite 303."

"No messages, madame, but checkout is at eleven. If you want a late checkout, you need to let us know the day before."

"We ain't checking out until tomorrow."

"Unfortunately not. Your reservation was changed. You are leaving us today. The manager has gone to speak to your colleague."

Catinca was too furious to wait for the lift so ran three flights of stairs and pelted along the corridor to their suite, almost colliding with the manager as he reversed out.

"What the hell is going on?" she demanded, her breath short.

The manager gave her a slight bow, but his expression remained intractable. "Good afternoon, Ms Radu. I have explained the circumstances to your colleague. You need to vacate this suite immediately. A car will collect you at 14.00 and take you to the Eurostar terminal. You are returning to London today. I apologise for the change in arrangements and wish you a safe journey home."

"Bollocks to that!" yelled Catinca and pushed past him to get into Suite 303. At first, she couldn't find Beatrice – not in the living-area or in her bedroom – until she heard a voice on the balcony. Still in her bathrobe, hair contained by a towelling turban, Beatrice was on her mobile phone.

Her eyes met Catinca's but the sunlight behind her meant her expression was unreadable. She continued speaking into her handset. "I don't know what you mean by false identities. We are exactly who we said we were."

She listened for a moment, shaking her head. "No, that is just ridiculous. We are interested in two branches of your operation, not the entire family. Why on earth ...?

Beatrice went very still. "I'm sorry, but did you just threaten me? You are perfectly entitled to throw us out of your hotel, but I think deporting us from the country is a step too far. My colleague and I ..."

Her jaw dropped and she ended the call. She put her finger to her lips and tugged at her ear. She typed a frantic message into her phone and showed the screen to Catinca.

THEY KNOW. NO IDEA HOW. THEY MUST'VE BEEN LISTENING. JUST KEEP SPEAKING NATURALLY.

"Catinca, what on earth have you said to these people? They are convinced we're spies!"

Catinca followed Beatrice into her bedroom, protesting loudly. "I ain't said nothing! They know who I am. My face is all over my feed! Why they kicking us out?"

"God knows! Whatever the reason, we have to pack up and ship out. Go and get your things."

"Something weird is going on. Anastasia cancelled lunch. I really wanted to buy that line for the shop. Look at my outfit. Hommidge to that marine print design."

Beatrice scribbled on the pad by the phone. *Don't mention Naïade!!!*

"Yes, yes, you look very nice. And it's pronounced *homage*. Come on, we have to get packed and go. They've cancelled our flights and are sending us back on the Eurostar. A car is coming at two."

"They can't do that. We'll go when sodding ready! And they can stuff their car. I'm gonna call reception and book a taxi."

"To where? We have nowhere to stay. My feeling is to give this up as a bad job and go home. Now will you please go and pack? Your wardrobe will take ages."

"Takes me two minutes to pack, mate. You got all your potions in bathroom and that's what's gonna take ages. So the case stops here? After all we done? Can't believe it."

"I'm afraid to say, yes, the case stops here. We did our best.

Other projects demand our attention, such as your shop, so let's return to London and write this off as a jolly. At least we had some decent food and stayed in a five-star hotel."

"Never got to go to flea markets after all. Can't we stay one more day? Find our own hotel? We ain't seen half of it yet."

"There'll be other occasions," said Beatrice. "Right, I'll be ready in fifteen minutes. You'd better do the same. Please don't be late, Catinca. You know how much that bugs me," she said, with a wicked grin, and closed her bedroom door.

Chapter 28

As Beatrice had predicted, neither woman was ready when the phone rang to announce their car. They finally emerged from the lift at 14.35, heads held high and completely ignoring the fussy manager. Catinca dropped their key cards onto the reception desk as if they were soiled tissues and they emerged into the Parisian afternoon.

Beatrice approached their black sedan with a haughty expression, which was no match for Delphine the driver's. The snooty female barely gave them a chilly glance while stowing their luggage. In character, Beatrice waited for her to open the door and spotted the second car. So, not only were they being driven to the airport, but they had an escort to ensure they left Paris. Rather than grumble to each other, they posed for selfies against the backdrop of the square, causing a further delay.

Once inside the car they did not speak a single word to one another. The driver confirmed that they were going to the Eurostar terminal and received a nod in reply. Beatrice watched the streets of Paris pass by, half saddened, half relieved to be leaving. Her mind raced, trying to imagine how they could continue to pursue the case while back in London. Whatever steps they took from here on had to be subtle and under the radar of the family de Marsault. It was only too clear they were being watched. Had they actually bugged that hotel room? It was absolutely outrageous.

Catinca spent the entire journey pressing buttons on her phone, huddled into the corner. Beatrice asked no questions and simply waited for their arrival at the train terminal. The driver took their bags and escorted them right to the check-in desk. She clearly had no intention of letting them escape. She handed over their tickets, they thanked her and proceeded to passport control and security. She stood there watching them leave, so Catinca turned round to give her a supercilious wave. Then Beatrice spoke.

"Right. Listen to me, we're going get on the train and we get off again. Then we go find the Metro to Montparnasse and take a train to Bordeaux," she muttered from the corner of her mouth.

"What you talking about?" asked Catinca, walking along behind her, dragging her monstrous suitcase.

"We aren't going to London!" Beatrice hissed. "We're going to Bordeaux to find out what these people are doing. Trains go every hour and we are going to be on one by tea time."

"That's mad, boss! Them lot are still watching us and they gonna know if we get off the train." Catinca resisted looking over her shoulder. "And what we gonna do in Bordeaux?"

"Get to the heart of the matter," said Beatrice. "If all roads lead to Madame Agathe and that lovely château, we should pay another visit. I just have to avoid that puffed-up little PA git, Denis Hugues, and her fragrant son Yves, as they might remember me. Shame about Yves, I wouldn't mind sipping another glass of sauvignon blanc *avec lui*."

With a charming smile she approached the conductor and showed him the tickets. "Excuse me please, can you tell me where we are sitting?"

He pointed down the line of carriages, smiled and urged them to hurry. "You only have five minutes!" Thanks to their tardy departure they were only just in time to catch the Eurostar back to London.

Beatrice took the opportunity to look behind them at the ticket barrier. The driver and two other men stood with folded arms, all wearing sunglasses. Beatrice was tempted to snigger. Instead, she thanked the conductor and followed Catinca down the platform to their appointed carriage. They scurried down past three more doors and then boarded the train at the point where the long line of carriages curved around the platform.

Beatrice bumped and apologised her way down the aisle through two more carriages until she decided they were sufficiently out of sight. Finally she opened the door and got down onto the platform dragging her bag after her. Catinca followed suit and both women scuttled into the shadow of a stairwell. They waited until the huge leviathan of the Eurostar had departed. Catinca took off her distinctive white hat and poked her head out of the stairwell.

"No one coming. Let's change clothes and go find the Metro," she said, with some satisfaction. "You keep watch while I put on something boring."

Beatrice squinted up the platform as Catinca pulled off the eye-catching garments she had specifically chosen to attract attention. When Beatrice turned around, she was wearing a grey hoodie and jeans. She even changed her Converse trainers to black. With some relief, Beatrice changed into ordinary slacks with a dull jumper. They had a brief argument over whether Beatrice should wear a beanie hat, which Catinca won with ease. Beatrice's hair was legendary for its distinctiveness. They could do little about the suitcases, but both being black and blue, they could have belonged to anyone.

Beatrice was hot, nervous and stressed. Why could she never just leave things be? She followed Catinca up the stairs and across the walkway to the main concourse. Her pulse pounded and she wished she had not indulged in quite so much caffeine that morning. With the coolest and slightly irritating nonchalance, Catinca led her to the Metro station, bought two tickets and they boarded the Line 4 in the direction of Mairie de Montrouge. They squeezed into a recess beside the doors. Neither said a word as the Metro rattled south, but both assessed every other passenger as a potential stalker.

After an age, they emerged at Montparnasse Bienvenüe and some app on Catinca's phone directed them to the main railway concourse. Trains to Bordeaux left every hour, there was no one on their tail, so no hurry.

Beatrice pitched for a refuelling stop, her stomach already violently complaining about the lack of a proper sit-down breakfast. "What we do now?" she asked, "Probably the safest place for us to hide would be in a restaurant. Not to mention providing essential sustenance."

Catinca's gaze roamed the platform. She gave a slow nod. "Yeah, mate, I'm hungry and all. Let's hang about here for a couple hours. Eat first, and then find hairdressers. You got to look completely different to last time you visited that château. Wanna get some pasta and redesign Beatrice Stubbs?"

"You can do whatever redesigning you like so long as I get some food in the next fifteen minutes. Otherwise I may faint."

"Right put your glasses on and let's go. After two days of posh nosh, I'm ready for some well dirty junk food. Pity Paris doesn't do Cornish pasties."

Two and a half hours later, Beatrice emerged from a hair salon, in a mild state of shock. Her wild curly mane, part stamp of identity, part bane of her life, lay on the black-and-white tiles around her feet. Catinca and the stylist had chosen to transform her hair into a platinum helmet. Raw and exposed, her face displayed all its flaws without its protective frame. Up until that moment, she had no idea how attached she had been to her hair until she saw it, lifeless on the floor around her, about to be swept away. She wondered if she could ask the stylist if she might keep it, like one did with teeth or gallstones.

She took another look in the mirror, horrified and enthralled in equal measure, at the woman she did not recognise. "Yes, well, thank you very much, and how much do I owe you?"

On hearing the extortionate amount a cut, colour and blow-dry cost, Beatrice pulled a shocked face at Catinca. She paid and followed her assistant back into the bowels of the train station, reluctantly agreeing that it was indeed worth it. Whatever would Matthew say?

"Right. Now we split up. See you on the train at half seven," Catinca whispered.

"Keep your eyes open," Beatrice replied.

"You too, specially for bargains," Catinca said and melted away into the crowd.

At 19:15, Beatrice entered the Bordeaux train from the first class doors and made her way to her seat. She parked her suitcase overhead and settled in at a table beside the window, leaving Catinca, aka Ms Fidget, the aisle. She took out her papers and the iced tea she'd bought for the journey and got comfortable. People moved past as the train began to fill up and without warning, a sense of being watched crept over her. She looked around the carriage for any sign of the men in suits but saw no one resembling their escorts. A mother with two children, a stylish blonde woman, a group of teenage girls and two elderly couples were all occupied with phones, food or quiet conversations. Beatrice took a moment to check out the blonde's colour co-ordination. Now she had platinum hair, perhaps she could get away with some bright pinks and purples. The woman lifted her head, her green eyes returning Beatrice's stare. Embarrassed, Beatrice dropped her eyes.

Ten minutes later, Catinca arrived and to Beatrice's surprise, sat opposite, her excitement visible on her face. Neither spoke, waiting until the train left the platform to provide them with some sense of security. As the Parisian suburbs flashed by and no one joined their table, Catinca unzipped her rucksack and withdrew two little bottles of champagne.

"Time for celebration, mate," she whispered. "I even got glasses!"

"Did you steal those from the hotel?" Beatrice followed her lead, keeping her voice low.

"Yeah. And that's not all. That bath robe was well comfy."

"Oh, Catinca," Beatrice laughed. "They broke the mould when they made you."

"So tell me again, what are we going to do in Bordeaux?" Catinca asked "I went along with your idea simply to piss off those heavies, but I got no clue what we do when we get there."

Beatrice pulled a pen from her jacket and started drawing on a napkin. "Picture the elements of the MdM organisation. Each one represents one strand of the family business: the perfumery, the fashion line, the hotel, the vineyard, the property portfolio, the restaurant chain and fast food business. Each one is run by a family member – some openly, some hidden behind legal constructs. The family's centre is Madame Agathe de Marsault. The reclusive matriarch who may not appear in public but controls the family business with a steely grip."

Catinca tapped a nail to the central hub. "Are we gonna meet her?"

"Not sure that is a good idea. I believe they know everything we said in that hotel room. They know what we know. They know we're onto them. This puts us in a very vulnerable position and although I'm glad they were not able to chase us out of the country, I'd rather not walk into their open jaws. But maybe we can uncover another detail or two. The additional knowledge we gained meanwhile justifies another close, albeit cautious look. Their feathers are ruffled, so they are more likely to make a mistake. We need a piece of concrete evidence, rather than just a dessert and photo of a boat, and then we can hand over to law enforcement, such as Interpol. There comes a time when one has to realise one's weaponry is no match for that of one's opponent."

Topping up the glasses, Catinca thought for a moment. "OK. Let's start by going to vineyard. Just like tourists. Having a nose around, keeping our eyes open and not getting recognised. Hair sorted, so all you need to do is wear shades and stylish clothes. No one will think it's the same person."

"Fine. We can do that. Just to add detail to the dossier and certainly not to get ourselves seen. On that note, it seems the bug I planted on Xander has successfully transmitted some recordings. I got a note from my associate in Naples. He will have to translate the audio file and then provide me with an English transcript. Let's hope it will be more than scent meanderings by pompous Monsieur Le Nez. Now I'd like to freshen up, then I suggest a visit to the buffet car. I love eating on trains."

Catinca emptied her glass. "Mate, you love eating anywhere."

Chapter 29

Hacking the Wi-Fi at the visitors centre had presented him no more difficulty than a child's puzzle and accessing the security guards' mobile phones had been the work of an afternoon. That was how he discovered a beekeeper would be in attendance on Tuesday morning to tend to the château's hives.

It took him forty-five minutes to send a virus to the beekeeper's computer, ensuring he was out of action for the entire morning. Instead Davor himself, complete with beekeeping gear, was welcomed at the château. He spent no longer than quarter of an hour wandering between the hives before placing his equipment behind some recycling bins and returning to the security gate. He informed them more sophisticated equipment would be required and that he or one of his colleagues would return later that afternoon. There was the slimmest of risks the beekeeper would apologise for his late arrival, but due to the shift changeover two new guards would be in place. Then all Davor needed to do was park his motorcycle out of sight, scale the wall, retrieve his equipment and climb the ladder to the tree-house under the cover of darkness. Not that this revealed any conversation inside the house. But it got him this lookout in the trees.

She had convened the entire family. Presumably they would stay the whole weekend. He watched from his vantage point as one by one, each in a flashier vehicle than the last, they arrived. It was time to test his theory.

Ever since he had done the first job for the de Marsault family, he was convinced that some members were privy to more information than others. The chain of command was clear and the orders came from on high, but certain people were kept out of the loop. For what reasons, Davor could not be sure. Madame de Beauvoir aka Daria and Monsieur de Maupassant aka Xander were clearly in the inner circle. She had been his handler since he first began working for them exclusively. Yet Parisienne airhead Anastasia Kravets seemed to be excluded from that particular line of business. For one thing, the girl had no literary pseudonym. Where did the viniculturist Yves, or Monsieur de Saint-Exupéry, fit in?

So why summon the entire family to Château Agathe? To discuss his transgressions? What other reason would she have to demand their presence? In which case, she would have to reveal some of the less salubrious elements of the family business. Davor would like to be a fly on that wall.

Actually, he'd like to be a fly anywhere at all. Hours of sitting still in the children's tree-house played hell with his knees. The view, however, could not be beaten. Obviously designed to enable parents to watch their offspring, it worked equally well in reverse. He could observe every arrival and departure, watch Madame move around her quarters or potter about in her private garden, study each visitor and be aware of anyone approaching his tree-top hideaway. An expert in conserving energy and maintaining stillness in cramped conditions, he found the tree-house comparative luxury. He was able to stretch out and sleep for a few hours each night while the security guards performed a perfunctory patrol at ground level. Creatures of routine, they never deviated in either route or timing. When they got to the furthest point of the grounds, Davor could descend, access the visitors' toilets to relieve himself and refill his water bottle. The system worked well.

Even so, his frustration built as he had no way of knowing what was going on inside the house. What decisions were being made, how much information was revealed and what that meant for him. He took another bite of dried meat strip and assessed the daylight. In around twenty minutes, the setting sun would radiate its brilliance on this side of the family house. As every day, a member of the household staff would draw down the awnings to protect the family from the afternoon glare. Only then did he dare to open his laptop and attempt to penetrate the communication system of the main house. At any other time of day, he would not risk the blue light of the computer screen giving away his hiding place.

Three days and nights this tree house had been his home. He had no plans to check out before Monday. After all, he had work to do.

Chapter 30

Whether it was the relief of escaping Paris, the satisfaction of making progress in the case or the three glasses of claret she had consumed with dinner, Beatrice enjoyed a deep and dreamless sleep. When she awoke on Friday morning, that particular golden south-of-France sunshine lit their twin room like the reflection of a thousand sunflowers. Catinca's bed was empty and she could hear the sounds of tooth brushing coming from the small bathroom. She sat up and lifted the blind, eager to see the view by daylight.

The wide muddy expanse of the Garonne river stretched away in both directions, spanned to her right by a honey-coloured brick bridge. On the opposite bank, church spires and towers rose above the city buildings. The sky, in its morning baby blue, held the promise of depth and intensity. Her gaze dropped to their side of the riverbank and she watched cyclists, scooters and joggers speed along the broad promenade alongside meandering tourists. Closer still, the traffic stopped and started along the boulevard, while trams whizzed up and down the central reservation. Right below their hotel were a strip of pavement cafés. A waiter delivered a cup of something to a smartly dressed woman at a pavement café and hung around to chat for a moment. On the corner stood a group of bearded men, arguing in a language Beatrice could not understand.

To her, it seemed life was happening out there and she should join in. Just as soon as she'd had breakfast. Beatrice ran a hand through her hair before realising it was no longer there. A full-length mirror hid the wardrobe door. She stood in front of it and examined herself. Crumpled face, spotty pyjamas, bare feet and shiny skull cap of blonde hair.

Someone knocked at the door. Beatrice checked the peep hole and saw it was a waitress with a breakfast trolley. She opened the door with a wide smile, for once in her life unafraid of frightening people with her just-out-of-bed hair. The maid greeted her with a '*Bonjour!*' and indicated the tray.

"Oh, she ordered room service? Thank you so much! Would you like me to sign for that?"

"No, madame, that's fine. I will bring it in."

"No need, I can manage. Just a tick." She reached behind her to where she had dumped a handful of coins, receipts and ticket stubs on arrival. She gathered up a couple of Euros and handed them to the woman with the short black bob.

"Thank you very much, madame, and I wish you a very nice day."

"Same to you," she said, returning her smile and wondering if those fabulous green eyes were contact lenses.

She wheeled the trolley inside and placed the juices, coffee pot, milk jug and pastries on the little table. By the time she was ready, Catinca had emerged, having affected yet another complete transformation. Hair slicked back into a tight plait and dressed in a pale green jumpsuit, she looked like Lara Croft.

"Sorry to be so long in loo, I had work to do. Mate, your hair looks fab! You aren't freaked, are you?"

"That's all right, I've only just got out of bed. No, I'm not freaked. To be honest, I'm rather delighted. And I have to say, you look extraordinary. Like some sort of action woman."

Catinca plumped herself onto the window seat beside the table and sank her teeth into a croissant. "Which is what I am. I been up for two hours. Sorted out wine tour at Château Agathe for this afternoon. You know they got a restaurant? That's where we're having lunch."

"Good idea. About time we had some *spécialités culinaires Bordelaise.*"

"And have a nose around. You want coffee? There's warm milk and them little jam pots I love. French breakfast is the best. Good idea to order it for room." She poured coffee into two white china cups as Beatrice came to sit opposite. "You OK, really?"

"Yes, I am. Really." Beatrice sipped coffee and helped herself to a croissant. "I had no idea what a difference a dramatic haircut could make. You wouldn't understand, being the Queen of New Looks on a weekly basis, but I've looked the same for the last forty-five years."

"About time for a change then. And you look sodding fabulous." She picked up a little pot of jam. "What the hell is quince? I'm not touching that, I'm vegetarian."

Beatrice snorted with laughter. "What time is the wine tour?"

"Coach picks us up in forty-five minutes. You better get a shift on."

"Forty-five minutes is ages. Unless you intend to 'style' me again."

Catinca gave her a stern look down her nose.

Beatrice sighed, finished off her croissant and headed for the bathroom.

Public tours were something Beatrice detested, being firmly of the belief that 'Hell is other people', regardless of what Sartre originally meant. On this occasion however, she knew it was the most innocent way of arriving at Château Agathe. Now they had left Paris, she assumed she would be able to dress as she wished. Her travelling companion thought otherwise.

"We gotta be boxed, see? People wanna put a label on us. Mother and daughter, lesbian couple, travel journalists, we got to look the part."

"Which part?" asked Beatrice, rather alarmed at the idea of playing any of the above.

Catinca, who was reapplying severe eyebrows at the vanity unit in the twin room, lifted her shoulders almost to her ears. "What do you think? We are a pair of wine critics, which ain't far from the truth. Wear them linen trousers with that asymmetric top. Espadrilles, subtle jewellery and I'll do your face."

In character, they entered the hotel foyer and joined the vineyard excursion. Other than polite smiles, they had little interaction with the other tourists as they boarded the coach and listened to the tour guide prattling on about the Bordeaux region. Both Beatrice and Catinca had heard it all before so devoted their attention to the passing scenery. It was a beautiful part of the world, Beatrice had to admit. As far as she could see, swaying wheat fields speckled with poppies covered the landscape, only giving way to sunflowers, their golden heads the size of serving platters all lifted to the sun.

Catinca nudged her in the ribs, pointing to the château just visible beyond the sunflower fields. A buzz of enthusiastic appreciation rippled up the coach and almost everyone turned to the window to take photographs. Beatrice turned in the other direction, her mind occupied by broader, darker views.

The tour was typical, basic and held neither Catinca's nor Beatrice's interest. They affected interest, made notes, took photographs and paid a great deal more attention to their surroundings. A simple photograph of a rosebud could, with some refocusing, take in much of the detail around the house. While Catinca posed for an image against a covered bower, Beatrice took a series of snaps identifying security cameras. Catinca returned the favour by snapping a shot of Beatrice admiring the main château building, ensuring all vehicle registrations were visible. Naturally the tour ended with a wine tasting. Their bland but efficient guide led them back to the main building where a stone outhouse, furnished with oak tables and benches on an outside patio, offered a selection of samples. They were supposed to taste, identify their favourites and make a purchase in the building itself.

Beatrice thanked their guide, slipped him a five-Euro tip and asked him, quite unnecessarily, for the direction of the restaurant. It was signposted, as was everything else around the grounds. But the distraction did allow Catinca to plant her cosmetic bag behind one of the patio's fig plants without being seen. After another effusive round of thanks, she and Catinca left the party and headed across the lawns to Le Chalet. Once again, Beatrice had the surest feeling they were being watched. She threw a glance across her shoulder, yet no one had followed them from the outhouse. Nor could she see any faces at the windows of the château. But that didn't mean no one was looking.

The wine list, as one would expect of an on-site restaurant, featured a rich portfolio of the château's vintages. The food menu on the other hand was disappointing. Classic tourist pleasers such as French Onion Soup, Boeuf Bourguignon and Crêpes Suzette left Beatrice unimpressed. Perhaps five-star hotels in Paris had spoilt her.

Twice they asked the waiter for more time, making a huge pantomime of being subtle. Both wrote in little notebooks, studying the menu with exceptional concentration. On his third attempt, Catinca announced they would like to speak to the sommelier. The young man's confusion was evident and he summoned the head waiter. Catinca asked various questions, all of which sounded plausible to Beatrice, and eventually accepted his advice of a light chalky sauvignon blanc vintage to accompany their entrée, a shared platter of seafood. Purely as a matter of principle, they rejected the idea of the aged grand cru offered as wine pairing with main courses of ratatouille and minute steak and selected instead a younger and more boisterous variant of the estate's second label. Their fastidiousness had the correct effect and once they returned to the serving station, Beatrice watched the head waiter whisper in the young man's ear. The waiter became more solicitous with every visit to the table.

As rehearsed, Catinca announced a visit to the bathroom the minute they had finished their seafood starter. Naturally this required a search through her bag for her cosmetics – which were missing – stuffed behind that fig plant not one hour before. With much fuss and kerfuffle, the two women determined to themselves and any watchers that the cosmetics were indeed lost. Catinca got to her feet, dropping her napkin on her chair. With another of her signature shrugs, she looped her bag over her shoulder and went in search of her make-up. Content that her assistant could manage the job alone, Beatrice motioned the waiter and advised him to serve her steak.

The little one with the jumpsuit and trainers came out of the restaurant alone. With that classic head swinging, 'I'm looking for something' affectation, she retraced her steps back to the tasting outhouse. But she didn't stop there. She walked past, taking the right fork, dodging behind the bushes which guarded Madame de Marsault's private garden.

Davor slid his hand into his combat trousers and pulled out a pair of binoculars. He'd spotted these two the minute they got off the bus. Hadn't he spent the majority of his life blending in, looking ordinary, and becoming one of the crowd while taking in every detail? He knew the routine; he'd honed it for decades.

These two were neither amateurs nor pros, he could see that even at this distance. Good surveillance skills, he acknowledged. Obvious spies to anyone with a security background. This ruse was as old as they came. She would search, look exasperated, retrace her steps, take a wrong turn and find herself in an area forbidden to visitors. If challenged, she would explain her reasoning and persuade the guards to help her look.

He had seen her slip that patterned purse into a plant pot. Once the guards found that, she would seem as sweet and innocent as the character she played. Davor was not fooled. She and the other woman were far from ordinary tourists. The question was, who were they? And what did they want? The family or him?

In some ways, Catinca's absence while Beatrice enjoyed her rare steak with duchesse potatoes was a good thing. Rivulets of blood on white china would make Catinca nauseous. On the other hand, her little Romanian companion had been gone far too long for comfort. As tension increased around Beatrice's windpipe, swallowing grew increasingly difficult. Just as the waiter poured her second glass of wine, a familiar figure accompanied by a uniformed security guard approached the doorway. She saw Catinca shake his hand and chirrup a cheerful goodbye. As she caught Beatrice's eye, she held her cosmetic bag in the air and waved it in triumph.

"Thank goodness," said Beatrice, beckoning the waiter to bring Catinca's meal.

Once Catinca began digging in to her ratatouille, Beatrice muttered under her breath. "No problems? You weren't seen?"

Catinca shook her head. "Nah, mate. Nobody saw me, I got away with it. But didn't see anything spectacular either. Large private section further back, with view across fields, but all rooms I could peek through windows were deserted. Security believed me and even walked me back here. What do you reckon? Little wander round the grounds after lunch and catch a bus back to the city?"

"So long as we keep our heads down, fine. Now, I'm ready for pudding. Today feels to me like a chocolate mousse day, wouldn't you agree?" Beatrice twisted over her shoulder to find the waiter, who had already materialised on her other side. He was angling his head to read her notebook and stopped immediately she noticed.

She slapped the cover shut and ordered her dessert and coffee with a sharp stare. At that moment, a handsome man at a corner table caught her eye. Yves de Marsault, dressed in a blue-black suit, got to his feet, clapping his companion on the shoulder with a laugh. She bent her head, convinced he would recognise her despite the change in hair colour, and pretended to make notes on her pad. She rested her brow on her palm, shielding her eyes from view. The two men brushed past the table, conversing in lively French.

The change in Beatrice's behaviour had not escaped Catinca, who was smart enough not to speak until they had left.

"Whoozat?" she asked, eyes on the receding backs.

"That," said Beatrice, "was Xander's brother, Yves de Marsault. The one who runs the vineyard." She saw the waiter approaching and smiled as he placed a pretty bowl of chocolate mousse decorated with a violet in front of her.

"Excuse me? I'm probably mistaken, but would I be right in thinking that man is Yves de Marsault?"

The waiter hesitated, his unfortunate complexion colouring. "You are not mistaken, Mme. That is indeed Monsieur de Marsault and his guest."

Beatrice gazed up at him, wide-eyed. "Really? That is a wonderful endorsement of this restaurant, if the family dines here."

"Monsieur de Marsault is a regular client. He lunches here at least once a week."

"Well, what luck we had to be here on the same day. Tell me, do any other members of the famous family frequent your establishment?"

The waiter bent down, his tone confidential. "I served M.

Xander de Marsault on several occasions. Also his sister-in-law one time. She came here with her niece, the model, Anastasia Kravets."

"Oh I would love to have seen her. In all the pictures she looks quite lovely. What about Madame de Marsault? Does she ever eat here, being a local and all?"

"Sadly, no. She almost never leaves the house."

Catinca dipped some bread into her ratatouille. "Almost never?"

"Only once a month, when the family have their monthly meeting. That always falls on a Sunday, which is the busiest day of the week with this restaurant, so they have Sunday lunch in the Hotel de Marsault in Bordeaux. They own it, you see." The waiter looked over his shoulder, and Beatrice spotted the head waiter's stare.

"How absolutely fascinating!" said Beatrice. "Not only excellent service, but well-informed background."

"I must get back to work. Enjoy your meal, ladies."

Beatrice took a mouthful of her mousse. Airy and creamy, it melted on her tongue. But the half of her mind which was not obsessed with her dessert, chewed on a problem.

"Which one was Yves?" Asked Catinca. "The one with nice bum?"

"I can't say I noticed his bum. He was the one without the briefcase."

"Good-looking bloke. Very nice bum. All pictures I seen of the older brother, he seemed pretty tasty too. Is the youngest one like that? 'Cos I'm still in the market for a sugar daddy."

Beatrice shook her head and ate the last spoonful of her mousse. "Believe me, he's not your type. Pretentious, snobbish, arrogant and fake. Precisely the opposite of you."

"Aww," Catinca grinned. "You love me, don't you? Tell you what, by Christmas I'm gonna be Employee of the Month."

Beatrice burst into a loud guffaw.

Breaking cover was an extreme risk. Davor was not stupid enough to put himself in a situation without an exit. If you get in, you need to know exactly how to get out. His exit strategy was based on his knowledge of night-time security patterns. Now, he was exposed to bright afternoon sunlight, crowds of tourists, guides, security staff and CCTV cameras. Somehow or another, he had to find out who those two women were and where they were going. He considered his options. His drone was armed with a camera, not a microphone. Sending that to photograph them, their credit cards or anything else which might identify them would be madness. Equally insane would be to descend from the tree-house, follow them and try to eavesdrop on their conversation. He focused on the door of the restaurant, waiting for them to appear, and applied himself to the problem.

Facts: they had arrived on a tourist bus. Therefore, he could assume they would depart the same way very soon. These buses, he knew from experience, picked up and set down from various city centre hotels. Even if you were able to place a tracking device on the bus, how could he know at which hotel they disembarked? He needed to either get on the bus or follow it on his motorcycle. But how could he get from the tree-house to his bike before they left, without being seen?

The afternoon light turned from apricot to peach, signalling the setting of the sun. Small clusters of tourists returned to board their coaches, most clutching Château Agathe shopping bags. The two who interested him were some of the last to wander out of the grounds. They scurried across the gravel and boarded the huge bus. He was going to lose them and he cursed under his breath. Then an idea occurred. Deploying the drone inside the grounds was a risk he could not countenance. But just outside, still within range, he could at least narrow down the choice of hotels.

He scrambled to ready his device as he heard the engines below rumbling to life. With great stealth, he sent up the remote robot, navigating the tree canopy until it emerged onto the road. Using his thumbs to manipulate the control pad, he let it hover over the thick green hedge opposite the grand pillars marking the entrance. He kept enough height to conceal the high-pitched noise of the propellers. Its colour and camouflage allowed it to completely disappear against the backdrop of the sky. Once the coach made its creaking, lumbering way between the august stone pillars, indicating left in the direction of Bordeaux, Davor struck.

The drone dived in a sharp line to the vehicle's front, above the sight line of the passengers and driver, to take pictures of the destination board. Davor zoomed in, noting the names of each hotel and taking a series of high resolution photographs. Then he directed the drone to the back of the vehicle, capturing licence plate and coach company. That would have to suffice. Unwilling to take further risks, he decided against bringing the drone back into the grounds, and instead parked it behind the hedge where he had concealed his motorcycle. He would find a moment to descend and catch up with the bus, now that he knew its route.

To Davor's immense annoyance, Friday evening seem to involve far more security guards than usual, including several non-uniformed men who looked like management. Discussions took place as the group took a slow stroll around the house. Gates checked, cameras examined, angles discussed, notes taken, it was clear they were increasing security measures. None of the family made an appearance, but that officious little Blondie bloke peacocked his way in front of the troupe.

When the charade was finally over, with handshakes and promises and mimed mobile phones, the main security team return to their vehicles and departed, leaving the normal shift of four men. These four chose to debrief in the security lodge and

Davor saw his chance.

He slipped down the tree, careful to keep his body in the shadows, and hit the mossy undergrowth with no more than a silent puff. Crouching, he waited and listened for any response to his descent. After a full minute had passed, he crept into the shrubbery, crawling five paces, waiting five breaths and crawling five more. He pressed himself flat against the wall until he was convinced he was unobserved. Only then did he begin to scale the mossy wall out of the château. Outside, he checked his watch. The bus had left twenty-seven minutes ago. With heavy evening traffic, his bike could catch up before they reached the city centre.

Chapter 31

Dear Beatrice

Here's what I transcribed. The contents cannot be verified and accuracy is unreliable. You couldn't use this in court. Sound was poor and there were a few gaps. Inaudible elements in parentheses with guesswork as to content.

TRANSCRIPT OF RECORDING
PHONE CALL
Single voice of Man A: Yes? – What do you mean? – When? – How (did she) know? – Son of a bitch! I'm coming!"
General noise, Man A shouting at someone to get his car. Instructs driver to take him home. Angry cursing at traffic. Instructs driver to wait. Sound of keys and shouts at some people to get out of his office.

CONFERENCE CALL
Man A: Maman, are you OK?
Woman B: Her name is Madame Colette. Always use the names, Guy de Maupassant. (inaudible, perhaps sounds of irritation – tut/tsk?)
Man A/Guy de Maupassant: Of course. Sorry. How do you feel, Madame Colette?
Woman C/Madame Colette: How do you think I feel?

Threatened, unsafe and let down. Le Fantôme was here. Again! He put a picture of my perfume on the Internet. That (brute?) has been in my room. I have never seen the man, but he has seen me. You and Simone de Beauvoir are supposed to protect me but I feel more vulnerable than ever.

Woman B/Simone de Beauvoir: (He is to die soon?) I sent people to retire him. He won't come back.

Guy de Maupassant: Can you be sure, Madame de Beauvoir? (inaudible – man is eating something) Getting inside Madame Colette's room is too (inaudible). That son of a bitch is sending us a message.

Simone de Beauvoir: I got his message, loud and clear, and he will get mine, don't you worry. There's another complication. Monsieur de Maupassant, you had a visitor today, no? At Parfums Parfaits?

Guy de Maupassant: What? Yes, Anastasia asked me to meet her. Something to do with an influencer she wants to impress. She's a British perfumier.

Simone de Beauvoir: No, she isn't. She and her fashionista friend are investigating our business. They're staying as our guests at Hotel de Marsault Paris and I took the precaution of listening to their conversations. When I realised they weren't who they said they were I sent their photographs to the team to find a true ID. Monsieur Hugo called me instantly. The woman who visited you today is the same one who came to the château, asking questions about the Budapest incident."

Guy de Maupassant: That old witch was undercover police? (inaudible due to rustling noises)

Simone de Beauvoir: Wait, Guy, please. It seems they are not police, but they are investigating the death of (Señor Geres?). They made the connection via (Sharl?).

Guy de Maupassant: Not police? What then?

Simone de Beauvoir: Private detectives, possibly with a police connection. The woman's name is Beatrice Stubbs, the same one who caused us all the problems in Naples. In my opinion, she needs to be frightened off.

Madame Colette: I agree. Both of them. I don't want them on French soil. Can you and Guy have them removed as soon as possible?

Guy de Maupassant: I'll kick them out tonight! Staying in our hotel, eating our food ...

Simone de Beauvoir: No, let them stay till Friday as planned. But we listen to every word they say. We must find out how much they know. It's possible it may require something stronger than a deterrent.

Madame Colette: That is acceptable. I want you to take care of this once and for all. You will present your plans this weekend. I am calling a family meeting, here in Bordeaux. On Sunday, we will have lunch together. Everyone must be present.

Guy de Maupassant: Really? Including Yves? Sorry, Monsieur de Saint-Exupéry?

Simone de Beauvoir: (angry cursing)

Madame Colette: Of course not! Nor does he know anything about Le Fantôme. I did inform Monsieur Hugo, who is increasing security. The *rosbifs* are not an immediate threat. In my view, it is best to deal with them from a distance.

Simone de Beauvoir: OK. We'll send them home as planned. We have copies of their passports including home addresses. I will arrange for that problem to be handled in Britain.

Guy de Maupassant: They could get stabbed. People get stabbed all the time in London.

Simone de Beauvoir: Guy, please shut up! I said I'll deal with them. Listen, Colette, I am going to travel down on Friday, once I'm sure the Brits are on the plane. In the meantime, I will send a second agent to find Le Fantôme.

Madame Colette: I want him exorcised.

Simone de Beauvoir: I know.

END CALL

Much rustling and long silence. Man took jacket off? No more dialogue for remainder of recording.

That's all there was, Beatrice, and I'm not really confident of its accuracy. My French is reasonable, but the sound quality was very bad. I just hope you find it useful.

I'm worried about you. What they say sounds threatening. Although I really want to find out what happened to my uncle, I don't want to put you in danger. I would prefer to cancel the job than take any risks. Could you give me a call? My number is below.

Kind regards, Bruno.

Beatrice read the whole thing again, aware of Catinca's eyes on her. Then she handed it to her colleague, grabbed a sheet of hotel stationery and began making notes.

Guy de Maupassant = Xander de Marsault
Simone de Beauvoir = Daria de Marsault
Colette = Madame Agathe de Marsault
M. de Saint-Exupéry = Yves de Marsault
M. Hugo = Denis Hugues
M. Geres? = Gennaio Colacino?
Sharl = (charles)
Le Fantôme?

"I don't get it," said Catinca, her face pale. "This was Wednesday afternoon, right? They say they will let us stay till Friday. But next morning, we get kicked out of hotel and taken to Eurostar."

Beatrice pointed to a line in the transcript: 'we listen to every word they say. We must find out how much they know. It's possible it may require something stronger than a deterrent.'

"Whassat mean?" Catinca asked, eyes wide.

"Think about it. When I got back from the perfume house

and you got back from the fashion designer, we discussed the case in detail. Then that night, after dinner, we made the connection to the Naples case. We revealed that we know far more than they expected. That's why we were hustled out of there so fast. There was no way they could let us stay any longer."

"And what about 'something stronger than a deterrent'? You think they mean ...?"

Beatrice took a deep breath. "Having overheard how much we know about their operation, there's no doubt in my mind they want us silenced. Permanently. As she says, they know where we live. Thank God we didn't go back on the train. They might have had people awaiting us at the other end. Thing is, they'll know by now we didn't get on that Eurostar."

"And they gonna be looking for us. What do we do now?"

"Call for the cavalry. And keep our heads down."

Chapter 32

On Saturday morning, Beatrice badly wanted to get rid of
Catinca. She needed time and space to make two essential phone
calls, on top of which, she recognised that low hum of tension
indicating she required some time alone. The transcript detail
had finally given her the push to involve Interpol. She put an
emergency request to Lyon and was waiting for the call from
Fisher, her senior contact. The fact that the family thought them
to be out of the country reassured her. Still, she had to act fast.
From the little chat with the waiter she knew where the Sunday
meeting would be held. If she could convince Fisher to strike
then, the cabal could be taken in before sending their thugs after
Beatrice and Catinca. As for this "Phantom", she had no idea of
his agenda.

By nine o'clock no trolley had arrived, so they descended to
the restaurant. Beatrice preferred it, actually. More choice. As
they ate, she proposed her assistant take a trip to the wine
museum. Catinca's protests ran along the lines of not going on a
jolly while she was at work. Beatrice countered by saying it was
in fact Saturday and even private detectives deserved some time
off.

"And as a matter of fact, I would like to talk to my Interpol
contact with no one else around. He and I have a certain amount
of history. Listen, if I pay the entrance fee, will you go and

explore?"

Catinca scooped up another spoonful of berries, eyeing Beatrice across the table. "Course I will. Didn't want to leave you in the lurch, is all. But if you want me out the way, I'm happy to piss off. Even better if it's a wine museum. Thing is, I'll be gone for a good few hours. You gonna be all right on your own?"

Beatrice nodded, sipping at her cappuccino. "I'll be fine. To be honest, I'd appreciate some thinking time. At my age, brains need a little longer to process information. By the way, have you given any thought to when you should get back to London? I understand you only took a week off. That means you're due at work on Monday."

"I know," Catinca grimaced. "But we not finished, are we? Can't leave things like this."

They ate in silence, listening to the clatter of cutlery and chatter of voices around them. Finally, Beatrice poured herself another coffee and folded up her napkin. She dropped her voice.

"We may have to leave things like this. Depending on what Interpol says, we could book ourselves a flight home tomorrow morning and let them deal with the rest. It's frustrating I know, but part of a detective's skill includes knowing when to hand over to the experts. I'd like to prove we found who was behind the Budapest incident, otherwise we don't get paid. That said, if it's a case of endangering ourselves, letting them get away with it or blowing the thistle, I'm going to blow with all my might."

"OK, boss," Catinca grinned. "I'll get out of the way and let you get on the blower. Depending on what Interpol bloke says, I'll call Adrian and report for duty."

Beatrice only wanted to speak in public places after what happened in the Paris hotel. She'd find a spot with people but discreet enough to have a private conversation on the phone. And it wasn't just Interpol. This morning, recognising her symptoms, she had also requested a telephone consultation with her counsellor. At such short notice, there was no guarantee he would fit her in. His secretary had promised to do her best to slot her into his schedule, but could not say precisely when he would have an opportunity to ring. James's Saturday morning surgery was frequently fully booked. She decided to check her emails.

To add to all her concerns, the Luxembourg law firm had sent a vague threat of legal action on behalf of Xander de Marsault and the management of Papillion. Since she and Catinca had gained access to their respective companies by fraudulent means, they should be warned. If any of their products or company information appeared on Catinca's feed or any other public platform associated with her name, they would sue. For what, they didn't say. She told herself it was nothing more than sabre-rattling and dismissed it with more confidence than she actually felt.

The second unwelcome email came from Tanya.

```
To: admin@beatrice-stubbs.com
From: tabail_y12@gmail.com
Subject: Advice
```

Hi Beatrice, hope you're enjoying Paris and having fun with Catinca. Wish I was there, for two reasons. One, I want to be in Paris with the pair of you! The other thing is that I need to pick your brains.

It's Marianne and her new boyfriend. Something's not right. Not just little sister helicoptering, because Gabriel sees it too. Joseph Gibson is dodgy as hell. Charming on the outside, but this guy has an agenda. He 'forgets' his wallet and Marianne ends up paying. The nice bottle of wine he gave Dad came from Marianne's wine rack. He's borrowed money from her on a short-term basis and when I asked if he'd repaid it, she bit my head off. We've been out with them twice and he's not spent a single penny. It's not just the fact he's tight as a gnat's chuff, I think he's got bigger ideas. When he came round ours for dinner, Gabe saw him photographing our post. WTF is that all about? I've done some digging and found bugger all online – he doesn't exist. In my shoes, what would you do? Don't say talk to Marianne, she's in lockdown. Mum and Dad both broached the subject and she flounced.

Sorry to bother you while you're on a case, but Dad, Gabe and I are so worried she'll get hurt/scammed again.

Any advice welcome. Love to you and say hi to Catinca.

Tanya xxx

PS: Luke says will you bring him some real French fries back from France?!?

Beatrice pressed her fingers to her eyes and tried to concentrate on a summary of the de Marsault situation for Interpol. Domestic drama must wait. Now, she had to go.

Leaving the hotel, she marched for a few streets, heading for the stone bridge over the wide Garonne river that separated the entire city into north and south banks. It was Saturday lunchtime on a sunny day, so there were plenty of dog walkers, tourists, runners and the occasional homeless person asking for a Euro on her way. She turned a corner and approached the silty, fast-moving river. This would do. No cars were allowed on the bridge so all she had to contend with in terms of sound was the occasional tram. She stopped around a third of the way across and checked if she had been followed. People wandered by, stopping to take photographs, pointing out landmarks and moved on towards the old town. A bulky man carrying a weather-beaten rucksack, in a classic French beret and old-fashioned Walkman earphones, settled himself at the entrance to the bridge to plead for coins. .

The melody of her mobile phone made her jump.

"Hello?"

"Hello, Beatrice, it's James here. Is this a good time?"

"James! Thank you so much for calling. It is the perfect time. I really appreciate you fitting me in. I know your Saturday mornings are busy." She leaned backwards against the railing on the bridge and checked if she could be overheard. No one was in earshot.

"I'm happy to be able to help. Are you outside? There is a constant background noise, like a waterfall."

"Yes, indeed, I am just crossing the Garonne river. If you don't mind, can we keep talking?"

"Of course. I assume there is something particular you like to talk about?"

"Yes, there is. I'm feeling a little discombobulated and out of sorts. The case I'm pursuing turns out to be rather more far-reaching and complex than I had anticipated. I believe we might be talking about organised crime. If I pursue this myself, accompanied by my brand new assistant, I would be putting us both in an extremely dangerous situation. If I hand this over to higher authorities, they may dismiss it and regard me as an interfering old biddy. Alternatively, they may take it seriously and I would be side-lined, not to mention unpaid. The question is, am I giving up too soon on account of my assistant? Is my sense of responsibility making me risk averse?"

"Let's pick up on that one phrase 'sense of responsibility'. Why are you pursuing this case? Take a moment to think about the real answer to that question."

Looking down and up the bridge, she focussed on the question. Her view also flicked over the big homeless man sitting at the start of the bridge, tampering with something that looked like a black umbrella from this distance. Finally, she stared at the water and replied.

"The reason I am pursuing this case is to find out who killed Gennaio Colacino. That's why I was hired."

"And have you?" asked James.

"No, not exactly. I don't have the name of the man who committed the murder, but I do suspect it was a professional killer. Most importantly, I know who arranged and paid for it. The same people who kidnapped me and threw me off a boat into the Bay of Naples."

"After such an experience, no one would blame you for being risk averse. Now you have identified the organisation behind all this, do you feel capable of bringing those people to justice yourself?" James's voice always had the strangest effect on Beatrice's mind. She had described him as a balm, a hosepipe, a cold shower or fresh air to her friends. Today, he was gravity. She was a helium balloon, bobbing, bumping and blown in all directions until James's voice brought her down to the ground.

"No. This is out of my league. That's why I've called Interpol. What worries me is that they will see me as a dotty old bat, playing detectives as a hobby. I'm waiting for a call from a senior officer, possibly the most patronising arse I've ever had the misfortune to meet. He will either pat me on the head and say 'there, there, dear' or take over the whole case."

"If the case is, as you say, out of your league, why would you not want them to take over the whole case? You mentioned your concern that these ex-colleagues of yours might regard you as 'a dotty old bat'. Beatrice, can we address the issue of your ego in this situation?"

She closed her eyes, incredulous at herself. Same pattern every time. Furious with James, outraged at his assumptions, insulted by his reductive analysis of her mindset, offended by his suggestion that the problem might lie within, not without. After a long inhalation of breath, she accepted the truth of his insight.

"I was about to protest the financial angle," she admitted. "That's not going to wash with you, is it? After all these years, all these sessions, it's still all about me. I want the glory, the recognition. And yes, the cash. How am I supposed to pay an assistant when I'm not earning any money?"

"We can discuss the business acumen behind your decision to employ an assistant in our next session. Currently I think we have more pressing problems. Did I understand you correctly? You have informed Interpol regarding the scope and risk factor of your investigation?"

"Not yet," Beatrice replied. "I'm waiting for him to return my call. But when he does, I intend to tell him everything. They can't just brush this off, although I think they might try. We are talking about a very powerful family in France who ..."

James interrupted. "Please give me no more details of the case itself, for both our sakes. My concern is you and your health. Apart from the immediate stresses, can you give me an overview of how you feel?"

It was a question Beatrice asked herself at least twice daily; on waking and while cleaning her teeth before bed. Her night time routine included taking a mood stabiliser and jotting a few lines in her daily journal. While brushing her teeth, she would assess herself and her moods with a realistic eye. Then she would sit on the bed, write her analysis, swallow her medication and get into bed.

"Right now, I find that question hard to answer. I've been in constant company in recent days and that always makes it harder for me to think clearly. Overall, I'd say I'm fine, but there is that little internal whine of panic. My assistant has gone out for the day, which I think will do both of us good. Sometimes I forget how important it is for me to be alone for a few hours at a time."

James did not respond immediately. Although Beatrice could not hear it, she knew he was writing. She waited, finding even his silence soothing.

"We know when we are hungry, our bodies tell us. Same with thirst, rest and cleanliness. Some signals are loud and clear. Others, more subtle, quieter. Your desire for solitude, which you described as a whine of panic, needs to be attended to before it gets to that stage. Whatever you're doing, factor in some quiet time. Make that non-negotiable. We all have special needs, and learning to cater for them makes us healthier and happier. I appreciate the fact your job is unpredictable and hard to plan. But every day, you make time for the essentials: eating, showering, sleeping. Solitude should be one of your essentials. How are you getting on with the mood stabilisers?"

Beatrice opened her mouth to answer when a beeping noise in her ear announced an incoming call. "James, I'm so sorry, I have to go. This is Interpol. Thank you so much for today, it's been a huge help. See you next month!" She rang off and answered Fisher.

Of all the versions of the conversation she rehearsed, it was nothing like she expected. Fisher listened to all her evidence, the detail of the transcript, without interruption. Once she had finished, he was professional, interested and surprisingly well informed. The family de Marsault had been on Interpol's radar for some considerable time, in particular Xander de Marsault and his perfume operation. The Sûreté were convinced the company was involved in some less media friendly business such as narcotics. In typical Fisher fashion, he mentioned 'associated activity'. Beatrice didn't need him to spell it out. Where there were drugs, there was prostitution. He asked perceptive questions regarding Daria de Marsault, her connections to the Naples incident and her standing in the family hierarchy. They had very little to incriminate Yves de Marsault although he seemed guilty by association, living at the château with Madame. Fisher agreed with Beatrice that the old lady was in fact the mastermind of the operation, which also came out clearly as she read him the transcript.

"All very interesting and very good work. Unfortunately, the question of legality raises its head. None of this can be admissible in court as you planted an illegal bug. That said, with a criminal organisation of such a calibre, we may be able to find a reason to ask these people some questions. To which end, I would like you to send me everything you have via secure comms. Why ever did they let you walk off, I wonder?"

Beatrice shared their experiences in Paris including their ignominious escort from the city. On relating their escapades at Gare du Nord, he actually chuckled.

"My word, Beatrice, you do have some adventures. Nevertheless, I am going to ask you to retreat instantly, mainly to keep you and your assistant safe. With the information you have provided, we will essay an arrest at Château Agathe during Sunday lunch, taking the entire family into custody."

"No, that's not where they'll be. Family meetings take place in Hotel de Marsault in Bordeaux. There's a private dining room. I winkled that out of a waiter. Once a month, they have family meetings in the hotel which bears their name. Always on a Sunday."

He chuckled again, a strange sound, as if he were hyperventilating. "Rather perfect, on a Sunday afternoon. Trying to scramble their legal team from Luxembourg is going to prove quite the challenge."

"Yes, sir. I wish you every possible success. I regret 'not being in the kill', as it were, but it is probably best that we get out of the way and leave you to it. I'll send you all the details I just described and will be happy to make a statement if required. When my assistant returns, we will check out and head to the airport."

Fisher did not reply, the silence at the other end of the line telling Beatrice she'd been put on mute. She waited with no sense of resentment, more a glowing sense of relief. The family de Marsault were no longer her problem.

"Beatrice? Sorry about that. Just got some interesting intel. Our observers tell us the family employ a number of freelancers to handle some of the less salubrious jobs. The individual they refer to as "Le Fantôme" is one such, who appears to have gone rogue. I shall revert with all the details, as we suspect he is likely to target the family. My point being, if you are watching them, and he is watching them, he will be watching you. Be exceptionally careful. My advice is to stay where you are, keep to your rooms if possible and wait until I give you the all clear before returning home. If all goes smoothly tomorrow, I might come and find you in person. We owe you a decent lunch at the very least. Can I just say I am enormously grateful for your sharing such intelligence? Obviously, a lady detective in her senior years ought not to tackle such people alone, but you always were headstrong. I'd say you did the right thing by calling us. Older and wiser, eh? Thank you, good luck and I'll see you once this is over. Goodbye."

"Goodbye, sir." Beatrice ended the call and turned around to look at the water, her mind replaying the last twenty-four hours, wondering if she and Catinca had shown their hand. She doubted it. At Château Agathe, she was 98% sure that Yves de Marsault hadn't seen her and the only other person they had spoken to was the young waiter. It was good of Fisher to warn her, but she was confident no one was watching. On the other hand, that flare of irritation at his supercilious tone sparked a new idea. With responsibility handed to Interpol, Beatrice and her assistant definitely deserved a little treat before leaving France.

Fisher didn't actually know where she and Catinca were

staying, so if she shifted herself, they could relocate this afternoon. Then they would stay in their rooms, as instructed, while enjoying a grandstand view of events unfolding at Hotel de Marsault. Beatrice powered her way back to the hotel, mentally preparing to pack. She hurried across the bridge, passing the homeless umbrella man and with a twinge of conscience, dropped a few Euros into his empty hat. His eyes lifted, his expression unchanged, and he placed his hands together in a gesture of gratitude. No one else seemed to even see him, rushing past as if he were a ghost.

Chapter 33

La Cité du Vin lay on the banks of the Garonne river, its sensual curves shimmering and shivering in the reflections of sunlight on the water. It was a touristy way to do it, but Catinca didn't care. She had made up her mind to approach the building from the river in order to appreciate the remarkable design.

Created to resemble the swirling of wine in the glass, the huge space looked like a carafe from one angle, a wave from another, and from still one more, a fat sleek serpent. She took the BAT 3 boat from the Stalingrad stop, travelling past some of Bordeaux's most beautiful architecture. Yet La Cité du Vin drew the eye due to its extraordinary shape and the textures of its walls, which gave the impression of a constant shifting fluidity. All in the bright blue morning of a Saturday in Bordeaux.

The rest of the tourists dawdled and dithered and took photographs with the building as a backdrop. Catinca could see how this would work to her advantage. She overtook her fellow passengers, striding into the foyer with her prepaid ticket already visible on her mobile. With a glance over her shoulder, she noted how most of her fellow travellers were only just reaching the front door. Determined not to get stuck behind the crowds, she pattered up to the second floor, accepted the multilingual audio device and entered the permanent exhibition, wishing Adrian was by her side.

The museum had a bit of everything. History of wine,

vinicultural regions around the world, types of wine, sound bites from expert oenologists, wine and erotica, literary references and Catinca's personal favourite, the five senses experience complete with scents you could try for yourself. She lost herself, delighting in this beautifully designed environment, absorbing titbits and background on a subject she thought she knew very well. By the time she arrived on the eighth floor to survey the city panorama and sample a glass of the product itself, she was surprised to see it was already one o'clock. No wonder she was peckish.

Leaning on the railing to survey the city of Bordeaux and sipping at her glass of white, she decided it was time to switch her phone back on. No messages from Beatrice, which could be good or bad news. Best to wait and see. There was a message from Adrian in response to her earlier photograph of her location. He sent a photograph of himself holding a bottle of Prager in brilliant green glass, with the caption, 'This is the colour of envy. Ax. PS: see you Monday?'

Catinca smiled to herself and looked out across the vista. A shadow moved in her peripheral vision and she took out her phone, just like everyone else in the room. She held the device at the best angle to catch a panorama of the breathtaking view, but reversed the camera so that she could shoot what was directly behind her. Her skin cooled, and she refocused her gaze from the city under the midday sun to the air-conditioned room behind her. It was the same woman she'd seen before. Leather jacket, jeans, short dark hair and biker boots. She had been one of the few to get off the boat and walk directly to the entrance, forgoing any selfies.

Catinca had seen her again when she chose to retrace her steps and listen once again to a feature on Romanian wines. That was not surprising. Just as in a supermarket, the museum guided the visitors in a slow spiral upwards, from the dark roots of the vine to the full-fruited harvest of the upper areas. Because they had almost collided, Catinca gave her a brief smile of acknowledgement as she stepped aside. She couldn't see her eyes behind her tinted glasses but she did nod, as if to say 'you're welcome'. Was she getting paranoid? She moved behind a pillar to take another shot. On her camera phone, the woman came into view. Catinca's stomach dropped as if she was in mid-air. She needed to get out and fast.

She left her half-finished glass on the bar and made for the lifts, pressing 0. Once she got in, she jabbed at the Close Doors button, hoping no one would join her. The lift doors shut noiselessly and took her to the ground floor. She trotted upstairs to the first floor and wandered around the foyer of the temporary exhibition. If that woman wanted to find her, she'd have to search the snack bar, toilet, gift shop and ticket area first, before rushing off to the boat. Which was due to leave in the next three minutes.

By the time she twigged her target wasn't aboard, Catinca would be long gone. On a tram from the other entrance. When she judged the boat must have left, Catinca sauntered downstairs. Checking over her shoulder every thirty seconds, she browsed the gift shop for presents: one for Adrian, one for Beatrice.

Her phone vibrated. Beatrice.

"Hello, boss. All sorted?"

"Hi, Catinca. I think so, yes. I'm on my way back to the hotel, ready to make some arrangements. How is the museum?"

"Nice, but to tell naked truth, I'd rather not be on my own right now. What arrangements? Do I tell Adrian I'll be back on Monday?"

"Well, that's the question. I can fill you in later, but the authorities were already watching these people. Therefore, they are grateful for our input and happy to take over completely, with immediate effect. We're supposed to stay in our room until it's all over. But I was thinking ..."

"What was you thinking?"

"We could change hotels once more, then stay in our room and observe the action as spectators. Enjoy the performance as our private grand finale to this case. All perfectly civilised with a view, champagne, nibbles and giggles."

Catinca exploded into a laugh. "Woman, seriously! I am on next tram back, it's faster than boat!"

"Listen, it's just started to rain. Take a cab directly to Hotel Garonne. No need to come back here. I'll pack, leave the cases with reception and potter off up the road under an umbrella. You order tea and I'll check us in. Then we send a courier for our cases. Just in case anyone is watching."

"Got it. Then home tomorrow?"

"Home tomorrow. Just as soon as our targets are under arrest. See you soon!"

Catinca made straight for the checkout to pay for the silk scarf and three-jar set of confits she'd chosen for her friends. While she waited, she planned the captions to so many of the photographs she'd taken that afternoon. It was the most gorgeous way to spend a few hours and when she got home, she would insist Adrian and Will plan a visit. She checked her watch. No wonder she was hungry. She handed over her purchases to the cashier and counted out the requisite amount of Euros. With a smile, she returned the wishes for a nice evening and began placing her purchases in her handbag.

For some reason she looked up. Standing by the door, apparently busy on her phone, was the same woman who had followed her all day. She was waiting for Catinca to return to the boat, to the hotel, to Beatrice.

Enough was enough. She slung her shoulder strap over her arm and took fast determined strides towards the door to confront this nosy cow. The woman had disappeared. Catinca peered into the wine store, the smoking areas outside and returned to the gift shop. Her tail was nowhere to be seen. She was about to scurry off in the direction of the taxi rank, when a hand rested on her shoulder.

She squeaked in alarm and whipped around. A security guard in uniform stood behind her, holding a package of confits.

"I think these belong to you," he said. "You forgot them at the cash desk."

Catinca's breath was short, and the pound of her pulse made it difficult for her to understand anything other than the fact she was not being assaulted. She stared up at the uniformed officer, still scanning the room behind him for the woman in a leather jacket.

"Oh, right, yeah. Thank you. You want to see my receipt?" she asked.

He shook his head. "Not necessary. I saw you pay. Are you all right?" His dark bearded face creased into a frown. "You don't look good."

Catinca saw a chance and took it. "Is there somewhere I can sit down?" she asked. "I don't feel so well."

He placed a hand on her back and the other under her elbow, guiding her to a door hitherto hidden behind one of the pillars. He swiped at a console with a card and the door swept open. A small staff area, complete with lockers, led into a storage facility. The light was dim, only sufficient to light a few chairs and a low table. Her saviour guided her to a chair, smacked a switch on the wall and poured a glass of water, directly from the tap over the sink.

He crouched in front of her and offered her the glass. She took it, with a weak smile. After several thirsty gulps, she rested it against her forehead. "Thanks. You're very kind."

"I can call a doctor?" he offered, his piercing eyes searching her face.

She shook her head. "That's not necessary. Nothing serious. Didn't eat all day, drank wine, got dehydrated and dizzy. My own stupid fault."

With the jerk of his chin, he indicated she should drink more. She obeyed, studying him over the rim of the glass. He was a fine looking man, with thick black hair, a neat beard and lovely warm eyes. Only problem was his height, at least two metres tall. By his side, she would look like a little girl, lifting up a hand to hold Daddy's.

Gorgeous as this bloke was, he was only good for one thing. She handed back the glass.

"Cheers, mate. Is there another way out of here where I can get to a taxi?"

"Yes, no problem." He unfolded himself to his full height, placed the glass on the counter and indicated a fire door at the back of the room. "You can go out this way. Straight across the road turn left and taxi rank is 200 metres ahead. Will you be safe on your own?"

"Sorted. Thanks very much. I really appreciate it. Should let you get back to work." She held out her hand.

He took it, enclosing hers completely in his large, warm palm. "You're welcome. How long do you stay in Bordeaux? Maybe I should take your number? Just to be sure you're OK?"

She broke into a smile. "No offence, mate, but I don't give my number to strangers. Can I take yours instead?"

He reached into his top pocket and retrieved a business card. "Here. My name is Didier. And you?"

She took the card, read it and tucked it into her handbag. "Nice to meet you, Didier. I'm Catinca. You're a decent geezer. If I get the chance, I'll give you a call."

He pressed the metal bar to open the fire door. Catinca slipped out, and with a wave at Didier, walked away from La Cité du Vin, unable to repress a smile.

Chapter 34

Never in his life had Davor suffered a crisis of conscience. Well, only once. When presented with a potential job, he only ever asked himself two questions: How much? How dangerous? In essence, was it worth it? He had little experience with moral dilemmas.

Raindrops smeared his visor as he rode his motorcycle out of the city, forcing himself to look outwards, maintaining his cautious scrutiny of his environment to keep himself safe. The time for introspection would come when he went to ground. Not the tree house, not in this weather. He had something more comfortable in mind.

By the time he had parked his bike under the wisteria, clambered through the greenhouses and emerged into the private garden, the sky had brightened and a rainbow embraced the château. He stood in the shade of a plum tree and watched the sun hit the French windows of Madame's private quarters. That was his moment to slip into the summer house.

He waited, still and silent until he was sure he had not been followed. With minimal movement, he dumped his rucksack, dried off, changed clothes and lay on his front to observe the house through the crack in the door. Only then could he turn his mind to the matter at hand. Davor dealt in realities, not hypotheticals. Action and reaction, nothing more.

That woman on the bridge. A private detective who had

enough information and all the right connections to bring the family down. He had heard more than enough while listening to her conversations via his remote microphone to see that time would soon be up for the family de Marsault. One part of him applauded. Justice was long overdue, so long as they didn't drag him down with them. Another part of him resisted. Loyalty, history and a sense of always opposing the law bound him to the family forever. Until they sent someone to kill him.

Here was an opportunity. Sunlight sparkled off blades of grass and spiders' web, filling him with optimism and a tiny spark of hope.

He could walk in there, talk to them in person, explain what he knew and assist in their escape. What greater proof did they need of his undying loyalty? A promise of release should be automatic. But he needed a shield. If he appeared in Château Agathe, they might shoot him before he could open his mouth. The way to do it was to use Madame Agathe de Marsault. After all, she'd used him all these years.

Forty minutes passed until the lights came on in her quarters. Gauzy curtains hid the figure within, but Davor's binoculars showed him there was only one person in the room, bent over the desk. He slipped out of the summer house, alert for security lights, gliding across the lawn like a phantom. The patio doors would be impossible to access without triggering lights, so Davor did the practical thing and snipped the wires with the pliers on his knife. He picked the lock in seconds and lifted the security chain with the thinnest blade of his knife. He was in.

The breeze lifted the curtains and Davor concealed himself behind the heavy drapes. He heard a chair creak and rapid steps crossed the room to check the doors. That was not Madame. Her steps were languid and arthritic. When Davor could see the blond head peering from one side to the other, he took his chance and stepped into the light.

The fussy little blond let out a gasp and reached for his phone. Davor clamped a powerful hand around his wrist and shook his head. "Bad idea." Some instinct told him to address the man in English. Probably because he had awful hair.

"I know who you are!" the idiot spluttered.

Davor did not blink. "I don't know who you are and I don't care. Where is the family?"

"You cannot come in here and expect to talk to ... ow!"

Davor placed his hand around the man's wrist and squeezed. "Listen, my friend. I have crucial information that will save the family de Marsault. I will speak only to Madame."

Blondie's face grew sweaty. "No! You can't. They do not want to see you and your information is worthless. We're far ahead, in actual fact."

Davor relaxed his grip. "Take me to the family. Now."

A combative light enlivened Blondie's eyes. "Soz, no can do. You are persona non grata and I'll thank you to leave via the front do...argh!"

Davor pushed the man around, wrenching one arm up behind his back and clamping his own muscular forearm across the squeaking fool's throat.

"The family are being watched, imbecile. Do you want the facts or not?"

"Not! We already know. When did we ever employ you for your brain? Never. You are nothing more than muscle. You know nothing. We're aware of the Brits. They checked into Hotel Garonne less than an hour ago. We own it! Of course we got the notification they'd booked the penthouse. *Et voilà!* Your special secret is worthless and so are you."

Davor released him and looked into the man's highly coloured face. At the same time, he became aware of floodlights illuminating all the grounds, shadows running across the lawns and a net closing in.

Blondie hadn't finished. "The women are a threat to the

entire organisation and will be dead by Sunday morning. You, on the other hand, must leave us tonight. *Adieu, Fantômas!*"

He took a pace away and pressed a device, an expression of such self-satisfaction on his face, Davor would have killed him anyway. The metal shutters ground down, trapping everyone inside.

In the second Davor's attention had been drawn to the windows, the blond had reached the door. With one unhesitating move, Davor snatched the bottle of perfume on the dresser and aimed it at the idiot's temple. The man cried out and fell onto his right knee. Davor was on him before he even hit the ground. He pressed his foot on the man's back, caught him by the hair and snapped his neck. The body went limp in his hands and he kicked the carcass under the bed.

He pressed himself flat against the wall, releasing the safety catch on his weapon and listened. He could hear nothing. This was a trap and they had all exits covered. This much he knew. The chances of him leaving this room alive were Butch Cassidy and The Sundance Kid. But he was better than that. He was Le Fantôme, who could disappear at will. He inhaled and drew on the strength of his mind.

The metal shutters were a panic system. If someone broke into the grounds, Madame would be alerted and close herself in. Of course she had a door to the main house, through which that idiot had tried to escape, but that could not be the only exit. If intruders entered the property, they could be in the grounds *and* in the house. The only way of guaranteeing Madame's safety was another way out. But where was it? Many of these châteaux had underground tunnels to another part of the estate. Davor would bet his life, no, he had no choice but to bet his life, there was such a passage somewhere in this room. All he had to do was find it.

He opened his eyes and scanned the room. For a reason he could not explain, his gaze fell on the dresser. A black china object rose from the glass top, a simulacrum of a female forearm with long pointed nails, bearing rings, necklaces and other trinkets. He stared at it in disbelief. There, dangling from the thumb was a lapis lazuli bracelet he hadn't seen for twenty-five years.

Time was against him. Just outside the windows came the sounds of readied weaponry. The trap was triggered and shooting an intruder would be understandable. Particularly with a dead body in the room. He had to make his move. He snatched up the bracelet and zipped it into his jacket pocket.

Then he studied the room: fireplace, tapestry, wardrobes. In his observations from the tree-house, he'd seen maids take and replace items from the armoire on the left. Its twin was never used. That must be the entrance. Moving with all the stealth he possessed, he dropped to the floor and crabbed his way towards it. The only question now, was whether it was locked. He ran his hand around the door, pulled it softly open and crept in. Empty. With the pads of his right fingers, he tapped the back wall. Sweat ran into his eyes as he tested the wood for the faintest sound of hollowness. From outside, he heard someone demanding his surrender through a megaphone. That didn't make his task any easier.

His fingers found it. It was subtle but he detected a different resonance and by exploring the area, found a single groove delineating a doorway. No handle, no lock, not even a keypad to enter a combination. He stood up and pressed the door with his right hand. Nothing. He replayed all the times he had watched Madame feeding her dog, brushing her hair, applying her make-up. She used her left hand. He tried again and the door stayed closed. He recalled an image of the woman, her stooped posture, her diminutive body. He reached his left hand to knee height, gave one sharp press and released.

The door gave a click and opened inwards to a black space. Davor tested the ground in front of him and switched on his torch. Below him, a set of stone steps, as if heading to a cellar. At the bottom, a low stone corridor which looked disused, but Davor had to take the risk. He pushed the door closed, descended the steps and began to jog, his mind evaluating the distance and trajectory compared to his knowledge of the château. If the security people knew of the passageway, he would have a lethal welcoming committee.

The tunnel ran for over a kilometre at a steady upward gradient and halted at a wooden door, the type seen in country gardens. He switched off his torch and listened. After several seconds, he heard the engine of a vehicle. The sound went from left to right, the driver changing gear to take the curve. Davor knew where he was. Outside Château Agathe on the lane leading to the entrance. His motorcycle would be less than 200 metres away on the other side of the road. If he could get out.

He shone his torch around the door and the surrounding walls. In a small recess around elbow height, he spotted a large wrought-iron key lying on a dusty shelf. He inserted it into the lock, turned it with imperceptible increments and heard the tumblers fall. Then he flattened himself against the wall as he eased it open. Nothing, only the sounds of the night.

In less than ten seconds, he slipped out into the summer evening air, locked the door behind him and tucked the key into his jacket. With great caution, he crept along the wall until he found his spot. He began to climb. It would take mere minutes before the château would be surrounded by security and very likely police, all of them trying to prevent him from getting out. The last thing they'd expect was for him to go back in.

Chapter 35

In the flurry and fuss of relocating to their new penthouse, Beatrice packed their suitcases as fast as possible. Her excitement reached almost childish levels and she dismissed any guilt about booking such an expensive suite by convincing herself it was her well-deserved reward. She planned to take a taxi directly to the new hotel, then she and Catinca would stay inside until checkout time on Sunday afternoon, watching events unfold over the road.

Once she was ready, Beatrice called Matthew and assured him that she had handed over control of the case to higher powers and therefore was out of danger. Once again her confidence was more bravado than belief. She promised to keep him informed and expressed the conviction that she would be home for dinner on Monday evening.

"I do hope that comes to pass. Your advice is required on another topic. My eldest seems to have attracted another undesirable."

She chose not to mention Tanya's email. "Oh dear. The minute this is over, I will devote all my energy into supporting Marianne. Just one more day and I'm all yours."

"I would appreciate that. You see, the man is in desperate need of emergency funds."

Beatrice dropped her face into her hands. "Tell me everything in fifteen minutes, because I really must go."

Matthew began.

In their new penthouse, Catinca took a shower while Beatrice made two stiff gin and tonics and took them onto the balcony overlooking the street that separated them from the entrance to Hotel de Marsault. She sat with a heavy sigh.

Catinca emerged in her fluffy stolen bath robe, face scrubbed of make-up and shiny with skin cream. She sat opposite and lifted up a glass. "Tell you what, mate, I needed this."

They sat for several minutes, sipping their drinks, soaking in the view and allowing the tension to seep away. Even at this hour of the day, the sun's strength should not be underestimated and Beatrice welcomed the glow upon her face as she closed her eyes.

She took a long soothing draught of gin. "Things are getting complicated. According to Fisher, a hired killer called "Le Fantôme" has gone rogue and might be targeting the de Marsault family. I don't know the details, but the concern is that we may have crossed his radar. Of course he doesn't know we were actually after the family in the first place. Fisher is concerned he may have noticed us sniffing around. Personally, I think it's unlikely, but I do not want to take too many chances."

Catinca rotated her wrist, swilling ice cubes around her glass. "Do we know," she asked, "what this rogue agent looks like?"

"He didn't say. And even if he had, these people can disguise themselves and blend into the background so we wouldn't recognise him, or her, even if he delivered our breakfast."

"Funny you should say 'her'. You know I said I didn't fancy being on my own? That's because I thought someone was following me round the wine museum. I saw her several times and once, when I turned to go back, I almost bumped into her."

"Did you get a look at her face?" Beatrice asked.

Catinca shook her head. "Not really. She was wearing sunglasses. But she was youngish, quite slim and wearing jeans and leather jacket. Short black hair."

"Fisher definitely said 'he'. But that does sound odd. One other thing I wanted to ask. Yesterday morning, did you order room service for our breakfast?"

"No. I thought you did that."

"It wasn't me. If you want breakfast in the room, you have to specify what you want the night before and leave the order hanging outside. I certainly didn't do that and I was surprised you would do that without asking what I wanted. So why did a young woman with short dark hair and green eyes bring us a continental breakfast on a trolley?"

They lapsed into a thoughtful silence. "I don't get it. What's she want with us? If she's pissed off with the family, why follow me?"

Beatrice gazed into her glass, her face thoughtful. "I don't know. We can't be sure it is the same person, to be honest. But if it was, my best guess is she wants to know who we are. I can't imagine for one second she suspects us of being operatives, but maybe she just wanted to see for herself."

"Good job we changed hotels then. She doesn't know where we are now."

Beatrice waved her head from side to side in an I'm-not-sure gesture. "Not unless she followed your taxi. One thing is for certain, we are not going out this evening. Room service it is."

"That's no hardship, mate. Have a look at this menu!"

After some faintly ridiculous shenanigans involving a note on the door instructing the waiter to leave the trolley outside, checking the peephole and Beatrice sticking her head out to check the coast was clear, they managed to retrieve their dinner. Over a meal of sage polenta with roasted Mediterranean vegetables and a bottle of St Emilion, Catinca described as best she could the delights of the wine museum, with the additional highlight of a handsome security guard in shining uniform.

Since Catinca had been so forthcoming Beatrice decided to

share one of her own worries, unconnected to the current situation. "The email from the lawyers wasn't the only one I got while you were away. Tanya wrote to me. She's worried about her sister."

Catinca stopped in the act of spearing a red pepper. "Marianne? What's the matter with her? Not more men problems?"

"Marianne doesn't have much luck with the opposite sex. I'm sure Adrian told you about the incident in Portugal, when her Mr Right kidnapped Luke to make a point. If Will hadn't been there, I don't know what we would have done. Anyway she's been Internet dating and met someone she really likes. Perfect in every way, apparently. Then a couple of hours ago, Matthew told me that Mr Perfect had asked Marianne…"

"… for a loan?"

Beatrice's head snapped around. "How on earth did you know that?"

"Let me guess. He's going through a divorce, but when he and his ex-wife sell the house he's gonna be minted. Or, his poor dear mum needs help with her care home fees in the twilight years of her life, but when she dies, he's gonna be minted. Maybe there is no fake wife or fake mum, just a fake idea. He's got a brilliant concept for a start-up and simply needs some seed capital. Once the business takes off…"

"… he's going to be minted. So your thought processes follow the same pattern as mine. I thought I was being cynical. I know romance fraud is a huge subject for the Met and wondered if my outlook as an ex-copper made me jaded."

"Listen, mate. Western Europe has no monopoly on scamming bastards. Plenty of them shits everywhere. Romania, Nigeria, America, Russia and probably here and all. She has actually met this bloke right? Not just Internet chats?" She poured them both another glass of wine.

"Thank you. She's definitely met him and even introduced

him to the family. So far, he has won them over. But when Matthew asked if they would babysit Luke one Sunday afternoon he refused, saying it was too painful to be around young children since he was fighting for access to his own young son. Tanya and Matthew are suspicious and want me to look into it."

Catinca soaked up the oily juices of the vegetables with a piece of bread. "Right then, boss, we are stuck in here till tomorrow lunchtime. We got computers, we got Internet access and we got a fine pair of minds. Let's do it! What's this bloke's name?"

Beatrice beamed at her. "I rather hoped you'd say that. As assistants go, you aren't half bad. His name is Joseph Gibson."

Chapter 36

Only one way to get over being hunted: go hunting.

Armed with the man's name, address, job description and photograph scraped from Tanya's Facebook feed a shot of the four of them at dinner – plus any details Gabriel, Matthew and Tanya could provide, Catinca prowled the net to find the man who called himself this Gibson geezer.

Reverse image search showed a couple of possibilities in Britain, the first being Eddie Graham on Tinder. Looked quite a bit younger than the picture Tanya had sent, but didn't everyone use younger versions of themselves on dating sites? She studied the image with care, blowing it up to get a good look at the detail and comparing every feature to the grinning man with his arm around Marianne. Something wasn't quite right. Jimmy from Ayrshire had hooded eyes, whereas Joseph's lids were clearly visible. Catinca moved on to the next.

Carlton Joseph, personal trainer, profile on LinkedIn. The photograph was a full-length shot, focused on the man's buff body rather than his face. His hands were on his hips and Catinca noted the wedding ring on his left hand. The face did look exactly like Joseph Gibson, so if it wasn't the same man, Gibson had a doppelganger. She opened the profile and dug further. The personal trainer had worked at several gyms and as a fitness instructor in a Taunton college of further education.

"How far is Townton from where you live?" Catinca asked.

"You mean Taunton? About an hour. Have you found someone?"

"Maybe. Give me a few minutes." Fingers flying across the keyboard, Catinca accessed the websites of both gyms and the college. The second gym had an impressions page, showing the staff at work and at play. There was Carlton, crouching beside some muscleman doing a bench press, wearing a tight T-shirt and tracksuit bottoms. Another picture showed him with three other men, arms around each other's shoulders, red-faced and laughing in a pub. The face was an exact match for Joseph Gibson. Then Catinca struck gold. Near the bottom of the page, there was a photograph of Carlton holding a young woman's ankles while she was doing a sit up. On his left shoulder, there was a tattoo. She zoomed in and crossed her eyes. A crow. How original.

Beatrice spoke. "Right, this looks interesting. His job checks out; he is a PE teacher at a comprehensive just outside Exeter. According to his biography, in his free time he likes to complete triathlons and plays the guitar. But the photograph makes it very difficult to identify his face. It was obviously taken at the end of one of those 'get as dirty as you can' fun run things. His face is all splattered with mud. Interesting choice." She tilted her laptop to show Catinca. The man was smiling at the camera, holding up the medal which hung around his neck, his face, hair, and T-shirt smeared and speckled with coffee-coloured mud. "The other thing is that his previous employment is very ambiguous. It says he has worked as a fitness instructor, lists his qualifications but makes no mention of where he worked. I find that rather odd. The other thing is that Joseph Gibson seems to have no profile on any social media site. His prerogative of course."

"Joseph Gibson might not but let's have a look for Carlton Joseph." She showed Beatrice the images from the gym, pointing at the tattoo. "I'll trawl Instagram, you take Facebook."

Nothing under Carlton Joseph, Carl Joe, Carlton Crow, Joseph Crow, Triathlon Man or any other combinations Catinca came up with. Beatrice had no luck either. They sat in silence, trying to think of another way of gaining information.

"Maybe we don't need to," Catinca said. "Just show Marianne this website and ask her if he has a tattoo. If he has, he's got some questions to answer."

"Hmm. It's rather inconclusive and with some quick thinking, he can probably explain why he's changed his name and moved cities. I'm going to do some searching on the name Carlton Joseph and see if there's anything on the legal register. Have a look at those pictures again. Is there a caption under that one in the pub? He might have a nickname we can use for a social media search."

Catinca checked again and shook her head. "No captions, no names on any of the pictures. Just photographer."

Beatrice leaned over to look at the pictures and frowned at the one of the woman doing sit ups. "Can you zoom in on that one? You know, I don't think that's a crow. It's too small. That's either a blackbird or a starling. See if either of those throw up anything on social media." She went back to her own computer and started tapping.

With a yawn, Catinca began another search, with little optimism. "Whassa starling, anyway?"

"Wild bird with speckled plumage and a distinctive song. Great flocks of them make fabulous patterns in the sky. They have a talent for mimicry and blending into their environment."

"Oh yeah, I seen them on YouTube. Didn't know what they were called, though. Only starling I know is from *The Silence of the Lambs*." On a whim, she typed in the words 'C. Starling' and checked all the profiles with a man's face. There he was. C. Starling, with the face of Carlton Joseph. Catinca whooped and started scrolling through his photographs.

"Gotcha!" she beamed at the screen.

Beatrice came over to look. "Oh, well done! Now, let's have a look at what he's been up to."

Teaching classes in beachside locations, posing with students, all of whom female. Holiday snaps in Machu Picchu, Aspen, Bondi Beach and the Maldives, each with a different lady companion. Restaurants with spectacular views and bejewelled women. None whatsoever of school PE fields, but plenty of his six-pack belly, tanned torso and muscular arms, the left one sporting a tattoo of a starling. He branded himself as 'Your Personal Trainer with an emphasis on the Personal'. Just to ram home the point, was a picture of him massaging a slender woman's naked body, with only a folded towel covering her buttocks.

"Sodding hell, mate! He's a ... what do you call 'em?"

A huge sigh escaped Beatrice. "Gigolo. Or to put it another way, expert at the three Fs. Flattering, fleecing and, well, you can guess the rest. Poor Marianne. How the hell do we break something like this?"

"No easy way to tell her. Thing is, Beatrice, she could have checked him out herself. I always do! Every sodding bloke I meet gets a background investigation. Some people prefer not to know and I reckon Marianne was happy to go along with fantasy. She should be more like her sister. Tanya's got her head screwed on."

Beatrice shook her head. "Only because she got screwed. Luke is the result of a liaison with a married man who promised to leave his wife. Guess how that turned out. He now lives with his wife and two charming daughters in Brittany, selling gîtes to gullible Brits. This is why I think Tanya is so concerned. Her liar-detector is set to eleven."

Catinca blinked, surprised by the news of Luke's parentage. "So what do we do now?"

"I don't know. I'm going to have to sleep on this. The last thing I want to do is tell my god-daughter she's picked a wrong 'un. Again."

Catinca made a decision. "Look, mate, get some sleep. We'll work something out in the morning, don't worry. Between us, we got this."

"Thank you. And even more thanks for helping me root out this shitty charlatan. See you in the morning."

Distracted by the email she was composing in her head, Catinca said, "Goodnight, Beatrice and don't forget your pill." Then she turned her attention to her laptop.

Chapter 37

It was two in the morning by the time Yves de Marsault returned to his quarters in the Garden Wing. Davor heard the crunch of feet on gravel and sent a prayer that the man would be alone. No voices, one set of steps, it sounded good.

In the hall, he dropped his keys and phone into the brass bowl on the sideboard, the clatter a brash assault on the peace. From the first landing on the wide staircase, Davor watched the man as he headed straight into his study, selected a glass and poured himself a good measure of something dark. Good idea. Make it a double.

Seven minutes later, Davor eased his way down the dozen carpeted stairs and evaluated the situation. Yves de Marsault had flopped into a wingback chair beside the unlit fire. His glass rested on the little card table to his right. Without seeing his face, there was no way of telling if he had fallen asleep. Davor released the safety catch and pressed the muzzle behind the man's ear.

"Please don't move, monsieur. I apologise for interrupting at such a late hour, but we have very little time to act. Allow me to begin with a confession. I was the man who entered the château this evening and disposed of the young man in Madame's quarters. I give you my assurance I did not come here tonight to kill anyone; not him, not Madame, not you. But he tried to trap me when I had come to deliver a message in good faith."

After a moment's hesitation, Yves answered. "A message?"

His voice sounded even and calm.

"It's a long story and I've had one hell of a busy day. I would like to sit and join you in a glass of cognac, if you don't mind. Can I just say, the slightest hint that you are trying to signal for help, attempting to overpower me or lying, I will not hesitate to shoot you. Believe me, Monsieur de Marsault, because I do this for a living."

Davor collected the decanter and a glass and moved into the man's line of vision. Yves nodded as if they had just met in a gentleman's club. Davor nodded back, while the gun remained aimed at his forehead the whole time. He poured a drink for himself and added more to Yves's dregs.

"I'm going to tell you my name. Not my real one, that would be unprofessional. Your family, my employers, know me as Le Fantôme. I want to tell you three things. Then I will quit this place and leave the decision up to you." He drank, the fiery fluid waking his passion.

Yves did not touch his glass, his attention fixed on Davor's face.

"One, your family have been running drugs from the Ukraine to Western Europe since 1991. Ever since your brother married Daria, actually. They launder the money through the restaurants and the perfume business. How do I know? Because I have worked for Daria since 1986. Now things have changed and I'm not the only one to know. Tomorrow afternoon, at your family hotel, Interpol will arrest your brother, your sister-in-law and your mother and launch an investigation into your family's business. Drink some cognac, my friend, you're going to need it."

The man reached for his glass and took a sip, his face pensive. "How do you ..."

"Let me finish. Two, I came here tonight to warn Madame about tomorrow's trap. It was an enormous risk because she wants me dead. No time to go into that now, but your mother and that blond imbecile sent people into the field with the express purpose of killing me. Even so, I wanted to warn them about the hotel sting. This was supposed to be my bargaining chip. I help them evade arrest and they let me live. But tonight I found this and I changed my mind." He reached into his pocket and placed the bracelet onto the card table beside Yves.

The young man hesitated for a moment then examined the tiny thing between forefinger and thumb. His focus returned to Davor's face.

"She was six years old. Her life should have been perfect. As the song goes, wealthy father and good-looking mother, no need to cry. Her father managed a shipping operation in Odessa and Madame Agathe wanted to buy it. He refused. She ordered me to apply pressure, to make it personal. Daria and I kidnapped his daughter, only planning to hold her a couple of days." He swallowed, the pain dragging him into a whirlpool of regret. "We put her into a little room in a cellar. She had food, drink, even books to read. It wasn't supposed to take too long. Her father was stubborn, but he gave in, eventually. When we went back to release the little girl ..." He bit his inner lip, reminding himself he was holding a man at gunpoint.

"She was dead," said Yves.

Davor took another large gulp of cognac. "Not enough oxygen. Daria and Madame took the body out into the Black Sea and dropped her into the ocean. I kill people, monsieur, sometimes without a second thought. Carrying that little girl out of the cellar and into the daylight, her limp arm bouncing at every step, came close to breaking me. I couldn't look at her face. All I could see was her silver bracelet, inlaid with lapis lazuli." He indicated with the gun. "That bracelet. The one I just found in your mother's bedroom. The one that came from a dead child's arm."

Yves passed a hand over his face and spent several minutes staring at his knees. Eventually, he looked up, his gaze steady.

"You said there were three things?"
    "I did. You may need more cognac."

Chapter 38

There was something of the consolation prize in unearthing the truth about Marianne's boyfriend. It wasn't the main objective of the case; more grief and upset was on its way to Matthew's unlucky daughter; plus Beatrice had to find a way to exonerate the rest of the family. The only realistic way of doing that was to step up to the plate and take the blame. Naturally nosy, ex-cop, interfering godmother, professional private investigator, she had taken it upon herself to make sure Marianne did not get hurt again.

Even if Beatrice did play the human shield, deflecting attention from Matthew and Tanya, Marianne would indubitably get hurt again. The emotional cost weighed heavy on Beatrice's heart. Lying awake as the sky grew lighter outside the curtains, she did her level best to accentuate the positives.

She and Catinca had exposed the man as a fraud in little under than two hours, simply by astute manipulation of the Internet. The girl was a gold-bottomed asset and Beatrice had already made up a mind to offer her a full-time position. Whether she could afford her was a question she would consider at a later date.

Marianne might not be defrauded of her life savings or find herself in debt as well as heartbroken, but the facsimile of love in which she had tried so hard to believe, was about to disappear. Once again, it was Beatrice's fault.

The rats' nest of the de Marsault family was no longer her problem. In a few short hours, they would be incarcerated in a police station for questioning. And there were a whole lot of questions. Another pang of regret tensed her jaw. Was that lovely man, Yves de Marsault, likely to spend the rest of his life behind bars? She could scarcely believe he was as toxic as the rest of his relatives, but she knew better than to trust in surface charm.

Past failures rose from her subconscious and she rolled over, away from the dawn, away from sour memories and recollected embarrassments. She might as well get up rather than lie there, subjected to a slideshow of her regrets. She closed her eyes, cuddled her pillow and wished it were Matthew.

Three hours later, she was woken by Amy Winehouse. 'Back to Black' was playing in the living area, and a small, slim female with a black beehive and a feline flick at the corner of each eyelid stood in her bedroom doorway, her hands on her hips.

"You ever gonna get up? I had breakfast, wrote to Marianne and prepared viewing gallery on balcony. Come on, mate, it's half past ten. I saved you some crêpes but they gonna be soggy by now. Shake leg, innit?"

Beatrice did as she was told, stumbled into the shower, dressed and joined Catinca on the balcony. To her delight, a breakfast tray held a pot of fresh coffee, a bowl of berries, a basket of croissants and a silver cloche covering some pancakes. She noted Catinca's large sunglasses and dug in her handbag for her own. While eating and murmuring in a low voice, she watched the street and surrounding buildings. Familiar with surreptitious operations, she soon spotted the unmistakeable signs of a police sting. It was a Sunday morning, yet regular road maintenance crews had set up at one end of the street and two alleyways in between.

She checked her watch. 11.20. They had an hour and ten minutes before the family were due to arrive. She watched

Catinca thumbing her phone. Her chameleon of an assistant wore a checked bustier, black pedal pushers and scarlet lipstick, and the rose in her hair had been plucked from the hotel suite's flower arrangement. She looked ready for a photo shoot.

An image popped into her mind. Catinca in her bedroom doorway, talking about soggy crêpes. "Did you tell me you wrote to Marianne or did I dream that?"

The girl's expression was hidden by her huge bug-eye shades. She glanced up and her forehead creased like corrugated cardboard as she lifted her eyebrows. "You only just remembered that? Yeah, I wrote to her. One of us had to do it and you're too close. She'd hate it coming from either you, Matthew or Tanya. I got nothing to lose, mate. We found out what a shit that bloke is, so I sent her details. Gave her facts, told he is a bloodsucker and left it up to her. Well, mostly."

"Can you explain 'mostly'?" asked Beatrice, her mouth drying.

Catinca took off her glasses. Her eyes always reminded Beatrice of a Siamese feline. Now, with her 60s style eyeliner, the comparison seemed stronger still.

"She's in love. She's looking for any excuse not to believe what I told her. Course she is. So if he's kosher, test him. Her money, she can say, is in joint account with Matthew. Any release of dosh must be signed by both. Why not sit down with her dad and explain situation?" Catinca showed her little white teeth. "Can't argue with that, can you?"

Beatrice rolled up the final crêpe with her fork. "No, you can't. The reason I overslept was because I was awake half the night worrying about how to handle this mess. Now I wake up, find you have resolved the entire thing and yet again completely transformed yourself. You really are an extraordinary talent."

Catinca grinned and returned her attention to her phone.

Breakfast completed, Beatrice checked emails. Confirmation from Fisher's assistant that arrests would be made shortly before one o'clock. No press, no publicity, no photographs. The second email, from Fisher himself, suggested a meeting after the event, depending on the outcome. Just under an hour to go. She called Matthew to inform him of his eldest daughter's likely trauma. Rather than concerned he sounded relieved.

"Tanya and I have been beside ourselves with worry. I cannot thank you and Catinca enough for your efforts. We will stand by for the fallout. Do you have the vaguest idea when you might come home, Old Thing? The creatures and I miss you dreadfully."

Catinca's head poked through the gauzy drapes. "Mate! It's on!"

"Everything depends on the next sixty minutes, but I do believe we will be back in Britain by tomorrow night. I'll keep you informed. Matthew? Please tell Marianne we did this purely out of concern for her. I have to go. I'll call you when the bust has settled."

She donned her sunglasses and large floppy hat, then returned to the balcony to watch the family de Marsault finally face justice.

For a long time, nothing seemed to happen. Expensive cars came and went, depositing their finely dressed cargo and departing once again. From the penthouse, Beatrice and Catinca had difficulty observing individual faces, but could see enough to be sure that none of the arrivals was a member of the family. A black range Rover cruised up to the covered portico and a doorman paced smartly to welcome the occupants.

"That's her!" hissed Catinca.

Three people got out of the vehicle. Beatrice recognised Xander de Marsault as he aided his mother along the carpet. It was the first sight she'd had of the matriarch. From this distance, she looked frail and delicate, leaning on her son's arm. They were followed by his sister-in-law, Daria, wearing a piece from the Papillon collection, a bubble-gum pink trench coat. There was no sign of Yves de Marsault, a fact which puzzled Beatrice. Perhaps he would arrive later or was already waiting inside. It seemed inconceivable that he would miss the family meeting. The group ascended the carpeted steps and disappeared into the hotel foyer.

Catinca turned to Beatrice, pulling her sunglasses down her nose with her forefinger. "She don't exactly look like Lucrezia Borgia, but did you cop a look at them rocks? The woman is wearing more jewellery than Marie Antoinette."

Beatrice scanned the length of the street, seeing nothing that could indicate an imminent arrest. "I felt rather sorry for her," she said. "She looked awfully old and weak."

"So did Nazi war criminals when they came to trial," said Catinca. "Just remember, it was that 'old and weak' evil sow who ordered the murder of Gennaio Colacino. That sweet little old lady sues anyone who doesn't comply with her iron rule and employs hitmen to deal with the rest. Don't you go bleeding heart on me, mate. She gotta face justice. No sympathy from me no matter how old she is. Ooh, look!"

Beatrice looked down at the street to see two silver Mercedes Vianos moving at speed along the street. They pulled up and reversed into position either side of the hotel portico, to be joined by four silent police cars. Doors opened, plainclothes officers jumped out and armed police took up positions all around the street. A team of twelve, four detectives, eight uniforms, entered the hotel.

Beatrice and Catinca craned their necks to look over the balcony. Moments passed in silence and Beatrice had to remind herself to breathe. She shot a sidelong glance at Catinca who showed her trembling hands, but said nothing. They waited for any sign of movement, from the police, from the hotel, from the 'road workers'. Even the pigeons seemed to be held spellbound.

Without fanfare, the doors to the hotel lobby slid open and out came a plainclothes detective followed by Daria de Marsault, flanked by uniformed officers. They escorted her to the first Mercedes van, where she was joined by her mother-in-law, similarly guarded. Last came Xander de Marsault, who was separated from his female relatives and guided into the other Mercedes. The doors closed, the police returned to their vehicles and the convoy moved away in the direction of the city centre. The street reopened and the ersatz road works packed up and disappeared.

"Glad I didn't bother buying popcorn," said Catinca. "No car chases, no shootouts, no fighting. What happens now?" She stretched her arms above her head.

Beatrice's phone rang. "It's Fisher," she told Catinca. "Hello, sir. Yes, we are both fine. As a matter of fact, we saw the whole thing. The penthouse suite of Hotel Garonne. Yes, I know, but we did stay in our room. Very well, good idea. See you soon."

"Has he got the hump with us?"

"He was surprised to hear where we were and he's coming over for a chat. I'm going to check my emails."

"Me too." Catinca jumped to her feet. "Tell you what, mate, this is still better than serving olives and breadsticks to pretentious posers in Shoreditch."

Ten minutes later, a knock sounded at the front door. Instantly, Catinca looked at Beatrice, her eyes fearful.

With the back of her hand, Beatrice motioned that she should return to her bedroom, pressing a finger to her lips. Catinca did as she was told and Beatrice tiptoed to the door to check the peep hole. The man standing in the corridor was well-dressed, clean-shaven and with slicked back hair. For the first time in her life, Beatrice was pleased to see Fisher.

She opened the door.

"Beatrice! Good gracious! You look like a new woman. It's been too long. May I come in?"

As a highly respected Interpol senior officer, Andrew Fisher had mingled with international diplomats, organised criminals, niche experts and politicians keen to burnish their credentials in the area of law enforcement. However, for all his experience, Fisher had evidently never encountered someone quite like Catinca Radu. It seemed he could not decide whether to patronise, charm or ask for her autograph. Beatrice observed his confusion with some amusement until her impatience for answers took precedence. Anyway, it was past lunchtime. She interrupted Amy and Andy.

"Sir, are you able to join us for lunch? We can order room service if you wish. Although I think my assistant and I might be keen to stretch our legs after twenty-four hours within the same four walls. In your assessment, would we be safe enough to have lunch in the hotel restaurant?"

"I think that sounds like a jolly good idea." Fisher smiled. "We have much to discuss. As a token of our gratitude, we'll pick up the tab for this place and my assistant will arrange flights home for you tomorrow morning. The only reason I ask you to stay another night is simply to be available for questions from our local agents. You can invite them here if that suits you better. First things first, food. One works up an extraordinary appetite after putting a stop to institutionalised corruption. Shall we go?"

As the senior member of the party, Fisher requested a corner table some distance from the remainder of the guests. That made sense. Their conversation was likely to involve confidential information and much codification of the names involved. They selected their choice of lunch, ordered wine and asked questions.

"What happens now?" asked Beatrice.

"The family will be questioned and unless we have enough to charge them already, which I doubt, they could be released by tomorrow, I should say. An investigative team is already on the case, which is why they want to speak to you, in order to bring charges against the family, or its individual members, with their respective crimes. Bread roll, anyone?"

Catinca's brows furrowed. "They gonna get out? Tomorrow? What stops them popping our clogs? They know it was us what tipped you off! We are pig squealers."

Thankfully, Fisher had not yet taken a mouthful of bread, because his laughing fit would have choked him. After several seconds of nasal huffing, which Beatrice recognised as amusement, he took a sip of water, closed his eyes and inhaled.

"Popping your clogs? Pig squealers?" He started laughing again and even Beatrice had to chuckle at the effect her assistant had on anyone and everyone.

Catinca spread butter on a seeded bun and shrugged. "Not my mother tongue, mate. Thing is, we safe here? We gonna be safe back home? What if that bloke follows us to London, Le Fantômey fella?"

With a linen napkin, Fisher dabbed his mouth. "Le Fantômey fella, as you describe him, is after the family, not you. His objective was simple. You see, we've been watching. They communicate via a social media site. He posted a picture taken from inside Madame's bedroom. That was the message. Leave him in peace or suffer the consequences. He could have terminated Madame de Marsault, but he didn't. Back off, leave him alone and he would do them the same favour. His interest in you ladies was down to self-preservation. He must have known they would send someone after him. He had every reason to suspect it might be you two."

The waiter offered a bottle of St Julien for Fisher's approval. Without even acknowledging the label, he made a beckoning gesture to pour the glasses.

"Hang on a minute!" Catinca interrupted. "I wanna taste it first. Gotta be a bit careful with this vintage." She smiled up at the wine waiter. "Is that OK?"

The man nodded his assent and poured a sip of the wine into Catinca's glass. She held it by the stem, revolved the liquid around the bowl and sniffed. Only then did she take a taste. Everyone waited, watching her reaction.

"It's good. Let's have it."

Over Bouillabaisse with Gruyère croutons and a Salade Niçoise, Fisher explained why, how and how long they had been watching the de Marsault family.

"The piece we were missing was that of Daria de Marsault to the drug-running business via the Ukraine. To be honest, we dropped the ball there. Had we checked in greater detail the registration of the yacht Naïade and discovered the Odessa connection, we would have understood the link far sooner. Our intelligence services are truly grateful for the fact you have shared your discoveries. Can I refresh your glass, PI Stubbs?"

Beatrice accepted the top-up. "What I would like to know, where is Yves de Marsault? How come he skipped the family meeting?" She scooped up a black olive and chunk of tuna. "Or did you arrest him separately?"

"We have not arrested Yves de Marsault. There is simply not enough evidence to do so. However, we have invited him to talk to us on an informal basis. We think he will cooperate, once we have allayed his concerns regarding his mother's welfare. Off the record, we think he was excluded from the shadier sides of the business. He certainly wasn't invited to Sunday lunch today, for example. From all the intelligence we have gathered, the man seems to be something of an ingénue."

That comment caused Beatrice pause. She recalled the friendly, pleasant man she had met at the vineyard who smelt of lemon groves, and agreed with his analysis.

Catinca, however, had other concerns. "Whatever that is. But what about that phantom bloke and that woman stalking us? Now family are arrested, will they leave us alone?" she demanded, wagging her fork at Fisher. "I got no plans to end up dead in the river."

"You are unlikely to be the object of any operatives' attention any longer. After their bosses' arrest by an organisation such as ours, they will have hightailed it out of the country. Le Fantôme is a seasoned professional. It wouldn't have taken him more than two minutes to realise the pair of you are not contract killers. I say, this wine is the business, don't you think?"

Beatrice nodded her assent, studying Catinca who seemed to be wrestling between relief at not having a hired killer as a stalker and offence at being considered an unlikely hit woman.

Chapter 39

Regardless of Fisher's assertion that they could be interviewed at the hotel, the Bordeaux police were taking no chances. They interviewed Beatrice and Catinca separately in an anonymous looking police station a good twenty minutes' drive from the hotel. It took far longer than Beatrice deemed necessary, largely due to repetition and clarification on every single point. When her frustrations built, she breathed deeply, recollecting what it was like to be on the other side of the desk. As for Catinca's patience, she could only hope.

Eventually, they were free to go. An unmarked vehicle returned them to the hotel where they picked up their messages and returned to their suite. To Beatrice's surprise, Catinca was in an excellent mood, humming and singing as she packed, ready for the morning.

When she heard a helicopter thrumming overhead, Beatrice switched on the television searching for news of the arrest. Nothing, on any of the channels. She called into Catinca's room, interrupting a rendition of 'Valerie'.

"What do you want to do about food? I'd be keen to stretch my legs rather than order room service again. Should I ask the concierge for a local recommendation or we could even try that glitzy place downstairs, seeing as Fisher's picking up the tab. It looks awfully posh."

Catinca, dressed in a bathrobe, slunk into the room, her eyes on the carpet. "Mate, I gotta date. Just a drink, then you and me can eat after. I'll only be an hour. Do you mind?"

Beatrice opened her mouth and closed it again. "A date? How, who, when …? Are you sure this is safe?"

"Pretty sure. He's a security guard. One who rescued me at wine museum. I took his number and while I was waiting for you to get finished with the police I gave them a call. Quick drink before dinner, that's all. Just to say thank you. Good manners, innit?"

Beatrice nodded, torn between feeling impressed, neglected and hungry. "Well, good for you. I can always order room service if you want to make a night of it."

Catinca shook her head. "Nah, mate, it's just a drink. He's not my type. Told him I got a dinner reservation at eight. I'll be in the bar downstairs, and after he's gone, I'll come and find you in the restaurant, OK?"

Beatrice agreed and Catinca skipped off to prepare herself. For a date with someone who was 'not her type', she was going to an inordinate amount of preparation. With a determined effort of will, Beatrice stopped feeling left out and hard done by, choosing to see the hour Catinca was away as a gift of time. She ran a bath filled with glorious bubbles, smeared on a face mask, poured herself a glass of pink champagne and selected some Astor Piazzolla from the music menu. She lay wallowing in the scented water, relaxing for the first time in ten days. It was over. And even if she couldn't claim the victory as her own, she had won. She could also justify her decision to employ Catinca, despite the cash flow uncertainties, as she was the one who exposed Marianne's parasitic boyfriend. Tonight, she would dress in her best finery, aiming to impress Catinca with her newfound fashion sense, descend to the restaurant and order some light snacks while she waited. After all, lunch was a long time ago.

Just shy of two hours later, Beatrice entered the dining room, wearing amethyst earrings, lilac wedge-heeled espadrilles and a purple foulard over a cream shirt dress. Her usual preparation time had been cut by half, seeing she no longer had to manage her hair. Fragrant, relaxed and in the most positive mindset she had enjoyed for weeks, she settled herself by a window table and scanned the room in case Catinca had arrived first.

She had just finished ordering some olives and breadsticks when her companion flopped down into the chair opposite, her eyes sparkling and her cheeks pink.

"Well?" asked Beatrice. "How did it go? You look positively thrilled."

Catinca waved a finger up and down, indicating Beatrice's outfit. "Liking all this. You're learning. Yeah, well, he's nice, decent bloke. Unusual. Most first dates wanna talk about themselves this one was different. Asked loads of questions. His English is great, almost as good as mine. But…"

"What?" asked Beatrice.

They were interrupted by the arrival of the waiter with menus. He recited the specials of the day which included Moules Marinières with a pastis and white wine sauce. He got no further. Both women opted for the mussels.

"Certainly, mesdames. Would you like to see the wine list?"

Before Catinca could open her mouth, Beatrice interrupted. "Thank you but I have already ordered a bottle of champagne. We are celebrating, you see."

After the waiter left, Catinca unfolded her napkin and looked into Beatrice's eyes. "What we celebrating? All your brilliant work being nicked by Interpol? That don't qualify for a bottle of fizz, in my opinion."

"Which is exactly why I am the boss. This was a success. It wasn't all my brilliant work but yours as well. We make a good team. In time, we will be able to reassure our clients, Bruno and Chantal, that their uncle was indeed murdered and the people responsible will face the consequences. That makes us worthy of a Jeroboam of fizz. The facts of the matter are that we have dragged the de Marsault family from under their society parasols into the harsh light of justice. It will be a long and a bureaucratic road to the courts but you and I brought these people down."

The sommelier arrived with a silver bucket and a bottle of Pol Roger. With much ceremony, he uncorked the bottle and poured a glassful into each tulip-shaped vessel.

They toasted their first successful case and smiled across the table at each other. Beatrice sensed this was the perfect moment to announce her decision.

"Now, I have something to say. When you turned up at Adrian's flat that morning, I was not at all convinced this was a good idea. However, you have more than proved yourself as a fast learner with your own set of skills. Your performance on this case has convinced me that you're right. You would make the perfect assistant for a private detective. So if this case has not put you off the idea, I would like to offer you the job of my assistant. We do make a brilliant team."

Catinca's face broke into a smile, her little white teeth shining. She picked up her glass again and tapped it against Beatrice's own. "Thank you, boss. Means a lot that you found me useful. But probation period works both ways. I quit Adrian's employment because I was bored. I want to use my skills, my creativity. Private investigation is more interesting than selling wine, but you know what? I fell in love with my cover story. I really do wanna run my own business, all creative decisions taken by me. I want a shop in Spitalfields or somewhere like it. My dream is to create a collection people will love and I'm gonna do it. I'm gonna become a fashion designer. It's all I ever wanted to do."

Beatrice stared at her for several seconds, her mouth open, her brain processing what she just heard. Then she began to laugh, shaking her head. "I spend hours agonising over whether or not they can afford you, fretting about whether I have the skills to train a new assistant, arrange for you to have a trial run and when you finally prove yourself to be an asset, you don't actually want the job."

The little Romanian shrugged her shoulders. "Sorry, mate. But thanks for giving me a chance. To be honest, I don't think you need assistant." She tapped her temple. "You got it all, up here." The waiter arrived with a large enamelled tureen. "That smells gorgeous! Know what, I kind of like France. Nice hotels, classy food and some well tasty men."

The waiter's eyes widened momentarily as he placed a basket of warm baguettes between them. "Bon appétit, mesdames."

They tore, chewed, dipped, sipped and gnawed while discussing Catinca's prospects as a fashion designer and shop owner in London's East End.

They sat in comfortable silence for a moment, absorbing their environment. Familiar dialectics pulled at Beatrice. She wanted to go home. She looked up at the chandeliers on the ceiling and reminded herself that this was only one case of many. Most importantly, tomorrow she would be home, with Matthew.

Across the table, as if she'd heard, Catinca beamed. "It's great fun, all this adventuring and posh hotels, but tomorrow night, I'll be in my own bed again, planning what to wear to work the next day. Tell you what, I can't wait."

Chapter 40

One would think that after a relaxing bath, delicious meal, half a bottle of champagne and faced with the prospect of a queen-sized bed, sleep would come naturally. Not in Beatrice's case. It was as if the moment she closed her eyes, someone unlocked the worry box, releasing all her concerns and fears to plague her and keep her awake. Why didn't Catinca want to be her assistant? Was it due to something she had said or done? Beatrice had just got used to the idea of not operating alone and begun to appreciate sharing the workload. Maybe she should advertise for an assistant. The question was, could she afford one? Especially now that she wouldn't be paid by Bruno and Chantal after Interpol had taken over the case.

It would take months to come to court and in the meantime, the people who had decided to end Gennaio Colacino's life would be free to do as they pleased. Perhaps they already were. What if they blamed her and Catinca for their arrest? Surely they wouldn't come after them? If they did, it wouldn't be one of the de Marsault family, but one of their hired killers. For all Beatrice knew, there could be a hitman outside her bedroom window, training his gun on her sleepless face.

She scrunched up her eyes and rolled onto her side, turning away from the window to face the door. A silvery rhomboid of moonlight lay between the bed and the wall, evidence that she had not correctly closed the curtains. She sighed, telling herself not to be so ridiculous, to get out of bed and shut the drapes, that of course there was no one outside on the little balcony or hiding under the bed to grab her ankles. She simply had to get a grip on these night-time terrors. At her age, it was ludicrous to get so spooked. Still, she didn't move.

She closed her eyes again and took several yoga breaths, in through the nose and out through the mouth. In the carpeted silence of the room, she heard a click. A tiny sound, but one she could not explain. Her eyes flew open and the deep yoga breaths became shallow inhalations through her mouth as she listened. As she lay there, the door began to move. Slowly and silently, someone was pushing open the door to her room. Frozen in fear, she watched a huge black shadow fill the doorway. She opened her mouth to scream but her piercing howl was drowned instantly by the jangling, nerve-shredding blare of the fire alarm.

The lights came on and Beatrice's scream fell silent in shock. In the doorway of her room stood Batman, complete with cape and mask. In two strides, he reached the bed and bent down to speak to her. She couldn't hear a word over the cacophony of the alarm bells. He shook his head, yanked off the duvet and threw her over his shoulder. All her senses seemed to contract into her heart, expanding it to proportions that exceeded her ribcage. Shaking with terror, Beatrice kicked and struggled but his grip on her back and around her legs did not falter. He carried her out of the bedroom, through the living area and out into the empty corridor. He strode past the gaping lift towards the staircase, shoving open the door with his elbow. To Beatrice's surprise, he did not take the stairwell down but instead turned in the opposite direction heading upwards. He powered up one flight of stairs, carrying her over his shoulder as if she weighed no more than a blanket.

When Batman reached a fire door plastered with warnings not to open unless in an emergency, he opened it with one mighty kick at the metal bar. In the cold night air, they emerged onto the roof. The alarms, while still strident, were less overpowering outside and Beatrice's disorienting panic coalesced into fury. She pummelled her fists into Batman's cape, twisting and wriggling with enough force to make him stumble. He halted and put her down, grasping her wrists to prevent her from lashing out.

"Stop it!" He shouted over the alarms. "I'm here to help you, Beatrice Stubbs."

The use of the name made her pause.

He scanned the roof, and paced on, dragging her with him.

She resisted, throwing her weight backwards, but his superior strength pulled her in his wake. She cried out as her bare feet hit something on the rough surface, sending a vicious pain up her leg. Batman turned to see her limping and in one smooth move, swept an arm behind her knees and the other around her back, clutching her to his chest. Cradled like a child, she panted, winced and trembled, but ceased fighting. Even in her fright, she noted his smell. Her brain replayed a childish rhyme: Jingle Bells, Batman smells ... of freshly picked lemons.

He ran around the corner and across an expansive roof towards some kind of structure, accessible by iron steps. Once again, he hoisted her over his shoulder and managed to climb one-handed onto the platform. His breathing was heavy when he put her down. To Beatrice's astonishment, a helicopter stood in the centre of the landing pad. Less roughly this time, he took her hand and led her towards the machine. When he tried to guide her inside, she reared back like a pony.

"No!" she yelled. "Who are you?"

He looked down at her, reached a hand to his neck and peeled the mask off his head. Beatrice's mouth dropped open when she saw the sweaty face of Yves de Marsault.

Before she could speak, shrill screams rent the air and Frankenstein's monster clambered onto the platform, hampered by the writhing, kicking and struggling female over his shoulder.

He set Catinca down, clamping his arms on hers to stay the punches, and turned her around to face them.

She wriggled free from his grasp and ran towards Beatrice, who embraced her trembling body. The girl wore nothing more than a long T-shirt marked by patches of sweat. Both women panted with exertion and fear, watching their captors for any indication of what might come next.

The monster looked over his shoulder, turned back to them and said something unintelligible through the mask. No one moved. He clapped his big hands together and ushered them toward the helicopter. Beatrice and Catinca clutched each other, shrinking from his advance.

Yves de Marsault seemed to realise the effect his collaborator was having and shouted at the advancing monster. "*Merde! Le masque!*"

The Frankenstein freak hesitated, reached a hand behind his head and pulled the mask off. Catinca squeaked in fear, backing away. The man beneath the mask was well over six foot, bald and quite as terrifying as the mask he had just removed.

"Who are you!?" Catinca's voice wobbled.

As Beatrice stared at the man, her memory sparked. Where had she seen him before?

Yves de Marsault spoke, his voice authoritative and calm. "Ladies, I apologise for our crude and clearly frightening intrusion. Please let me reassure you. I and my colleague came here tonight to protect you. We have no time to explain because people who wish you harm are looking for you as we speak. You must get into the helicopter now or you will endanger us all. That I cannot allow. I'm sorry to say this, but if we are not able to persuade you to get in of your own volition, we will use force."

Catinca's grip tightened on Beatrice's forearm. "No! We ain't going nowhere!"

The huge bald man paced towards them. "Get in. For your own good." He pushed them firmly towards the machine, his hands on their backs like pizza shovels.

Catinca sprang away from the man's touch, but climbed into the aircraft. Beatrice scrambled in after her, banging her knees on the ledge, her whole body shivering with cold. He strapped them into adjacent seats and as an afterthought, grabbed a pair of blankets to wrap around each of them. The fabric was rough and scratchy, but the warmth welcome and the big spade-like hands surprisingly gentle. He slammed shut the side door and took his place beside the pilot, Yves de Marsault, who had already started the engines.

A small cold hand crept into Beatrice's and she squeezed it with as much reassurance as she could manage.

"I don't suppose you managed to bring your phone?" Beatrice murmured into her ear.

Catinca shook her head, her face pale and miserable. "Got nothing, mate. Not even a pair of knickers."

"Right, I have no idea what's going on or where they're taking us, so all we can do is listen and watch. On the bright side, if they wanted to kill us, they could have done that in our beds."

The *whump* of the helicopter blades grew louder while de Marsault checked his instruments.

Catinca leaned closer to Beatrice. "What if they don't want to kill us, but hurt us to get information?" There was a catch in her voice.

"Then we give it to them. No heroics, just give them what they need. I think what they ..."

The huge bald man was using a pair of binoculars to scan the roof. Without warning, he began shouting and gesticulating, all the while looking over his shoulder. The aircraft lifted, wobbled and took off across the city leaving the lights of Hotel de Marsault, their phones, IDs, and worldly possessions behind.

Beatrice clenched her hand around Catinca's and braced herself for whatever would come next.

Chapter 41

The flight lasted no longer than twenty minutes. Both women shivered throughout, but tried to pay attention to the landscape below, their direction and the conversations in front. Unfortunately, none of it made any sense. Before Beatrice could make any sort of strategy, the helicopter began its descent. As the ground grew closer, she could make out the guiding lights of a small airfield. De Marsault lowered the craft onto a small circle of cats' eyes, lit by floodlights. Three vehicles awaited them; two luxury sedans and a people carrier.

Once they were on the ground, the door opened, the rotor blades still whirring and creating a wind that buffeted Beatrice and Catinca. Figures scurried towards them from the vehicles, backlit by the vast hangar behind them. Two women waited at a safe distance, carrying long puffer coats and sheepskin slippers. The big bald man unbuckled them and guided them across the tarmac, into the care of the ladies. Gentle hands slipped Beatrice's arms into a cosy coat, eased her feet into warm slippers and beckoned her towards the lights.

The party crossed the airfield and entered the hangar. Inside, several private jets stood at an angle and in the corner, a Portakabin which presumably served as an office. Under the fluorescent lights, Beatrice could see the details of the guides' faces. Both women were a similar age to herself, with kind, sympathetic faces she instinctively wished to trust. She saw no sign of the bald man or Yves de Marsault. The ladies guided them into the Portakabin and offered them a seat on one of the six sofas surrounding a coffee table heaped with brochures.

Catinca sat beside Beatrice, zipped up in her long puffer coat so that she looked like a caterpillar. The women bustled around, one making coffee and the other packing some kind of bag. The lights stripped the scene of all nuance and Catinca's face, tearstained and white, reminded Beatrice of horrible tales of refugees. The first woman scooped the brochures into a bag and placed a tray in front of them, containing a pot of coffee, warm milk, a plate of madeleines and a bowl of sugar cubes. The second woman emerged from a back room with two nylon holdalls. She gave them one each.

"All you need," she said. "Until you have your own things. Please, if I forget anything, you must say." She gave both a gentle smile and she and her colleague retreated outside.

Several moments passed until either Catinca or Beatrice made a move. Eventually, Beatrice leant forward and sniffed the coffee. It smelt blissful so she poured two cups and added milk. Her feet were beginning to warm and the cold, nightmarish horror of the last hour began to recede, even if her heart rate still pounded in her ears. "Should we try a madeleine? They were perfect enough for Proust."

The question roused Catinca, who emerged from her catatonic state. "Nah. Not hungry." She unzipped her holdall and dug around the contents. She gave Beatrice a running commentary. "Bottle of water, toothpaste, toothbrush, moisturiser, ballet flats, deodorant, T-shirt, pashmina, hoodie, yoga pants and knickers! What they playing at? Who kidnaps people, gives them cake and coffee and a cashmere pashmina?" Catinca demanded.

Beatrice bit into her cake and looked out at the approaching figures. "I think we're just about to find out."

Batman and the monster were no longer in costume. Instead, Yves de Marsault wore a suit and tie while the bald man wore jeans and a sweatshirt and a black beret. In a flash, Beatrice remembered throwing coins into that hat on the stone bridge. The two men entered the room with what Beatrice presumed were meant to be reassuring smiles.

"May we sit?" asked de Marsault.

Beatrice nodded her assent and the two men seated themselves on the sofa opposite. Catinca eyed them warily, clutching her nylon holdall like a comfort blanket.

"Ladies, I cannot apologise enough for dragging you from your beds in the middle of the night and frightening you half to death. Please believe me when I say we had no other option if we were to save your lives. Perhaps I should begin by introducing myself and my colleague. Ms Stubbs and I have already met. My name is Yves de Marsault and this is Davor Vida, who has worked for my family for many years, a fact I have only recently learned. One of several facts I have recently learned. I presume, in your role as private detectives, you know about the other lines of the family business and the reasons for their arrest yesterday."

Again, Beatrice nodded.

"To cut a very long story short, I never saw eye to eye with either of my brothers or my mother on the subject of ethics. Their strategy, it seems, was to go ahead with their plans despite my objections and simply keep me in the dark. Some of their less legal activity required the assistance of Mr Vida. His role, that is to say, he used to be..."

"We know what he is!" snapped Catinca. "He's a hitman."

"Was. I was a hitman," said the bald chap, with a pronounced Eastern European accent. "Madame de Beauvoir and Monsieur de Maupassant decided I should retire earlier this year. The problem is that I know where the bodies are buried. They had no intention of letting me retire. They sent two younger agents after me to make sure I 'retired' permanently."

Beatrice frowned. "Mme de Beauvoir? Monsieur de Maupassant? You mean Daria and Xander de Marsault."

Davor Vida simply shrugged.

Yves de Marsault continued. "My mother has a great love for French literature. Everyone involved in the other side of our business was known by a codename. Apparently, despite my lack of involvement, I was known as Monsieur de Saint-Exupéry." He shot an unamused look at Vida.

The big man shrugged again.

"But that is not the point. The family sent to agents to eliminate Mr Vida, so he, well, he can explain."

Beatrice turned her attention to the large man and noticed his interest in the tray on the coffee table. Her classic old-fashioned politeness superseded her fear. "Would you like some coffee and perhaps a madeleine? Catinca, would you be so kind as to pass those paper cups from the water cooler?"

Catinca boggled her eyes but did as she was told. Beatrice poured coffee for the two men and pushed the tray towards them so they could help themselves.

Vida devoured a madeleine in one bite and added sugar to his coffee. "When I knew they had sent someone after me, there was only one thing I could do." he said. "Scare them into calling off the dogs. There was no point in running or hiding because they would find me. That's why I came to Château Agathe. I had to show them how close I could get."

"That's exactly what…" Catinca began.

Beatrice elbowed her sharply and now it was Beatrice's turn to boggle her eyes. Catinca closed her mouth and stirred her coffee.

"Go on," Beatrice encouraged. "Have another cake."

Vida didn't need asking twice. He swallowed the second madeleine and wiped his fingers on his jeans. "I got inside. I showed them what I can do. They knew I was watching, but still they sent no word. I expected two agents. That is why I noticed when you visited the château. At first, I thought it might be you. I followed you to your hotel and watched. That's how I overheard your conversation with Interpol on the bridge ..."

"I remember. The homeless man. That wasn't an umbrella, was it?" Beatrice asked.

Davor nodded. "No. It was a remote listening device. Not ideal in such sunshine, but I had very little choice. I knew what was going to happen at the family meeting on Sunday. I also realised that you uncovered one of my previous jobs. It had never happened before. I was shaken, and made a bad decision."

Catinca interrupted and clasped a hand to her throat. "So who was that woman following me at the wine museum on Saturday?"

Davor wagged his head from side to side. "Someone was certainly looking for you. It just wasn't me. I said I made a bad decision after I listened in on Mrs Stubbs. My decision was to warn the family about Interpol. Buy my peaceful retirement with a bargain. But it went all wrong. That stupid blond fool would not listen. That's when I knew he was the one who sent agents after you and me."

"You may remember Denis Hugues, Ms Stubbs?" asked Yves de Marsault.

A jolt of outrage shot through Beatrice. "It was that pompous little shit who set the dogs on us? Bloody hell! I don't believe it!"

"I'm afraid so. I'm not sure how, but when you came to the château to investigate the death of Gennaio Colacino, you got under his skin. Thanks to Mr Vida, I understand Denis Hugues was the one who gave the order to remove the Italian. Then you turn up asking questions. You upset him very much."

"Good," muttered Beatrice.

"He was so arrogant," Davor sneered. "He thought my big secret was the fact you two were still in France. Like a cockerel, he crowed when he informed me that you just checked into the penthouse of one of the family's hotels. You used your own passports," he said, with a regretful shake of his head.

Beatrice and Catinca both recoiled as if someone had slapped them in the face.

"He told me the British women wouldn't survive Sunday night and then I understood. Even if the family went to jail, he would still be running the agents. He was determined to see me, and both of you, dead. So I abandoned my plan and just got out."

"Get out of where? The château?" Beatrice asked, frowning at Davor.

"Correct. That idiot tried to trap me in Madame's quarters." A smile played across the big man's face. "It didn't work."

Yves de Marsault interrupted. "When Mr Vida came to me, it was to ask for help. He assumed, rightly, that I was not a party to their illegal activities. He gave me enough proof—" he glanced at Vida. "Enough proof to convince me my family will stop at nothing to defend their reputation. He warned me that even if the police arrested my entire family the next day, those 'agents' Denis sent after him would proceed with their task no matter what. But he was not the only victim. Mr Vida explained his conviction that you two were to be eliminated. We agreed there must be no more deaths. Therefore, we devised a plan to attend the hotel in fancy dress, as if returning from a party. The idea was to enter your rooms and remove you from danger. However, just as we arrived, they set off the fire alarm. They would have been waiting for you to clear the building, the perfect time to snatch you from the street. That meant we had only a few minutes to get you out and no opportunity to explain. I appreciate it must have been a terrifying experience, but I hope you understand why we had to act."

Beatrice looked from one man to another, trying to gauge the sincerity in their eyes. She considered this story and tested it for plausibility. She shook her head. "I do understand why you needed to be masked while walking through the hotel," she said.

"But once inside our suite, why not take off the masks so we could see who you are?"

The hitman nodded vigorously. "That was the plan. If you saw Yves de Marsault enter your room after you had just had his family arrested, you would raise the alarm. We checked one room each and when we knew who was where, we would unmask and explain. I was supposed to take you, leaving Yves with the lighter one. When the fire alarm went off, no time to switch. In her room," he pointed to Catinca, "no one in bed. I had to drag her out of the bathroom. Yves took you, so I took her. Sorry."

Beatrice scowled at the man and his reference to her weight. Catinca sat back and folded her arms, squinting at their captors.

"And you just happen to have a helicopter on the roof? That was handy."

A faint smile crossed Yves's face. "The family organised a meeting to which I was not invited. They often do this when I am out of town. I heard the news of their arrest as I touched down on this very airfield later yesterday afternoon. Mr Vida and I saw an opportunity. I flew my helicopter to the hotel, radioing ahead to warn the staff I wanted to hear what happened in person. We own the place, so we can fly in and out whenever we like."

"Not whenever you like. You will get fined for flying tonight," Vida warned.

The four sat in silence for several minutes and Beatrice noticed the lightening of the sky to the east. Sunrise was about to break. Her mind was so full of questions it seemed blocked. Twice, she opened her mouth to articulate a query and closed it again in confusion. Finally, it was her assistant who broke the silence.

"What now?"

Yves looked at his watch and at the retreating darkness. "As soon as it is legally permissible, we will fly you by private jet back to Britain. Before that, I need to check that the contract killers hunting you have been arrested."

Catinca piped up. "And Denis! 'Cos he'll hire new ones to get us."

"He is no more," said Davor. "He did not survive his last encounter with Le Fantôme."

A realisation formed in Beatrice's mind and she looked into the eyes of Davor Vida. He was the man who killed Gennaio Colacino. Ordered by Denis Hugues. Who died at the very hands of his own hitman. With the help of Yves, Davor saved her and Catinca's lives. She guessed she could call that quits. Her job was done.

"I see," Beatrice said. "How can we be sure those men are no longer on our tail? Even if we do fly out here on a private jet, what's to stop them following?"

Yves looked at the man beside him, whose mouth expanded into a long slow smile. Davor Vida blinked with all the contentment of a lazy cat. "For one thing, they don't know where you are."

"Which leads us to the second point," Yves continued. "When they cannot find you outside the hotel, they will search inside. That is when police officers will make their arrests. Detectives on the Bordeaux force have my full cooperation, except when it comes to Davor. He shall disappear and retire in peace; that is the deal. I'm sad to say, several members of my family will spend the rest of their lives incarcerated. But I want to thank you, Ms Stubbs, Ms Radu, for bringing this to…"

Someone wrapped sharply at the door of the Portakabin. Everyone jumped except Davor Vida, who stood up, stretched and grabbed the final madeleine.

"Relax, it's the pilot. Finally we have clearance to fly. Ladies, go and change. Make your calls, Monsieur de Saint … de Marsault. One hour before take-off. If all is well, the housekeepers will return with your luggage before we leave. If not, your bags will follow. I will escort you home."

Beatrice looked Yves de Marsault who was already scrolling through his phone. Somehow, she trusted this man. "You're not coming with us, Batman?"

His face smoothed into a smile. "Not a good move. Leaving the country in a private jet after most of my family have been arrested? I think not. As soon you have left French soil, I plan to present myself at the Bordeaux police station and offer them a statement which will incriminate my late ex-assistant."

Beatrice struggled to her feet in her coat which could be better described as a sleeping bag, collected her emergency supplies and followed Catinca through to the draughty toilets to change. As she locked the cubicle door, she rolled her eyes. Clean knickers and sportswear were all very well but what the hell was she supposed to do about a bra?

Chapter 42

Living at the beach, Davor had a routine he enjoyed. Get up with the light, make a smoothie and sit on the garden chair to watch the day wake. Since his second retirement, he'd given up coffee and didn't miss it at all. It used to be handy, keeping him alert and buzzing on the job, but it was a habit he no longer needed. When the caffeine urge niggled, he inhaled the air of Miami Beach and asked himself why he would put anything else but organic juice into his system.

While the morning remained mild, he watered his terrace plants with a sense of pride. The bell peppers and zucchini were almost ripe for plucking. Maybe he'd make a peperonta starter for Friday's guests. 'From my own garden!' he would exclaim.

Duties completed, he dressed in a turquoise kaftan, his yellow turban and just a touch of hummingbird eyeliner before applying mascara. Here, subtlety stood out. Flamboyance was the only way to go if you wanted to fit in. He added crystal earrings to reflect the Florida sunshine, slipped his blue-painted toenails into jewelled sandals and walked down onto Ocean Drive. Neighbours and shopkeepers greeted him with a wave and a smile, unaware of the effect their casual gestures had on the recipient. He loved them. Every smile, comment and handshake was an embrace, a welcome, an acceptance.

He waved, blew kisses, accepted invitations to brunch and promised Rico he would not miss the show tomorrow night. A horn blasted from the main drag and Davor saw Samantha and Jude cruising past in their vintage Mercury coupe. The turquoise matched his kaftan. He couldn't resist dashing over for a selfie as they sat in traffic. Many of the horns tooting behind them sounded like approval as they mugged for the camera.

Davor gave a gracious curtsey to the stalled vehicles and received a volley of toots and whoops. He sallied on towards the beach, aiming for the café where he met his friends, some for gossip, some for chess, and some for advice on designer sales. Yet his instinct would not be quelled.

Standing in the impatient traffic, he'd looked behind for just a second. Something had registered. What? He commanded his lazy morning brain to wake up. *What did you see*? He affected a limp and hobbled to a bench, where he slipped off his flip-flop and raised it to his face while studying the street from behind his shades.

There. A black Chevrolet Surburban crawling along the beachside boulevard, driven by a man wearing mirror shades, its tinted windows impenetrable. It stood out as sinister amongst the parade of showy Corvettes, funky Jeeps and classic Plymouths. He replaced his shoe, stood up and brushed himself off. Once again, they had found him, as they always would. He was tired of this constant cat-and-mouse game, and if he were honest, ready to retire for good this time. Rather than walking to the beach café, he walked directly to the sea. His friends called out and he waved. Not the 'hello, I'm excited to see you' kind of finger rain but more a long arcing sweep of the arm, the sort of thing you would see from the passengers of the Titanic. The kind of wave that said 'goodbye, because I don't know when I'll see you again'.

Davor walked out into the waves, lifting his kaftan to speed his progress. Laughter reached him from the beach café, his friends entertained by his eccentricity. He waded out still further, until only his head bobbed above the Atlantic waves and began to swim. He lay on his back, gazing up at the endless blue sky, cradled by the waves. Davor Vida intended to retire on his own terms. He took a deep breath and ducked under the water. He preferred not to alarm his friends.

Chapter 43

Beginning Christmas preparations the day after Bonfire Night might seem excessive to some and insufferably smug to others. For Beatrice Stubbs, it was absolutely essential. The amount of jobs she had lined up between now and the end of the year would keep her working flat out until she found a replacement for Catinca. And judging by the disappointing response to her advertisement, she had precious little hope of achieving that before January. Christmas week itself would be especially hectic, in spite of the fact that Matthew's daughters would have Christmas dinner with their mother this year.

Adrian and Will intended to celebrate their first anniversary in the village where they had married. Which meant that Beatrice and Matthew would be hosting an anniversary party on Christmas Eve, cooking Christmas lunch for four on the 25th and doing the whole thing again for the entire family party on Boxing Day.

Thus it was that Beatrice drove home from Exeter with a car packed to the gills with presents, decorations, ingredients and a whole raft of accessories she could use to gussie up one of her basic dresses for at least two of the events. She pulled into the lane leading to their cottage, her mind full of the PI tasks she needed to do before the end of the day. A large muddy vehicle came round the corner and she slammed on the brakes, causing several packages to slide off the back seat and hit the floor. The

Land Rover reversed to give her enough space to pass and she recognised the driver. She wound down the window.

"Gabriel, hello!"

"All right, Beatrice? Matthew said you've been Christmas shopping." Gabriel gave her one of his slow, shy smiles.

"Just call me Miss Efficiency. One well-planned morning and the festivities will be perfect. Are you on your own? Where's Tanya?"

Gabriel glanced into the rear-view mirror to check he was not blocking the lane. "At work, I suppose. I just wanted a word with Matthew. By the way, Huggy Bear is putting on weight. You need to be careful how much you feed her now she's been spayed."

"Tell him, not me! He's an absolute bugger for feeding them from the table. Unless I watch him…"

Gabriel interrupted. "Car coming behind you. I'd better get on. See you later." He gave a *peep peep* of his horn as he drove away.

With a wave, Beatrice put the car into gear and drove off towards their cottage, which sparkled brilliantly in the November sunshine. She lugged the first few packages into the hallway, trying not to trip over Huggy Bear and calling Matthew's name. On the third trip, there was still no sign of the man. She and the terrier made three more trips to carry on all her purchases and only then did he emerge from his study, blinking in surprise.

"You're back, Old Thing. Was your foraging a success?" Matthew enquired, his face flushed. "I have the most marvellous news. Let's go into the kitchen. Good gracious, you must have cleared out the shops."

"Yes, I have basically bought Christmas. And I could have done with a hand getting this lot in from the car… Matthew? Have you been crying?"

In lieu of a response, he took her in his arms, pressing his face into her shoulder.

"Matthew, what on earth is the matter? I just saw Gabriel..." She pulled away and looked into his eyes, goose bumps pimpling her skin. "Oh my God! He came to ask your permission, didn't he? He wants to marry Tanya, doesn't he? You said yes? Tell me you said yes!"

He nodded, brushing at his eyes and swallowing. "Of course I said yes. I find it hard to believe he even needed to ask. We may have had a manly embrace. As far as I'm concerned, Gabriel is the ideal husband for Tanya and the perfect father for Luke. I cannot believe my luck in terms of my first son-in-law. Huggy Bear, do get down, there's a good girl."

A squeal of excitement escaped Beatrice. "The best news! I must call her immediately."

"We've been invited to The Angel this evening for an official announcement. I'd say we let them spring the surprise. Now, we should find somewhere to store the excessive amount of shopping you brought home. Is there a present for me at all?"

"As if I'd tell you. Never mind the shopping, this calls for a glass of Prosecco."

He gave a knowing smile. "Never mind Prosecco, I think this calls for champagne. You might want to check an Internet news site first. Radio Four did a feature on the de Marsault case this morning. It has finally come to court."

Beatrice's jaw dropped and she ran into the study.

```
      INTERNATIONAL NEWS – De Marsault
                   Scandal
Paris: For many months, France has been
gripped by the allegations against one of its
finest society families. Today, in Paris, the
trial began with opening statements from the
prosecution and defence. Madame Agathe de
Marsault, her son Xander and daughter-in-law
Daria are accused of a range of criminal
```

activities from drug-running and prostitution
to extortion and even murder. The trial has
been delayed twice due to ill health of the
matriarch.
There has been much speculation as to the role
of Yves de Marsault, Madame Agathe's youngest
son. Gasps were heard from the gallery when
lawyers acting for the Sûreté confirmed he
will testify as a witness for the prosecution.
If found guilty, the three accused will face
jail terms of up to thirty years. A
spokeswoman for the Sûreté said this should
serve as an example for the rich and powerful.
'No one is above the law.'

Tanya and Gabriel's friends and family were far too numerous
for the snug, the back room at The Angel. Instead, they filled the
bar, squeaking, laughing and embracing each other. When
Gabriel finally made the announcement, the cheers practically
lifted the roof. Beatrice's eyes watered at the sparkle in Tanya's
and she squeezed Matthew's hand, leaning her head against his
shoulder.

Gabriel hadn't finished. "There's one other question I would
like to ask. Tanya has chosen Marianne as her bridesmaid and I
must decide on a best man." He looked around the room. "Next
year, I will promise to love, cherish and honour this woman for
the rest of my life. Someone else has done a pretty good job of
that so far. So I would like to ask you, Luke, if you will be my
right-hand man. Before you ask, you don't have to wear a suit."

A sob escaped Tanya and Beatrice realised this gesture was
unexpected. All eyes rested on Luke as he looked from one to
another and murmured something in Marianne's ear. She
whispered back and he broke into a huge grin, ran across the
room and flung his arms around Gabriel's waist. More than one
of the guests wiped away tears and applause resounded around
the room.

Tanya wrenched herself away from her fiancé and made her way via various well-wishers to Beatrice and Matthew. Amidst hugs, kisses and enthusiasm, they managed to convey their delight.

"He's a lovely man, in every way. Honourable, decent, and fantastic with Luke. He has a good source of income, his own car and is unreasonably handsome. If I was twenty years younger..." Beatrice laughed. "My number one question is, when? Please don't tell me this Christmas because I've got enough to do."

Tanya shook her head, wreathed in smiles. "Christmas? No way! Apart from anything else, it's going to take at least six months to make my wedding dress, according to my designer." She locked eyes with Beatrice.

"Good Lord," exclaimed Matthew. "You're having a dress designed? You really are going the whole hog, then?"

"Don't worry, Dad. This is not the Dark Ages and you are not expected to pay for my wedding. Everything will be simple, rustic and cheap. My wedding dress will be an original Radu, a gift from the designer herself. One thing, though. Luke can do most of the best man stuff, but he is still a minor. You will have to do is sign the register and write the speech. Ooh, there's Frankie. I must say hello."

"Speech?" said Matthew, but she had already gone.

Beatrice placed a peck on Matthew's cheek and peeled away to sit next to Marianne. They watched Tanya, Gabriel and Luke move through the guests, accepting congratulations and enjoying the moment.

"So what are you thinking in terms of a bridesmaid's dress?" she asked.

Marianne gave her a devious grin. "Obviously something fabulous, flamboyant and incredibly expensive, just to upstage the bride. Otherwise, what's the point?"

"Obviously," Beatrice laughed. "My mind ran along similar lines. Have you heard anything about your scammer?"

"No," Marianne shook her head. "I don't want to hear anything, other than more women are speaking up and exposing the cynical little shit for what he is. I'm giving up on men. After Christmas, I'm taking an extended break and going on a yoga and meditation retreat. If I'm going to spend the rest of my life alone, I'd better learn to love myself."

Beatrice rested her hand on Marianne's knee. "I'm your godmother. I will be here whenever required. Especially when you need me to chase off unsuitable men."

Gabriel popped a cork and began filling glasses and exchanging delighted glances with his wife-to-be.

"I know. You saved me twice from a shifty scumbag. Is there any chance you could go on the offensive instead of the defensive? Find me a decent bloke rather than shooting down the ones I dig up from under a stone?"

Beatrice thought about it while surveying the room. "To tell you the truth, I find you rather difficult to buy gifts for. So instead of a Christmas present, I'm going to set you up with at least half a dozen decent men. You will have to go into this with an open mind, otherwise it will not work. Marianne Bailey, will you or will you not allow me to fix you up?"

Marianne looked at her. "What have I got to lose? I will."

Floating on glasses of champagne, Beatrice linked her arm into Matthew's as they trudged down the lane towards home. Their conversation, elated and excitable, revolved around the impending marriage and the harmonious balance in the family. Chill November winds brushed their faces and without discussion, they picked up their pace towards home. The lane grew darker as they left the village and Matthew expressed his regret at forgetting to bring a torch.

Out of nowhere, hailstones descended from the night sky pelting their uncovered heads with bolts of ice. They speeded up, crunching across the surface of the lane, huddled into their coats and focused on the road ahead. The little pellets of ice stung Beatrice's cheeks and she focused on a large pan of looming milk into which she would break quarters of dark chocolate. Matthew covered his head with his hood and Beatrice pulled up her scarf to protect her head.

Just as Beatrice was about to suggest they return to the pub until the hailstorm had ended, headlights lit the road and a bright red Mini pulled up beside them. A young black man with dreadlocks jumped out, shielding his eyes from the weather.

"Beatrice Stubbs! Found you at last. Come on, I'll give you a lift home." He opened the back door and motioned for them to enter.

"Theo? What on earth are you doing here?"

"Looking for you! Get in!"

Beatrice hesitated but Matthew immediately took the young man up on his offer and clambered into the passenger seat. Beatrice got into the back and wiped her face with her scarf. Once she could see, she studied their driver's profile and tried to catch his eyes in the mirror but before she could even articulate a question, the young man swung into their forecourt and parked behind their own vehicle. He leaped out, opened Beatrice's door and guided her to the porch.

She unlocked the front door and the three of them stood in the hallway, brushing off the hundreds of tiny white pellets that covered their clothes while Huggy Bear dashed from one to another.

"Thank heavens for you!" Beatrice exclaimed. "That weather is atrocious. May I introduce you to my partner, Matthew? Matthew, our knight in shining Mini is Theo. He's a friend of Catinca's and a barman at Dionysus. Theo, this is Huggy Bear."

The man shook himself like a dog, scattering hailstones everywhere and grasped Matthew's hand. "Matthew, pleased to meet you, man. Beatrice, it's good to see you again. Hey, how much am I loving that hair?" He crouched to stroke Huggy Bear and scratch her ears. Then he stood to face them. "Listen up, people, I bring news. Me and Catinca have been talking. She's got ambitions for me, know what I'm saying? She reckons I'm wasting my talents. So I quit my job at Dionysus." He held out a hand. "Meet Theo Wolfe, your brand new assistant."

"I see." Beatrice took his hand in hers. "In that case, you'd better come in."

Dear Reader

From a quiet life in the country to being kidnapped by Batman in the wee small hours, PI Beatrice Stubbs finds private detecting unpredictable. Now with an impressive reputation, friends in high places and an unexpected new assistant, she is ready to take on the next case.

Passionate climate change activists are making waves and headlines in Finland, until their leader and her deputy disappear. Outraged media fingers point to their aggressive opponents, a triumvirate of well-funded energy giants. In attempt to get at the truth, one of the chief executives calls in Beatrice Stubbs. The clash between green and grey is about to get blood red.

The next in the series comes out in summer 2020.

Acknowledgements

As always, huge gratitude to my editors at Triskele Books: Catriona Troth, Liza Perrat, Jane Dixon Smith and Gillian Hamer. Thanks to Florian Bielmann for structural editorial input and focus. The book owes its look to JD Smith Design and its polished text to proofreader Julia Gibbs. Heartfelt appreciation to La Cité du Vin in Bordeaux and the research team: Julie, David, Tracy, Jane, Gilly and Ade.

Santé!

Message from JJ Marsh

I hope you enjoyed BLACK WIDOW.

I have also written The Beatrice Stubbs Series, European crime dramas:

BEHIND CLOSED DOORS
RAW MATERIAL
TREAD SOFTLY
COLD PRESSED
HUMAN RITES
BAD APPLES
SNOW ANGEL
HONEY TRAP

I have also written a standalone novel

AN EMPTY VESSEL

And a short-story collection

APPEARANCES GREETING A POINT OF VIEW

For more information, visit jjmarshauthor.com

For occasional updates, news, deals and a FREE exclusive prequel: *Black Dogs, Yellow Butterflies*, subscribe to my newsletter: jjmarshauthor.com

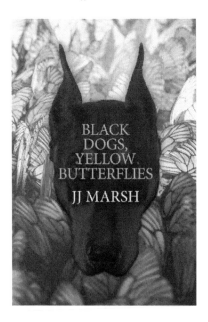

If you would recommend this book to a friend, please do so by writing a review. Your tip helps other readers discover their next favourite read.
Thank you.

Printed in Great Britain
by Amazon